"Welcome."
The deep voice was soft
as he gestured with his arm
at the open doorway.

Trembling, feeling as if she were stepping through an invisible barrier into another life, Nicole entered.

She was in.

She was going to do this.

Oh yes.

The next second her back thumped against the door and Sam Reston's entire weight was against her as he kissed her wildly. Not the fragile, tentative kiss in his car. Oh no, this was as if he were trying to inhale her. A deep kiss, wild, going on forever.

Oh God, his taste! Like a fresh mountain stream pumped full of male hormones, calculated to drive any woman wild. His mouth ate at hers, coming at her from various angles, as if one weren't enough.

And it wasn't.

INTO THE
CROSSFIRE

By Lisa Marie Rice

HOTTER THAN WILDFIRE
INTO THE CROSSFIRE
DANGEROUS PASSION
DANGEROUS SECRETS
DANGEROUS LOVER

Coming Soon
NIGHTFIRE

LISA MARIE RICE

INTO THE CROSSFIRE
A PROTECTORS NOVEL:
NAVY SEAL

AVON
An Imprint of HarperCollinsPublishers

AVON BOOKS
An Imprint of HarperCollins*Publishers*
10 East 53rd Street
New York, New York 10022-5299

First Avon Books mass market printing: December 2011
First Avon Red paperback printing: August 2010

Avon Trademark Reg. U.S. Pat. Off. and in Other Countries, Marca Registrada, Hecho en U.S.A.
HarperCollins® is a registered trademark of HarperCollins Publishers.

Printed in the U.S.A.

10 9 8 7 6 5 4 3 2 1

*This book is dedicated to the men
who have always protected their loved ones.*

Acknowledgments

A published author needs a lot of things, but above all, she needs time and space to write and the opportunity to be published. So I'd like to thank my beloved family for the time and space they give me and to thank my great agent, Ethan Ellenberg, and my wonderful editor, May Chen, for the opportunity.

Chapter 1

San Diego
June 28

Well, well. Look at that.

Sam Reston leaned his shoulder against the wall of the hallway of his office building and simply drank in his fill.

There she was.

His own personal wet dream, standing there in the hallway between his office and hers, desperately scrabbling through a huge, expensive-looking purse.

Everything about her was expensive, classy. Top of the line. Real high maintenance, too. The kind of woman he stepped right around without a second thought because he didn't have the time or the inclination, but shit, with her he'd make an exception.

Any man would.

Nicole Pearce. The most beautiful woman in

the world. Certainly the most beautiful woman *he'd* ever seen, hands down.

He remembered every second of the moment he'd first laid eyes on her. Two weeks, three days and thirty minutes ago. But who was counting?

He'd been under cover, infiltrating a gang of smugglers and thieves working the docks. His client, a big shipping company, had found it impossible to get a handle on the losses incurred during transhipment at the docks, which last year had totaled almost $10 million.

The police had gotten nowhere and the company suspected that someone somewhere was being bought off. Sam hoped it wasn't in the police department. His brother Mike was a SWAT officer with the San Diego PD and incredibly proud of it.

Someone had definitely dropped the ball, though. So the ship owner had decided to go private.

Smart move.

For a hell of a lot of money, Sam had gone under cover, working the night shift as a stevedore, spreading word around that he wasn't averse to some under-the-table money. He'd been contacted, and had quickly made his way up the hierarchy of the Bucinski gang, finally rising to the point where they had included him on two major hauls. He'd been wired to the teeth and had about a hundred photographs nailing gang members, their scumbag boss, and three corrupt Port Authority employees.

The fuckheads had not just been stealing cargo, they were involved in sex trafficking, too, bringing in kidnapped young girls hidden in the holds of legitimate ships, the owners of the ships entirely unaware of their human cargo.

The whole gang was going down. The shitheads deserved the needle but wouldn't get it. Each of them would, however, spend the next twenty to thirty being some gangbanger's newest girlfriend, which might even be better.

So Sam had looked like a scumbag the day he first saw her. *Being* a scumbag had been his job for the previous two weeks.

When San Reston did something, he did it well.

Going under cover wasn't like in the movies. You ate, dressed, acted and even smelled the part. While under cover, he rarely washed or shaved, and wore the same clothes for days at a time. He knew he smelled ripe and looked dangerous. Well, hell. He *was* dangerous—he was murderous with rage at the thought of fuckheads willing to rape little girls spending even one day out of jail.

He'd been up thirty-six hours straight and was just coming into the office after another all-nighter to shower, change and grab a few z's on his very comfortable office couch when he'd seen her.

Actually, he smelled her before he saw her. The elevator pinged, the doors opened and some floral . . . thing that traveled into men's heads through the nasal passageways and fucked with their brains reached out and walloped him.

He saw her a second later and froze. Simply froze. Later, when he'd untangled his head from his ass, he'd been amazed. He'd been a SEAL until his eardrum blew, and he'd been a damned good one.

SEAL training beats surprise right out of a man. You have to have good, solid nerves just to think of trying out for BUD/S. If you were the easily surprised type, you were weeded out fast.

Nothing took him by surprise, ever.

Except Nicole Pearce.

Sam had known that the tiny studio office across the hall had been rented out. The building's manager had told him. To a translation agency—though Sam had no fucking idea what that could be—run by one Nicole Pearce.

He hadn't thought more about it.

That particular morning he was more exhausted, filthy and pissed off than usual. He smelled, too, of sweat and beer. He was in a shitty mood, ready to cut the job short simply to get the top guys into the slammer fast. But he knew better. With the evidence he was getting, the entire operation would go down and that was worth a few extra days or weeks living with slime.

A second after that amazing, womanly smell chock-full of pheromones went straight to his dick, he saw her, and his entire body seized up. He was unable to move, unable to breathe, for a second or two.

Midnight black, glossy shoulder-length hair, enormous, uptilted eyes the exact color of the cobalt glass sculpture he'd turned down as too expensive for his office, eyes with lashes so long and thick they could stir up a breeze, slightly overlarge mouth with that Angelina Jolie dent in the bottom lip, perfect straight little nose, creamy skin.

Fuck-me shoes.

Incredible hourglass figure poured into a demure blue suit that exactly matched the color of her eyes and hugged curves guaranteed to make any male within a one-mile radius salivate.

She sure had the two moving guys salivating, as she directed them carrying in a heavy teak desk and a tiny antique sofa. They were doing her bidding like two puppy dogs hoping for a bone.

She turned to look at him directly, at the *ping* of the elevator, and Christ, all he could do was stare at the dazzler with the deep blue eyes.

Eyes that watched him warily.

Sam was exhausted, but a man would have to be dead not to have all his hormones wake up at the sight of the most beautiful woman on earth. And, hell, his hormones weren't the only thing to wake up.

Instant boner, right there in the upscale hallway of the very expensive building he'd chosen as headquarters of his new company.

Shit.

Thank God he had on his tightest jeans because she was already looking alarmed at the sight of him. Who could blame her? He'd put a lot of care into looking like a scumbag, walking like a scumbag, thinking like a scumbag, even smelling like one.

And he was enraged down to the bone at the sex trafficking he'd discovered. That was something that was hard to switch off.

A woman like this would have antenna way out there where men were concerned. She'd be able to read men like other women read fashion magazines. It was a fact of her life. She was stunning, with the kind of natural good looks that would carry her through from childhood to old age as a beauty. So she'd grown up with the background buzz of hot male attention and she'd have learned to filter out the bad ones, the dangerous ones pretty quick.

He wasn't bad but he *was* dangerous and he carried that with him, like a shroud. He'd had a brutal childhood and had learned street fighting before he could read. By adulthood, he was really good with his fists, with a knife, hell—with a rock. Uncle Sam had taken what he was by nature, refined it, armed him up and spent over a million dollars turning him into a killing machine.

He'd made his living as a soldier leading hard men, and now as a civilian he made his living being tougher than most.

He'd come straight into the office after working the night shift on the docks, then sharing a beer with the man who'd recruited him for Bucinski, Kyle Connelly. Sam had nursed one beer to Connelly's ten, and laughed while the pusbag told him about the perks of the job. Extra money, all the drugs you could snort or shoot up and sex.

Sam had had to listen while Connelly bragged about handcuffing a twelve-year-old Vietnamese girl to a steel post and raping her. Sam had even had to commiserate with the fucker, whining because he'd been sore afterward, after popping the girl's cherry.

Listening to this, laughing, slapping him on the back in sympathy, had been one of the hardest things he'd ever had to do in his hard life. His hands had literally itched to draw out the garrote wire in his belt and rip the fucker's head right off.

So he'd been fighting mad when the doors had opened and—*whoa*. The world's most beautiful woman, right there in front of him.

He'd actually had to rub his eyes, sure that what was right before him had to be some kind of vision, maybe some kind of compensation for the horrible night.

Her eyes had widened when she'd seen him. He knew what she was seeing—a very large, very strong, hugely pissed-off man, dressed like a bum and smelling like one, too.

Well, he couldn't shave, wash and change his clothes right then and there and there was nothing he could do to kill those deadly pissed-off vibes so he'd merely walked down the corridor and entered his office.

Her huge cobalt blue eyes had followed him warily every step of the way. She'd actually stepped back as he approached, which pissed him off even more. Goddamn it, the last thing he'd ever do was hurt a woman.

Though, in fairness, she couldn't possibly know that. Probably every cell in her single urban female body was screaming *danger*. He knew she was single because though he saw she had some fancy rings on those pretty hands of hers, none of them were on her left-hand ring finger.

She absolutely had to be single because Sam couldn't even remotely imagine a man married or even engaged to a looker like that who wouldn't put a rock the size of her head on her finger, to warn other men off her. And what husband or fiancé wouldn't be around to help his woman move into her new office?

She couldn't know that his rage wasn't in any way directed at her, of course, but at the system. He wanted to nail the gang *right now* and send them all into the slammer five minutes later, special treatment reserved for one Kyle Connelly, child rapist.

But what you want and what you can have are very different things. No one knew that more than he did. So he'd had to stay under cover, sick at heart, wondering if some other little girls were being raped while he put together enough evidence to put the fuckers away. And to do that he had to stay in Scumland for another couple of weeks.

So every time Nicole Pearce saw him, he'd been tired and grim and dirty, inside and out. Dealing with the scum of the earth was filthy work.

He knew that while he was on this mission, there was no room for anything else, certainly not something as beautiful as Nicole Pearce, so he'd waited.

But all that was now behind him and life had just handed him a big fat present all wrapped up in a fancy bow, to thank him for his patience.

Nicole Pearce, outside her office, looking as beautiful as ever, even with a ferocious scowl on her face, rifling through her bag and jacket pockets, looking for her keys.

The keys to the flimsiest piece-of-shit lock he'd ever seen. When he'd signed the lease on his office, he'd been happy with the space and the location and—though he ordinarily didn't give a shit about his surroundings—the classiness of the building. It was the kind of building that made clients relax, which was crazy to him. What the fuck difference did mellow earth tones and fancy designer junk make?

But to most people it made a difference. A huge one. He'd noticed that. Noticed tense clients start unwinding after entering the building, with its liveried doorman, elegant brass and teak fittings, slate floors, expensive floral arrangements scattered around.

The building supervisor had given him the name of some office designer, who'd come in, taken measurements of the huge space he'd rented and come back a week later and outfitted the office so it looked like a spaceship. A designer spaceship, sleek and comfortable. It all cost a fortune but it was worth it, to see his clients' faces as they walked in.

Anyone who came to Reston Security by definition needed relaxing, and it was good that his
office did the trick because Sam wasn't good at
putting people at ease. He had no charm and no
small talk in him.

When Sam came across a problem, he wanted
it solved yesterday. He became an arrow shooting
straight at a solution.

That attitude had worked real well for him in
the Teams, where problems and possible solutions
were clearly stated and no one's goddamned feelings ever came into anything.

Civilian life had been a bitch, as Sam found
himself tussling with clients who were afraid to
say what they wanted, who kept intel from him,
who had hidden agendas. Christ.

So the upscale, soothing premises had come in
real handy.

Not to mention Nicole Pearce, right across the
hallway from him, right now scrabbling for keys
that weren't there.

Well, he could do something about that. For a
price.

"Need some help?" he asked, and suppressed a
smile when she nearly jumped right out of that
gorgeous skin of hers.

"Need some help?" the scary lowlife who worked
for the security company across the hallway asked.

Nicole Pearce's head whipped around, heart
kicking up into a hard panicky beat in her chest.

Oh God, there he was, long and broad and dark and grim. And frightening as hell.

He hadn't been there a minute ago. Everyone on her floor came in well before her company's opening time of 9 A.M., so she had been sure she was alone as she scrabbled in her purse, quietly freaking out.

How could such a large man move so quietly? Granted, her head was completely taken up with the tragedy of *no key*, but still. He was huge. Surely he'd have to have made some noise?

Come to think of it, the times she'd seen him coming and going from what she assumed was his workplace across the hall, he'd been utterly silent. Frightening.

She looked at him warily, hands still in her large purse that often doubled as a briefcase.

He was standing with arms crossed, leaning back against the wall, looking completely out of place in the elegant hallway. Tall, immensely broad-shouldered, grim and unsmiling. Just perfect if Central Casting had sent out an urgent call. *One thug. Huge. Intimidating. Report to set.*

But it hadn't. Central Casting populated the Morrison Building in downtown San Diego with perfectly nice, perfectly tame office workers, some a little flamboyant if they were in the advertising business, but otherwise harmless.

Lowlife had absolutely no business here, staring at her out of dark, steady eyes, gaze still and unwavering, completely out of place in the context of the cream and teal accents, the expensive Murano wall sconces and the faux Louis XV Philippe Starck Plexiglas console with the very real calla lilies in the Steuben vase.

She'd chosen to pay premium rent for a tiny office in the upscale building near Petco precisely because its classy, elegant design had appealed to her and because, well, it shrieked success so loudly she hoped no one could hear the crackling sound of financial distress underlying her new company.

Everyone in the building bustled in and out in morning and evening waves, well dressed, well groomed and busy busy busy. Even after the stock market crash, they all made an effort to look sleek and prosperous and successful, which was why Lowlife was so out of place.

The rent took a big chunk out of the earnings of her brand-new company, and her office was the size of a thimble, but she loved it. She'd signed the lease half an hour after the realtor had shown it to her.

That was, of course, before Lowlife started haunting the halls. Every time she turned around, it seemed, he was there. Enormous, dressed like a biker. Or how she imagined a biker would dress— what would she know? Bikers had been scarce growing up in consulates and embassies around the world.

He had a uniform of torn, filthy jeans, a formerly black tee shirt washed so many times it was a dirty gray, and at times a black leather bomber jacket.

Overlong black hair and a heavy, scruffy black beard, nothing at all like the chic designer stubble sported by the guys working at the ad agency two doors down. No, this was a man with a heavy beard who didn't shave for weeks at a time.

But beyond not following the yuppie dress and grooming code, Lowlife was different in other ways from all the other people in the building.

She would never forget her first sight of him in the elevator, leaning one-armed against the wall, head down, looking like a warrior who had just come in from battle.

Only there was no war going on in downtown San Diego that she knew of. He'd disappeared into the office across the hall, passing some pretty fancy security, so she'd imagined he worked there.

As an enforcer?

She'd been aware of his scrutiny as she entered and exited her office. He never overtly stared, but she could feel his attention on her like a spotlight.

Now, however, God help her, he was definitely staring, arms crossed over that absurdly broad chest, unsmiling, gaze fierce and unwavering.

"Need some help?" he asked again. His voice matched his physique. Low, so deep it set up vibrations in her diaphragm.

Then again, maybe the vibrations were panic.

No key.

This definitely wasn't happening. Not on top of

the Ride from Hell in to work. Of all the days to lock herself out . . .

"No, I'm on it." Nicole bared her teeth in what she hoped he'd take as a smile, because she so *wasn't* on it.

What she didn't have—and what she so very desperately needed—was her office key. The office key on her Hermès silver key fob that had been a birthday present from her father, back in the days when he could work and walk on his own. The set of keys that was always, always, in the front pocket of her purse, except . . . when it wasn't.

Like now.

Nicole Pearce contemplated beating her head against the door to her office, but much as she'd like to, she couldn't. Not under Lowlife's dark, intense gaze. She'd save that for when he finally left.

He watched as she once more checked her linen jacket pockets, first one, then the other, then her purse, over and over again, in a little trifecta routine from hell.

Nothing.

It was horrible having someone see her panic and distress. Life had taken so much from her lately. One of the few things left to her was her dignity, and that was now circling the drain, fast.

She tried to stop herself from shaking. This was the kind of building where you keep up appearances and you never lose your cool, ever. Otherwise they'd raise the rent.

It was so awful, fumbling desperately in her

purse, sweat beading her face though the building's powerful air conditioners kept the temperature at a constant 62 degrees. She could feel sweat trickling down her back and had to stop, close her eyes for a second and regain control. Breathe deeply, in and out.

Maybe Lowlife would disappear if she just kept her eyes closed long enough. Realize that she deeply, *deeply* wanted him gone. Do the gentlemanly thing and just go.

No such luck.

When she opened her eyes again, the man was stiil there. Dark and tough, a foot from the console she wanted to use.

She looked at the slate floor and the transparent console and gritted her teeth.

Of the two horrible choices, getting close to him to dump the contents of her purse on the console was marginally more dignified than simply squatting and dumping everything in her purse on the floor.

Approaching him warily—she was pretty sure he wasn't dangerous, and that he wouldn't attack her in broad daylight in a public building, but he was so very *big* and looked so incredibly *hard*— she reached the pretty console, shifted the vase of lilies the super had changed just yesterday, opened her purse wide and simply upended it over the transparent surface.

The clatter was deafening in the silent corridor.

She had her home keys, car keys, a removable hard disk, a silver business card case, a cell phone, four pens, a flash drive—all of which made a clatter. And her leather bag of cosmetics, paperback book, checkbook, notepad, address book, credit-card holder, all of which made a mess.

In a cold sweat of panic, Nicole pushed her way through the objects on the console, checking carefully, over and over again, reciting each object under her breath like a mantra. Everything that should be there was there.

Except for her office key.

What a disaster. Construction on Robinson had forced her into a long detour, which was why she was opening the office at 9:15 instead of 9. At 9:30, she had a vital videoconference with a very important potential client in New York and her two best Russian translators, to negotiate a big job. A huge job. A job that could represent more than 20 percent of her income next year. A job she desperately needed.

Her father's medical bills kept rising, with no end in sight. She'd just added a night nurse for weeknights and it was $2,000 a month. A new round of radiotherapy might be necessary, Dr. Harrison had said last week. Another $10,000. It was all money she didn't have and had to earn. Fast.

If the conference call went well, she might be able to keep ahead of her money problems, for a while at least.

There was absolutely no time to cross all of downtown to go back home and get the keys. Not to mention the fact that she would upset her father, who was so ill. He'd be worried, be unsettled all day. Sleep badly that night. She absolutely didn't want to upset him.

Nicholas Pearce had a limited number of days to his life and Nicole was determined that they be as peaceful as possible.

She simply couldn't go back home. And she simply couldn't afford to miss this meeting. Her translation business, Wordsmith, was too new to be able to risk passing up this client—manager of one of the largest hedge funds in New York, looking to invest in Siberian gas futures and the Russian bond market, and needing translations of the technical data sheets and market analyses.

Sweat trickled down her back. She made a fist out of her trembling hand and beat it gently on the console, wanting to simply close her eyes in despair.

This was *not* happening.

"I can open your door for you." She jolted again at the words spoken in that incredibly low, deep voice. Heavens, she'd forgotten about Lowlife in her misery. His dark eyes were watching her carefully. "But it'll cost you."

This was not a good economic moment for her, but right now she'd be willing to pay anything to get into her office. Snatching up her checkbook from the clear surface of the console, she turned to him. He watched her with no expression on his face at all. She had no reason to think he was a decent sort of guy, but she could hope he wouldn't use her obvious desperation to make a killing.

Please, she prayed to the goddess of desperate women.

"Okay, name your price," she said, flipping back the cover, womanfully refraining from wincing when she saw her balance. God, please let him not ask the earth, because her checking account would go straight into the red. She steadied her hand. *Don't let him see you tremble.*

She looked up at him, pen hovering over her checkbook. "How much?"

"Have dinner with me."

She'd actually started writing, then froze. "I—I beg your pardon?" She stared for a second at the blank check where she'd started writing *dinner with Lowlife* on the line with the amount.

"Have dinner with me," he repeated. Okay, so it hadn't been an auditory hallucination.

Her mouth opened and absolutely nothing came out.

Have dinner with him? She didn't know him, knew nothing about him except for the fact that he looked . . . rough. Instinctively, she stepped back.

He was watching her carefully, and nodded sharply, as if she'd said something he agreed with. "You don't know me and you're right to be cautious. So let's start with the basics." He held out a huge, callused, suntanned and none-too-clean hand. "Sam Reston, at your service."

Sam Reston? Sam *Reston*?

Nicole couldn't help it. Her eyes flicked to the big shiny brass plaque, right next to the door across the hall, bearing the name of what she understood to be the most successful company in the building. RESTON SECURITY. He followed her gaze and waited until she looked back at him.

Maybe he was the company's owner's black-sheep cousin. Or brother. Or something.

It had to be asked. "Are you, um, a relative of Mr. Reston?"

He shook his head slowly, dark eyes never leaving hers. "Company belongs to me."

Oh. Wow. How embarrassing.

He was standing there, hand still out. Nicole's parents had drummed manners into her. She'd shaken hands with tyrants and dictators and suspected terrorists in embassies all over the world. It was literally impossible for her not to put her hand in his.

She did it gingerly, and his hand just swallowed hers up. The skin of his palm was very warm, callused and tough. For a moment she was frightened that he might be one of those men who had to prove his manliness by the strength of his handshake. This man's hand could crush hers without difficulty and she made her living at the keyboard.

To her everlasting relief, he merely squeezed gently for three seconds then released her hand.

"N-Nice to meet you," she stammered, because really, what else could she say? "Um—" And she so desperately needed to get into her office. *Now.* "My name is Nicole Pearce."

"Yes, I know, Ms. Pearce." He bent his head formally. His eyes were very dark and—she now realized—very intelligent. "So—as to my price, let's see if I can convince you I'm not a security risk."

He pulled out a slim, hugely expensive cell phone. One Nicole had coveted madly, both for its function and style, but had decided against as being simply way out of her current financial league. He pressed two buttons—whoever he was calling was on speed dial—and waited. She could hear the phone ringing, then a deep male voice answering, "This better be good."

"I've got a lady here I want to ask out for dinner but she doesn't know me and she's not too sure of my good character, Hector, so I called you for an endorsement. Show your face and talk to the lady. Her name's Nicole. Nicole Pearce." He waited a beat. "And say good things."

Nicole accepted the cell phone gingerly. The video display showed the darkly handsome face of San Diego's brand-new mayor, Hector Villarreal, dressed in a bright orange golf shirt, holding a golf club over his shoulder, out on the links, eyes crinkling against the bright sunlight. "Hello, Ms. Pearce." The deep voice sounded cheerful.

She cleared her voice and tried not to sound wary. "Mr. Mayor."

"So." He was smiling, eyebrows high. "You want to go out to dinner with Sam Reston? You *sure* you want to?" There was humor in the faintly-accented voice.

"Well, actually, uh—"

But it was no use talking to a politician, they talked right over you.

"Don't worry about it. Sam's a great guy, he'll treat you right, no question. But I really do need to warn you of something, Ms. Pearce, and it's serious."

Her heart thudded and she looked up into Sam Reston's hard, impassive face. He could hear perfectly, since Mayor Villarreal was talking at the top of his voice.

"Yes, Mr. Mayor?"

"Don't ever play poker with him. Man's a *shark*." A loud guffaw and the connection was broken.

Nicole slowly slid the phone closed and looked up at Sam Reston. He was standing utterly still; the only thing moving was that enormous chest as he breathed quietly. He had the extreme good taste not to look smug or self-satisfied. There was no expression at all on that hard, dark, bearded face. He simply watched her to see what she would do.

She held out the phone by one end and he took it by the other. For a moment they were connected by five inches of warm plastic, then Nicole dropped her hand.

They looked at each other, Nicole frozen to the spot, Lowlife—no, Sam Reston—as still as a dark marble statue. There was no sound, absolutely nothing. The building could have been deserted, there weren't even the normal sounds of air-conditioning or the elevators swooshing up and down.

Everything was still, in suspended animation.

Nicole finally took a deep breath.

Ooooo-kay.

Well, it looked like Lowlife—Sam Reston—wasn't a serial killer or a drug dealer. Actually, he, um, was the owner of a company she knew to be very successful. The success of Reston Security constituted a significant portion of the gossip machine that was alive and well in the Morrison Building. Reston Security was certainly much more successful than Wordsmith, which was clinging to life by the occasional IV line of new clients.

If the extremely dangerous-looking, seriously scruffy man in front of her, watching her quietly, was Sam Reston of Reston Security, then surely she could do this.

A deal was a deal. If he could somehow open her door and allow her to make her videoconference call, she would owe him far more than could be repaid by a couple of hours spent consuming a meal.

He was watching her quietly, and standing oh-so still.

9:23. She took a deep breath. "Okay, you have a dinner date, for an evening of your choosing." She gestured behind her. "But you're going to have to open my door, Mr. Reston, right now. I have a very important business call coming in at 9:30

sharp, and if I don't make that call, then our deal is off."

He dipped his head gravely. "Fair enough. And the name is Sam."

"Nicole." Nicole gritted her teeth, glancing at the big clock at the end of the corridor and wincing. However Sam Reston was going to get her into her office, he'd have to do it in the next six minutes or she was toast. "I wonder . . . is there a building super with a master key?"

"No." He shook his head. "So—we have the deal?"

"Um, yes. We do." Nicole barely refrained from tapping her toe.

"You'll go out to dinner with me tonight?" he pressed. At her look, he shrugged broad shoulders. "Ever since I left the Navy and became a business-man, I've learned to nail agreements down."

Actually, he looked like the kind of man who would enforce deals at the end of a gun. But she'd promised.

"As a new businesswoman myself, I've learned to keep my word. So, yes, I accept your invitation. Now, please open my door. And if you kick it open, I'll expect you to pay damages."

"Of course," he murmured.

Nicole shot a glance at her watch. Damn. It had taken her several days to set up this conference call. The client was a Wall Street "Master of the Universe," almost impossible to pin down to an appointment.

The "Master" in question was an anal retentive and when he said a 9:30 conference call, it would be 9:30 to the second, and she knew that he'd never call again if she wasn't on the line. In a harsh, nasal New Yawk accent, the words spilling out almost more quickly than she could understand them, he'd told her he couldn't have anyone wasting his time because his time was worth at least a thousand dollars a minute.

The message couldn't have been clearer. *Be at the end of the line at 9:30 or else.*

Nicole worked with two retired professors of economics, one of whom had been born in Russia and had come to the States as a teenager, and another who had studied in Moscow for ten years. They would be perfect for the big, long-term translation job and she had every intention of asking the Master of the Universe top prices. Her commission off the deal would go a long way toward paying for the night nurse.

Four minutes to go. She was going to lose this appointment, and probably the client. So much for . . .

She looked up from her wrist and blinked.

Her door was wide open, her tiny, pretty office beckoning beyond it.

She turned her stunned gaze to Sam Reston, who was straightening and moving away from her door. "How did you *do* that? Did you just pick the lock?" Surely picking a lock required some kind of effort? Some time? In the movies, the thief jiggled at the lock forever.

He wasn't looking smug or even proud of himself. In fact, he was scowling. "You haven't improved on the building security at all," he said, his deep voice making it an accusation.

"Um, no." Nicole felt like she'd fallen into a rabbit hole. The real-estate agent had stressed the excellent building security and had dwelled lovingly on the quality of the office locks. "Was I supposed to?"

"Well, sure. When it's as crappy as this." His scowl deepened as he pocketed something. Though she'd love to see if it was a lockpick, she didn't have time to waste.

Another glance at her watch and she hurried into her office. She was just barely going to make the videoconference.

She had less than two minutes to spare.

"Thank you, Mr. Reston. So I guess—"

"Sam."

"Sam." She gritted her teeth. A minute and a half left. "Tell me where to meet you and when."

His scowl grew deeper. "Absolutely not. I'll pick you up at your house."

There wasn't time to argue, not even time to roll her eyes. "Okay. Shall we say seven? I live on Mulberry Street. Three forty-six Mulberry Street. Is that okay?"

"Fine. I'll be there at seven to pick you up." A muscle in his jaw rippled, though the words were low and quiet.

Did he live far away? Well, if he had to drive across town, he'd asked for it. She'd been willing to meet him at the restaurant.

He turned away, she closed the door and the phone rang.

Nicole leaped to pick it up, heard the Master's nasal tones. She'd made it! The price had been high, but she'd made it.

Chapter 2

Well, that worked out just fine.

Sam Reston sat down behind his desk, looking at the day's reports, but all he saw in front of him was the delicious Nicole Pearce, with her exquisite face and hourglass figure, wrapped in classy clothes. An aristocratic wet dream.

He'd been waiting for this moment since he'd first seen her moving into that cubbyhole across the hallway from his own five-room headquarters.

He knew her office was small because it had been shown to him before he settled on his own quarters. Her office wouldn't have been big enough for his files. She ran a translation business. Sam knew exactly zilch about the translating business. Maybe you didn't need much space to translate French into English.

Or Spanish into Russian. Or Italian into German. Or Norwegian into Portuguese.

She covered them all, an amazing configuration

of languages, as her sharply designed website told him. He'd looked at her list of collaborators and it was 120 strong, each one with an impressive re-sumé, scattered all over the world. If there'd been translation work available on the space station, she'd probably have a collaborator there, too.

He'd nearly laughed at Nicole Pearce's expres-sion when he'd named his price for picking that ridiculous lock of hers—dinner out with him.

Granted, he thought, as he looked at his big, battered shitkickers now comfortably settled on his shiny, expensive desktop, he did look like a scumbag. Well, you wouldn't want to be his en-emy. But Nicole Pearce wasn't his enemy. Shit, no.

He'd been aching to touch that creamy white skin ever since he'd first seen her, and when he fi-nally got his chance, he'd make sure his hands were clean. And gentle. He had strong hands, but he knew when to curb his strength. The idea of hurting any woman made him physically ill, but the idea of somehow hurting Nicole . . . no, hurt-ing her was not in the cards.

Fucking her . . . now that was another matter.

The lock on Nicole Pearce's office door had been so easy to pick, it was embarrassing. It had taken two seconds, tops, while she'd been check-ing the time on that fancy wristwatch.

The memory of her slack-jawed surprise when she looked up to see him opening her door had him grinning as he bent forward to check his e-mail. This afternoon he'd get a haircut and a shave and then a half-hour shower before his date, but right now, he wanted to get some work out of the way.

He scanned the subject lines of his e-mails, giving a quick fist pump in the air when he saw NIGHTINGALE LANDED.

He scanned the e-mail, nodding with satisfaction. Twenty-four-year-old Amanda Rogers was now settled in her new life, under a new name and with a new job in Coeur d'Alene, Idaho.

The last time Sam had seen Amanda she'd been perched, trembling and terrified, on the edge of the client chair. A pretty girl, or at least he imagined she was pretty under all the bruising, and if you could ignore the puffy black eye and swollen jaw. One arm had been in a cast. The hand on the other arm clutched the arm of the chair with white-knuckled intensity. The uninjured arm was slender, with a delicate wrist. An enraged man would find it really easy to snap that arm, and an enraged man had. Her boyfriend, who terrified her.

Soon, it wouldn't be snapping a slender, delicate wrist. It would be a slender, delicate neck. Sam knew that. His two brothers, Harry and Mike, knew that. All three of them had grown up with men who loved nothing more than to beat the shit out of those weaker than themselves. Women and children top of the list.

As always, with Amanda, Sam had hidden his feelings under a business-like mask but inside he was seething with rage at the idea of her fuckhead boyfriend beating her to a pulp. The boyfriend was six one, two ten, gym strong, and now in jail. He'd screamed threats to Amanda every step of the way from arrest through booking to the moment when the barred door clicked shut behind him.

Mike had observed him carefully, then had contacted Sam.

Mike had then had a quiet talk with a terrified Amanda at the downtown station and given her a heads-up. The boyfriend had money and was going to make bail. She wasn't going to survive another round of Boyfriend TLC, so Mike quietly sent her to him.

This was what Sam loved doing. It was what he lived for. His brothers, Harry and Mike, too. The runaway success of Reston Security was gratifying. He couldn't have asked for a better outcome. He was his own boss and he was making money hand over fist.

But by God, what he and Harry and Mike got their rocks off on was this. His very own underground railroad. Having the money and the power and the knowledge to subtract women, often with their kids, from the brutal equation of violence. ·

Simply whisk them away to somewhere else where they could have a shot at living a life undarkened by terror. *Man*, it was a good feeling. The best.

The women came to him in trickles. Some brought by Mike, who was in Violence Central there at the SDPD headquarters. Most by word of mouth. The women were tall, short, blonde, brunette, pretty and plain. But they all had the exact same terrified expression and underlying hopelessness. As if they'd already been beaten to death and were just waiting for life to catch up.

Sometimes they were on their own, sometimes—tragically—with a kid or two in tow. Often the kid would be in a cast, or have blue-purple bruises or burns. And Sam would put on his expressionless mask and talk schedules and places and plans. While inside he was a beserker just dying to deal with whoever had broken the thin childish arm or put out a cigarette on tender flesh or swung a fist at a child.

You want to beat up on someone, fuckhead? Why don't you try me instead of a forty-pound child? Except I have spent a lifetime studying martial arts and I will rip your fucking heart out of your fucking body and feed it to you without breaking a sweat. Not so brave now, eh?

Sam never, ever allowed what he was feeling to show on his face. These women and kids had seen enough violence to last them a lifetime. So he quietly helped them disappear and reappear with a new life.

For Sam, it was as if the world had huge holes punched into it by monsters. He spent a lot of time and effort trying to close those holes.

Sam had set Amanda up with a new identity and carefully wiped her trail clean. If she kept her nose clean, she was home safe and free.

Setting her up in her new life with new ID had cost $10,000 and Sam had given her $5,000 in cash as start-up money.

Nightingale, in her new home and new life, had joined dove, falcon, finch, flamingo, gull, heron, hummingbird, ibis, macaw and mockingbird in theirs so far this year. Eleven women and seven kids, safe, because Sam had been able to provide that safety.

His clients funded it. They could all afford it.

Sam opened the file on his ship-owner client and added $15,000 in expenses with a great deal of satisfaction. He'd saved the ship owner more than $10 million; the ship owner could fucking well give something back.

Corporate America, via the US government, had spent millions of dollars training him, including SERE school. The US government had made him an expert at escape and evasion.

It gave him enormous pleasure to make corporate America pay for the lost ones, the weak ones, the ones who slipped through the cracks, the ones no one cared about.

Oh yeah, that felt good.

Man, Nightingale had landed, scumbags were going to prison forever and he had a date with Nicole Pearce. All was right with the world.

"Wow. Sam Reston, smiling. Jesus, break out the beer. What happened? You get word that Colonel Stewart got his balls caught in a thresher?" Colonel Roland Stewart, the sadistic son of a bitch who had been Sam's commanding officer for one and a half years of hell, had left a trail of hatred behind him as he slimed his way up the promotion ladder.

Stewart getting his balls caught in a thresher would definitely qualify for a smile.

"I wish. Son of a bitch's in the Pentagon now, balls secure."

His other brother, Harry Bolt, placed two crutches against the wall and leaned his trembling right shoulder against the door of Sam's office. Sam watched and said nothing. It had all been said before, over and over, loudly, by both Sam and Mike.

Harry had no business trying to stand without crutches. He had no business standing at all, since the last orthopaedic surgeon had said he had to stay in the wheelchair for at least another month while his bones knitted.

Harry was his own worst enemy. Sam had found him a small apartment in his own building in Coronado Shores so he could make sure Harry didn't do something terminally stupid.

Harry had come back from Afghanistan with a broken body and demons in his head only whiskey and, lately, some jazz singer he listened to endlessly in the dark could keep at bay. He couldn't be trusted with his own health. The more the doctors told him to take it easy, the more he rebelled. He'd already fallen badly twice, setting his recovery back by months.

Finally, in exasperation, Sam had asked him to come in to the office, simply so he could keep an eye on him. If Harry fell, at least Sam would be there to catch him.

Reston Security was expanding fast and it sounded natural for Sam to say he needed a hand. But then Harry turned out to be more than just an extra pair of hands—he was an enormous asset to the company. He was better with computers than Sam, a goddamned genius actually, and he had more patience with dumb clients than Sam did, so he was seconded to the array of latest-generation computers in a quiet room off Sam's office and to the Asshole Client Detail.

Harry tried looking nonchalant, bony shoulder pressed hard against the doorjamb for balance, but his legs were trembling.

Sam knew better than to protest. His brother had a head as hard as the steel that held his hip, right thigh and left shoulder together.

Harry ragging on him was brand new, though. Maybe it meant he was healing some. He'd come back from Afghanistan with barely a pulse, and had completely lost his sense of humor.

Sam and Mike were Harry's only family, down in Harry's file as the persons to contact in case of death. When Sam and Mike had flown to Ramstein to take him home, Harry had been more dead than alive.

Worse than the damage to his body had been the damage to his spirit. Like Sam and like Mike, Harry had come through a brutal childhood intact. Whatever had happened in Afghanistan—and so far he wasn't talking—had crushed his spirit.

So Harry taking the piss out of him was new and good.

Sam sat up, shuffled papers, wiped the smile off his face. "Wasn't smiling," he muttered. He rarely smiled. No one knew that better than his brother.

"Was, too."

Sam looked up into his brother's light brown eyes, as fierce as an eagle's and just as warm. "Was not."

"Was, too."

"Was *not*." Sam's jaw clenched at how childish they sounded. "Don't you have work to do? Weren't you supposed to prepare the McIntosh report?"

"Mmm." A corner of Harry's mouth lifted. "Did that last night, while you were having fun along the docks."

A joking Harry was good, but there were limits. "It wasn't fun," Sam snapped.

Harry's slight smile faded. He knew how heavily this two-week wait had weighed on Sam and he knew the reason why. Who knew how many girls were being hurt while Sam had to wait? "No," Harry said soberly. "I know it wasn't. I was just trying to get a rise out of you, God knows why. You've been walking around looking like the Grim Reaper lately."

"Not anymore," Sam said. "Job's done. I notified the client, who's already contacted the authorities. I'll write up the report today. It's over."

"Christ." Harry straightened. He put his crutches under his arms and hobbled into the room. "Wow, that's . . . that's great news. Did you get the evidence to back you up?"

"Damn straight," Sam said with satisfaction. "Photos and digital recordings and even some paperwork. Put those fuckers away for the rest of their natural lives. Which I suspect will be cut tragically short by a shank between the ribs in the prison showers. Nobody likes child rapists."

"Hey, man. Congrats. I'll call Mike and we can go celebrate tonight. On me. Bonus on that sucker'll keep us in tall corn for the next quarter."

"Can't." Sam's eyes slid to the computer monitor, staring into it. There was nothing there he had to see right now, but it kept his face away from Harry's intelligent, perceptive eyes. "Busy tonight."

"So cancel. The three of us need to celebrate."

Sam didn't share blood with Harry, or with Mike, but they were his brothers in every sense of the term. That didn't mean he'd miss his shot at dinner out with Nicole Pearce for Harry or Mike. Tonight was off-limits.

"Can't," he said, bending his head over a piece of paper, pretending to scrutinize it like it was a peace treaty between warring tribes. "Not tonight."

Harry jerked the paper out from under his hands and held it up. "Okay, I get it, you can't talk because you're way too busy with"—he glanced at the paper—"orders for paper and photocopy toner. Uh-huh. Okay, what's going on tonight that's so special?"

Sam glared at him. His very special Death Glare, guaranteed to terrify recruits.

Harry put his crutches to one side and carefully sat on the corner of the desk and looked at him, eyebrows lifted. Sam crossed his arms and set his jaw.

"Not talking, eh?" A corner of Harry's mouth lifted, Harry body language for a full-out grin. "That means I'll have to guess. Okay. I like guessing games. It's obviously not work-related, or you'd have told me all about it, so we're talking a date with a dame. And just as obviously that dame's someone you don't want to blow off, but if you don't want to talk about it, that means it's . . ." He snapped his fingers. "I know! That looker across the hall! The one you've been mooning over. Christ, how'd you swing *that* one? Who'd you have to kill?"

Damn! Sam hated it that Harry was so smart. He hunkered down in his chair, knowing he couldn't take Harry on. Harry's bones were just now resetting, Sam couldn't go breaking any new ones.

But, shit, he didn't want to talk about this. He'd never been one to blab about his sex life, mostly because there'd never been much to talk about. He had sex—lots of it in fact, though lately, work had gotten in the way—but it was never with anyone special. The sex he had was mainly a way to scratch an itch, like eating when hungry. Who wanted to talk about food once you'd eaten your fill? Mostly, one woman was just like another. They satisfied an appetite, and that was about it.

But . . . Nicole Pearce was different. He couldn't

really get a handle on why, but there it was. And he *wasn't* talking about it.

They stared at each other mutely, Sam not talking, Harry trying to crack him open but failing. Finally, Harry gave a big martyred sigh.

"Okay. This is what's going to happen. Right now, you look like a dockworker who's been scamming goods and you smell like one, too. No way in hell you're gonna get lucky with that babe looking and smelling like that. So you're going to get a shave and a haircut and take a long shower. Two of 'em, because *man*—" He waved the air in front of him as if someone had just let rip a massive fart. "You read me? And I'm going to go out with Mike for a beer and we're gonna wait for your report tomorrow morning on your evening out with Ms. Luscious."

"Out," Sam growled, rolling his eyes. "Get out now before I break your bones all over again, and I'll do a better job of it than some fucking Afghani RPG, trust me."

Harry gimped his way out of the office, a half smile on his face. It had been worth it being teased, to see Harry smiling. Sam wasn't much of a smiler himself, but Harry had been to hell and back. This was the first lighthearted exchange he'd had with Harry since he'd been blown up in the Hindu Kush.

Maybe it was the Nicole Pearce Effect. God knows, she had an effect on him, a massive one. Harry said he'd been mooning over her, which was crazy. Sam didn't moon. But he had been . . . interested. Real interested.

He'd timed his comings and goings to get a glimpse of her. Christ, just watching her walk down the hallway toward him had been enough to give him a boner he could use to hammer a nail into the wall.

He knew the basics about her, thanks to her website and Google. Daughter of an ambassador, grew up all over the world, attended the University of Geneva School of Translation, translated from French and Spanish, knew basic Russian and some Arabic.

That really impressed him. Language training was intense in SpecOps. Sam had aced just about everything in training except languages. He had a tin ear for languages, and it had been a real drawback. Still was, as he was starting to have foreign clients.

Though she was an ambassador's daughter, Nicole Pearce didn't live like a woman of privilege. She lived in a house that was worth about half the value of Sam's condo on Coronado Shores. Her income was one twentieth of his. She had founded her company only a year earlier, when she had moved to San Diego to live in the house her maternal grandmother had left her, operating the business out of her home until she'd moved into his building a month ago.

Before opening her own business, she'd worked as a translator for the UN in Geneva.

When, out of curiosity, Sam had looked up the job description, there'd been the income for her UN civil service pay grade. He'd whistled. In Swiss francs, tax free. It was an enormous amount of money. Why had she quit *that* to open a small business in San Diego, taking a huge cut in income?

She was single, which floored him. Never been married, either, which was even harder to believe. Actually, it seemed insane to him. Had she only lived in places where they put saltpeter in the water? Where all the men were gay? What was *wrong* with the men she came across? Because if he hadn't first seen her in the middle of an op when he couldn't break opsec, he'd have been on her tail the instant he caught sight of her moving in across the hallway.

Grew up abroad, owner of new business, single. Those were the facts he was able to find on her in public records. But what the facts on file didn't say was how mind-blowingly beautiful she was. She was the kind of woman who should probably come with a warning sign—*danger ahead*.

The Googleable facts didn't hint at just how fucking classy she was, either. The lady packed a double whammy Sam had never seen before. Throw-on-the-bed sexy and ice princess classy. Elegant, graceful, poised. He'd had to make a cage of his neck muscles not to swivel his head every time she walked by and had had to stop himself, through sheer will power, from sniffing after her like a dog, she smelled that good.

And shit, did she have the princess-to-peon thing down pat. One fulminating look out of those large, uptilted cobalt eyes with the ridiculously long dark lashes, and she could reduce any male to a whimpering mass of protoplasm. On days when he'd looked particularly reprehensible, he got looks that would have killed a lesser man.

But Sam was a tough guy. He liked challenges.

A corner of his mouth tilted upward.

Mostly because he always won.

Grand Port Maritime
Marseilles, France
June 28

Jean-Paul Simonet, an aging, lowly clerk in the back office of the Port of Marseilles, knew the shipping company Vega Maritime Transport well. It was a small one, running only three ships, if that's what you could call the rust buckets flying Liberian flags that plied the seas in its name. The company's ships were known among the port staff for cutting safety corners, sailing understaffed, even smuggling in crates of contraband goods. Cigarettes. Twice, arms shipments. Once, packets of white powder.

Which meant there was always money to get port authorities to look the other way.

The shipping company was owned by a consortium of shady dealers who would close the company down and disappear in a heartbeat if one of their rust buckets ever caused an accident.

Today, the *Marie Claire* was in port. The *Marie Claire*'s crew had changed numerous times over the years. It currently had a Turkish captain and crew from twenty different countries, and it was on its last legs. Somewhere, in some office in some third-world country, a group of men around a table had decided that they could wring some more profit out of these rickety single-hulled ships, reckoning that if they stopped paying for maintenance, they could run the ship until every last penny could be squeezed out of it, and when it was no longer seaworthy, it could be scuttled at night in the middle of the ocean, out of sight of surveillance satellites, and they could collect the insurance money.

Profit all around.

Simonet's boss, that *merde* Boisier, always looked the other way when Vega Maritime's ships came into port.

Simonet had no loyalty to the Port Authority. He was underpaid, was a year from retirement, and was heart-broken over the loss of his family. He didn't give a shit one way or the other.

He got the trickle-down effect from Boisier—ten cartons of Marlboros, a box of men's sweaters made in China, once a dozen bottles of Glenfiddich. He knew it was nothing compared to what Boisier pulled in to look the other way, to not raise a fuss over any safety inadequacies and to expedite the shipping company's passage through

Marseilles. That *con* Boisier drove a brand-new Mercedes S class on a civil servant's salary. Simonet drove a fifteen-year-old Citroen.

The way of the world was right there.

Taking care of the Vega Maritime shipments was Boisier's concern, but he wasn't here today. A violent case of the *grippe*, Simonet had heard. Served *le con* right.

The only thing was, expediting the company's ship's transit through the port was now his concern. The captain of the *Marie Claire* had failed to file an F–45 and Simonet had to go out to collect it because the captain wasn't responding to his cell phone. Without the form, the next port of call wouldn't accept the ship.

It was the hottest day of the year so far, with 100 percent humidity. It was almost half a kilometer from Simonet's air-conditioned office in the customs house to the bulk terminal where the stinking, rusty *Marie Claire* was waiting. For a moment, Simonet was tempted to just let it go. Fuck it. Fuck them. He could have a heart attack walking half a kilometer along the dock in the broiling sun, unless he could grab one of the electric carts the *fonctionnaires* used.

But if he didn't go, Boisier would miss out on his bribe and take it out on him. Boisier was a master of bureaucratic rules and could make Simonet's life miserable in any number of ways. Simonet was retiring in December, all he wanted was to keep his head down. So, okay, he'd make the trek out to the end of the dock, make sure the captain filled out the form and come back. He'd let Boisier know what he'd done. Boisier could pick up his bribe next time around and he'd better be grateful to Simonet.

Simonet only found a cart about a hundred meters from where the *Marie Claire* was moored. He stopped the cart on the dockside and looked up with disgust at the *Marie Claire*. It was a miracle she hadn't already sunk under the weight of the rust. She was scheduled to sail out at 1600 hours. Her entire crew should have been on deck, preparing the ship for departure, but Simonet couldn't see a soul.

Merde, he was going to have to do this the hard way. Grumbling to himself, he walked up the broad gangplank, looking around when he reached the deck. He was aft, near the forecastle, and completely alone on deck.

This was strange, and slightly eerie. Ship decks just before departure were hives of activity. Time was money, and docking at the harbor unnecessarily was expensive.

Simonet walked along the side of the ship, next to the huge containers that filled the mid-ship line. Doubtless there were double the number of containers belowdecks.

He finally reached the stern section, the radar tower and stack rising high above him. He still had not seen anybody. Simonet eyed the ladder leading up to the bridge and the chart room with loathing. It was steaming hot and this was way beyond the call of duty. Fuck Boisier.

But then again, Boisier definitely had the ability to make his life truly miserable in the remaining six months on the job. With a huge sigh, Simonet started climbing and was dripping with sweat and feeling faint by the time he got to the chart room, where most captains spent their time while docked.

Empty. *Merde.*

It was perfectly pointless calling out, because of the noise of the overhead cranes. He'd simply have to go through the ship looking for the captain.

Simonet found the ladder down into the hold and scurried down it, welcoming the slightly cooler temperature belowdecks. There was some noise at the end of a long corridor and he followed it, making no attempt to soften his footsteps. Men's voices, low and sonorous, concentrating on a task. He heard the sounds of hammers striking metal. Probably trying to repair the rust bucket themselves, without calling in the shipyard crew.

Simonet reached the end of the corridor—and froze. He took in at a glance a scene that sent ice through his veins, understanding it instantly. Heart thudding with fear, he backed slowly away, the form fluttering unnoticed to the deck.

He couldn't be seen! These men were heartless, utterly ruthless. Unworthy of the name of human beings. They didn't hesitate to massacre women and children. A low-level clerk was nothing to them.

Where he'd walked down the corridor without any attempt at quiet, he now flattened himself against the bulkhead, wishing he could simply melt into it, through it.

Oh God, he had to get out without being seen.

The longer he stayed, the greater were his chances of being discovered. Simonet moved as fast as he could back down the corridor, throwing frantic glances behind him. The men he'd seen were armed. He was totally defenseless in this steel corridor, an unmissable target. He had no idea what kind of noise he was making because he couldn't hear anything above the thudding of his heart in his ears.

By some miracle, by the grace of God, Simonet managed to make it up on deck and down off the ship without being seen. He found the electric cart where he'd left it, and ten minutes later, he was locking his office door behind him, sweating profusely, gulping in air, totally terrorized.

Oh God, oh God.

This was ten million times worse than cigarettes or contraband goods or even cocaine. This was *terrorism*. This was what had taken his two daughters, Hélène and Josiane, on that terrible day in Madrid. March 11, 2004. Nine hundred and eleven days after 9/11. The day his world ended.

He could still remember frantically calling the French Embassy in Madrid because his two daughters, his two treasures, were visiting Madrid, thinking—*my two darlings will call me and tell me they've been out shopping or visiting a museum or flirting with handsome young Spanish men.*

But it wasn't to be. Josiane and Hélène had been on the train coming into Atocha Station, and had been blown apart. Someone had pressed a detonating device that turned human beings into human hamburger, including his beloved daughters.

Simonet had travelled to Madrid and brought his daughters home in body bags that contained small body parts instead of bodies. And he'd come home to a wife whose broken heart had simply given out during the night.

The jihadists had cost him everything he held dear, everything he had in the world, and he made it his business to study everything about them. He bought books, read magazine and newspaper articles, watched Al Jazeera, attended night courses on the history of Islam. Over the past few years, he'd become an expert on Islamic terrorism.

So Jean-Paul Simonet had understood immediately the significance of what he'd seen in the hold of the *Marie Claire*. If he closed his eyes, he could see it as if he were right there again, standing terrified and quaking in the doorway.

Ten crew members working on the door to a secret cavity that had been cut out of one of the holds. Simonet could see into the cavity, see the air mattresses, the stock of bottles of mineral water and several large canisters with the black-and-yellow international biohazard sign.

And most terrifying of all, at least forty men, prostrate at prayers just inside the door. Forty men with *shaheed* jackets stacked on one side and lime green scarves around their shoulders, just waiting to become *shaheed batal*—martyr heroes.

Terrorists. Headed for New York with bombs

strapped around their torsos and access to radioactive material. Simonet's fingers trembled as he fumbled for the phone, dropping the cordless receiver in his haste. His hands were slick with sweat, he could barely breathe around the terror in his chest. His fingers punched in 17, the emergency gendarmerie number, but he hung up almost immediately. This information was too important to be given to a telephone operator.

His brother-in-law knew the *Commissaire de Police.* That's it—he'd plead a headache and leave early. There would be suspicions if the police swarmed his office building, people would talk, his name would be known. If there was one thing Simonet knew, it was that these people were vicious. He didn't have much to live for but by God, he didn't want to die at the hands of these *canailles.*

No, much better to leave early and go downtown to the *Commissariat* and speak with the *Commissaire* himself.

Having a plan calmed him down a little, until he heard footsteps coming down the hallway.

No one came to his office in the early afternoon. Were they coming for *him?* He stood, terrified, listening as the steps came closer, closer. Two sets, two men.

The information! He had to get it out!

His eyes fell on the list of files to be sent out for translation. Perfect. Simonet knew his way around computers and he knew steganography. Inside of five seconds he managed to hide the necessary information in a file. He pressed ENTER and turned at the sound of his door opening.

Two men, one small and armed, the other huge and unarmed, burst into the room. The big one stepped forward and with a contemptuous twist of his big hands, snapped Simonet's neck.

The big man opened his hands and Simonet's lifeless body collapsed to the floor. Simonet's last thought had been of the thousands, perhaps millions, of Americans he had saved from attacks he hoped he had stopped.

Chapter 3

San Diego

Nicole held up the eight-year-old Dior and the seven-year-old Narciso Rodriguez, one a flattering periwinkle blue, one a chic black. Blue, black, blue . . . she couldn't decide.

It was a very good thing that she hadn't lost or gained weight over the past few years because there was no way she could now afford a new Dior or a new Rodriguez. Caring for her father ate up every spare dollar and then some.

That was okay. She didn't miss her heady days in Geneva—young, single and rich. She'd had those years, enjoyed them, and now they were over.

She was a little less young now, still single and far from rich. Her life had changed beyond recognition. But she didn't mind. It was worth scrambling to be able to take care of her father.

Black, blue, black . . .

It wasn't like her to be so indecisive. And *late*.

When was the last time she'd been late for anything, let alone a date? No, not a date—an appointment. An agreement. Dinner-out-as-thank-you-for-unlocking-her-door. Whatever—just not a date.

And yet here she was, dithering about what she was going to wear, argh!

This was so crazy. What was she doing, going out with a man she didn't know? Had only exchanged a few words with? Would have crossed the street to avoid only yesterday?

It had never even occurred to her that the low-life she'd seen walking into and out of Reston Security might actually be the owner of the company. Clearly, security-company executives didn't need to dress for success. Every time she'd seen the man in the corridor he looked like he was coming off a drunk—incredibly scruffy, pissed off and none too clean.

As soon as she got off the phone with the hedge fund manager and her Russian experts, having happily negotiated an excellent contract, she'd checked out the website for Reston Security and had read the bio for Sam Reston. It was a long one. He was ex-military, a former SEAL, in fact. She remembered he said he'd been in the Navy. Well, that was modest of him. Being a SEAL was a little bit more than having spent some time in the Navy. SEALs were elite soldiers who underwent a gruelling selection process. As a soldier, Sam Reston had been the best of the best.

He didn't list his medals but there they were on his chest in the formal military photograph, for those who knew how to read them. Nicole was familiar with Special Forces. It was quite likely there were other medals in a shadowbox he would take to the grave with him for missions no one would ever know about, secret to the end of time.

He didn't have the Marine high-and-tight she was so familiar with from Embassies around the world, but his hair in the picture was definitely military-short and he was clean shaven.

The grim expression was the same, though. She'd been right. Take away the military trappings and he still looked like one dangerous dude. The kind of man she ordinarily wouldn't speak to, let alone spend an evening with.

But she'd given her word and that was that.

Still, it looked like there was much more to Sam Reston than met the eye. The medals, for one.

Nicole's father had always drummed into her enormous respect for the US Armed Forces. Her father had served in places where often the US military was the only thing that stood between civilization and the abyss.

The medals on Sam Reston's very broad chest weren't there for showing up on time or keeping his shoes and brightwork shined. They were medals of valor, for bravery under fire.

She'd swallowed heavily as she perused his website, letting the facts filter in, changing perceptions.

He'd been a very successful soldier and he was now a highly successful businessman.

Not an angry drunk, after all.

So she had to peel a layer of fear off the strong reactions she'd had to him every time their paths crossed in the Morrison Building's hallway, which had been often. Sometimes she'd wondered if he had some kind of radar. More often than not, when she'd turned around from locking up her office door, there he had been, behind her, just closing the door of the company he worked for. *His* company, she now had to remember. He seemed to have been just behind her or just in front of her every single time she moved from the building. And every single time, her entire body had gone haywire.

Every cell in her body had stood to attention in his presence. He often seemed to be going to the office when everyone else in the building was knocking off for the day. She'd been intensely aware of his presence even when he was behind her, as if she were made of iron filings and he were the lodestone.

This morning, it was only paralyzing anxiety that had kept her from sensing him behind her. At all other times, she'd had a sixth sense for his presence.

At the time, she'd thought it was fear. He *looked* so utterly frightening. Terrifying, actually.

She'd never seen male power like that up close before. His muscles were long and lean, not bulging, and looked as if they were used, and used hard instead of being for show, as most modern men's muscles were nowadays. It was as if Sam Reston belonged to another race of man.

Tougher, stronger, faster, bigger.

A bell rang downstairs and Nicole started. Oh my God! It was seven and she still wasn't dressed!

Luckily, Manuela would be there to open the door, since her father couldn't. It saved Nicole from having to run down the stairs in bra and panties with no makeup on and still-drying fingernails. Wouldn't that be a way to greet Mr. Sam Reston, former US Navy SEAL?

It wasn't like her at all to run late for a date, but she'd been running late all day. She'd only made it back home half an hour ago, craving a long, cool shower, but her father had waylaid her when she got in. He was agitated about an article on the government's response to the latest bombing in Indonesia.

Her father had spent three years as ambassador to Indonesia and was infinitely better informed than the hapless State Department mouthpieces or the hacks who covered the press conference on the bombing.

It was such a pity that his illness prevented him from sharing his experience and expertise. Nicole's heart ached for him. He had been planning a rewarding retirement of lecturing, writing newspaper articles, starting up a diplomacy blog. Finally finishing that book on the diplomacy of the Medici he'd been writing forever. The sudden onset of cancer had shot those plans down.

To Nicole, her father was the very embodiment of light and reason and goodness. The very best of humankind. She'd never seen him do or say a dishonorable thing. The world desperately needed men like him and yet his light would soon be snuffed out by illness. Even desperately ill, often in pain, he remained kind and considerate. Never complaining. It was breaking her heart.

Nicholas Pearce had always been her hero. Tall and handsome and smart and affectionate, the very best. A wonderful husband and father. She'd grown up feeling her family was blessed. Then they lost her mother in a car crash and now he had stage-four brain cancer, diagnosed a year ago.

That was when Nicole quit her job with the UN in Geneva to take care of him. It wasn't easy, taking care of a severely ill man, but there was no question in her mind. He'd been a wonderful father to her all her life. Taking care of him in his time of need was a privilege.

However, having a very sick father wreaked havoc on her love life. One whiff of what she was dealing with, and a lot of men who'd been very interested in a date suddenly lost interest.

It was her little test. As her philosophy professor in college would have put it, being able to deal with her father was a necessary but not sufficient condition for her to think of hooking up with a man.

If the man in question could deal with her life and all its troubles, fine. They might just take it a step or two further. If not . . . good-bye. If you wanted her, she came with her father. They were a package deal.

She'd had a lot of good-byes before the relationships even started, and now that her father was deteriorating so rapidly, she wasn't open to dating at all.

Not that tonight was a *date*, of course. It was a thank-you.

Blue, black, blue, black . . .

Blue, she finally decided. The periwinkle blue polished cotton sheath paired with a black linen jacket. After ten years of Swiss winters, San Diego's mild climate never failed to delight her.

Makeup! My God, there was no way she could go down with a naked face.

She glanced at her watch and shuddered. Twenty minutes late, unheard of for her. Nicole dressed and made up in record time and started descending the stairs when she suddenly stopped, transfixed.

There was her father downstairs, facing her, sitting in the fabulous wheelchair she'd bought with part of her severance pay from the UN. It did everything but make coffee and sing. He had a celebratory finger of whiskey in a crystal glass on the occasional table at his elbow and Sam had his own glass of twenty-year-old Talisker. Guests were few and far between and her father rejoiced at visits.

Sam Reston was sitting across from her father—she couldn't see his face but she could see his shoulders, so broad they overshot the chair back—clad in an expensive midnight blue suit.

But what had her blocked at the top of the staircase, one foot up, one foot down on the first step, was the expression on her father's face. He was . . .

happy. He looked animated and there was color in his cheeks. His eyes—the color so like her own—sparkled. No doubt he'd been telling one of his wicked jokes.

She hadn't told Sam Reston that she lived with her father and that her father was ill. She hadn't told him anything, in fact. So when he came to the door expecting to find a woman to take out to dinner, he'd been confronted with a visibly very ill man. An ill man he'd made smile.

Sam Reston just kept on moving up the scale. Lowlife to security company owner to guy who made her father smile. That last attribute was the best one.

Her father's gaze shifted and his smile broadened. "Hello, darling."

"Hi, Pops." Smiling at her father's expression, she walked down the staircase. If he was happy, even for a fleeting moment, then so was she.

Sam turned in his seat and their eyes met.

Nicole stopped. Everything in her stopped—head, lungs, legs. It was like taking a punch to the stomach. All the air left her system. His dark eyes were so intense, it was as if they were hands, reaching out to touch her. She could hardly breathe, hardly think.

She'd always seen him looking grim and dirty and dangerous. Now he still looked deadly serious, two hundred plus pounds of male potency, completely focused on her. His eyes made a quick trip down to her feet then back up to her face. With anyone else, she would have bridled at the blatant male once-over. Somehow Sam Reston managed to make it not insulting but . . . arousing.

At any rate, *he* was certainly aroused. Those dark eyes were full of heat; under the olive-toned skin of his sharp cheekbones was a faint wash of red, and it wasn't a blush of shyness.

There was pure sex in his look, powerfully potent, stronger than anything she'd ever felt from a man before. It sapped the strength right out of her knees and her hand went reflexively to the railing for support. She stood there for a long moment under his heated gaze.

It was only a lifetime's intense training in diplomatic circles where you never, ever showed your true feelings that got her feet moving again. She barely felt them as she descended the stairs, watched by the big dark man sitting across from her father.

It didn't help that he cleaned up fantastically well. During the course of the day he'd managed to make it to a barber. An expensive one. His hair—long, unkempt and greasy—was now shiny clean and beautifully cut, showing off the elegant shape of his head.

She'd never seen him in anything other than torn, grungy jeans and filthy tee shirts. Now he seemed like another man entirely, dressed in a well-cut midnight blue suit, white cotton shirt and burgundy silk tie. Now he looked like the businessman he was, and a highly successful one at that.

And that businessman watched her intently, step by step.

Her father, normally so astute and alive to the ways of the world, wasn't paying attention. He'd been caught up in the conversation and was excited at the company. Thoughtlessly, he reached for his whiskey and sideswiped the glass.

Oh no!

Nicole ran the few steps to her father, catching the glass just as it was about to shatter on the table.

Her father looked appalled, the high color of joy gone from his face. Nicholas Pearce, so graceful all his life, with an athlete's build and coordination, which had been a pure gift from the gods because he never exercised, had become clumsy. The tumors were robbing him of his fine motor control. The loss had come so quickly, he often forgot he couldn't control his muscles. He pulled his shaking hand back, stricken. He hated making a mess when it was just the two of them. In front of company it was even more humiliating.

Nicole's heart gave a hard squeeze in her chest. She knew very well how crushed he felt inside, to have almost spilled a drink in front of a perfect stranger, a stranger whose company he was enjoying. Company was a real treat these days.

How lonely her father must be. He spent his days alone in a wheelchair, with the housekeeper for company during the day and a tired daughter in the evenings.

Losing weight, growing weaker, day by day.

Dying was so hard.

She put a reassuring hand on his shoulder, picking up the glass, curving his hand around it. "Sorry to be so late," she said to Sam Reston.

He'd instinctively started to rise to help her father, but a fleeting touch of his shoulder as she passed by and he subsided. Smart man.

"That's fine," he said easily. "It gave me an opportunity to talk to your dad, here. We were both in Jakarta at the same time."

She casually held the whiskey glass to her father's lips, watching him out of the corner of her eye. A slight tilt and he took a sip. She placed the glass back on the table next to him, movements natural and unobtrusive. Her father had his sip without making a mess, and without being humiliated.

"Doing slightly different things," her father said.

"Yes, sir, that we were." An unexpected smile broke out on Sam Reston's hard face, the first she'd ever seen from him. She nearly did a double-take. It didn't soften that hard face but it did highlight the strong features, making him look almost . . . handsome. "Our doings were less respectable than yours, sir, but we were still serving the same guy. Uncle Sam."

Oh God, he shouldn't smile, Nicole thought. No, no, no. She had schooled herself to get through this evening purely as a thank-you for opening her door when she was so desperate, and because she'd given her word.

She didn't want to be attracted.

She didn't want this to be a date, not in any

way. This *wasn't* a date, not at all. She'd dithered over the dress simply because . . . because she always tried to look as good as possible, it was in her nature. And the sucker punch to her stomach when he'd turned to look at her? Surprise at seeing him in businessman mode.

She was perfectly prepared to spend a very boring couple of hours with Mr. Muscle as a thank-you, to pay off a debt. Drive with him to some bland restaurant, eat white-bread food, listen to him talk about himself—in her experience, men's conversations ranged from their jobs to their latest toys and back, seldom deviating—lock her jaw so she wouldn't yawn, be driven back home, fend off the gropes, say good night, be back in the house with a sigh of relief before ten.

Nothing she hadn't done hundreds of times before. Her standard date.

Spending an evening with a man who made her father laugh, and who had a charming, rakish smile in him—no, that wasn't in the program at all.

Not to mention a man who could punch all the breath out of her body with a mere look.

Nicole had no time for a man in her life. None. She had a very sick father. He was deteriorating almost daily. Each day brought some new heartbreaking loss.

Keeping a serene façade for him while she watched him die, slowly, inch by inch, was eating her alive.

Her entire life revolved around her father's illness, as she tried to keep them afloat.

There was no time for a man, for a love life. The only things she could allow into her life were caring for her father and work.

Sam needed to know that, as soon as possible. That look he'd given her meant business. He had to know that there was no possibility of anything between them.

He stood, bent over her father and briefly held his hand, pretending not to notice that her father's hand shook in his.

"It was a pleasure to meet you, Ambassador Pearce. I look forward to talking to you again."

Her father's cheeks were pink again with pleasure.

"The p-p-pleasure was a-all m-m-mine, I assure y-y-you." Pops was tired. When his scarce physical resources ran down, he started stuttering. Nicole went quietly into the kitchen and signalled to Manuela that it was time for dinner and then bed.

Manuela came into the room with a broad smile, wiping her hands on her apron.

Sam waited until Manuela was bent over her father and, with a nod of his head and a murmured "ma'am" to Manuela, he took Nicole's elbow and walked her out the door.

They descended the stairs and walked down the driveway in unison. Nicole realized he was shortening his strides for her. He seemed to be somehow attuned to her movements, though he wasn't looking at her at all. He was scanning the street ahead. Still, she got the distinct impression that though his attention was focused on the road ahead, he'd catch her if she were to trip on her very pretty and very impractical sandals.

Across the street, the curtains of the window of the living room opened and Creepy peeped out, then Creepier. She suppressed a shudder.

When her grandparents had bought this house in the early sixties, it had been an upper-middle-class area, the perfect place for a couple to bring up a family during the Kennedy years. Safe and ordered and prosperous. Nicole had heard her mother talk often and affectionately about life on Mulberry Street, among families that knew one another and socialized often.

But something had happened to the street after Meredith Loren grew up to marry Nicholas Pearce and spend the next thirty-five years abroad. Nicole didn't know whether it was because of demographics or economics or whether someone had put a hex on the area. Whatever had happened, it had turned the whole area into a receptacle for the lost and the hopeless, people on the last rung before falling into the void.

The big house across the street where her mother's best friend had once lived had changed hands twenty times and was now a run-down rooming house owned by an absentee landlord and inhabited by the saddest people imaginable. Poor single mothers barely scraping by, shabby middle-aged divorced men who had just lost their tenth job in a year, the odd illegal immigrant keeping his head down.

And, worse, it seemed to be Club Drifter—a place where angry, unbalanced young men congregated and spat their rage at the world. There were two in particular, one black and one white, both dreadlocked and heavily pierced, both with pant crotches down to their knees, both either high or drunk at all hours.

Both fixated on her.

If they happened to see her, it was like some inaudible signal had been beamed to dogs. They'd stiffen, start whistling, calling out obscenities. Nicole's only defense was to get into her car as quickly as possible, hit the locks, and pull out, fast. The other day, horribly, the blond had moved fast and knocked on the passenger-side window of her car just as she was getting in. She'd closed the locks with a *whump* and taken off as quickly as she could, heart pounding.

The whole thing was incredibly . . . unpleasant, to say the least.

And there they were, both of them. Just her luck. As if the door closing behind her were a secret signal, Creepy came out on the porch followed by Creepier.

Sam felt her stiffen, followed her gaze, and tightened his hand on her elbow.

They started with the cat calls and whistles, loud enough to pierce eardrums. Nicole watched her feet and walked as fast as she could. Experience had taught her that looking at them, acknowledging their existence, only made things worse.

She and Sam walked down the street together

as he calmly escorted her to his car, a late-model, dark blue BMW. He seated her in the passenger seat and walked around to the driver's side. He stopped for a second before getting in, looking out over the roof at the two creeps grinning and whistling from the porch.

She knew what they were seeing. A guy dressed like a businessman who . . . wasn't. When he'd seen the two, he had instantly morphed into the soldier he'd been. Amazing. She'd been standing next to him, thinking he was so very *big* when the air around him became supercharged and he grew even bigger.

The man had been a Special Forces soldier, a Navy SEAL, for God's sake, and had won a chestful of medals. He beat Creepy and Creepier on the male scale, hands down.

All she saw was a chunk of male torso through the driver's window but the two creeps must have seen more, because the whistling and cat calls stopped, as abruptly as if someone had put a hand around their throats and squeezed.

Males are, above all, animals. Herd animals, with a very keen instinct for the alpha male and when to keep out of his way.

Just a minute's look, and the creeps' eyes were on the ground in subconscious submission, another minute and they sullenly turned and slouched back inside, slamming the front door closed.

Never, ever, in a million years could Nicole have achieved that, not even with a gun in her hand, let alone with a look.

Sam got into the driver's seat, jaw muscles jumping. As soon as he was seated, he activated the locks.

"It's truly a man's world," Nicole said, sighing. "I could never quell them with a look."

"No, you couldn't." He shot a look at the front porch, then his gaze shifted back to hers. He reached over her, pulled down her seat belt, latched it. His shoulders were so broad they blocked out the evening light from the driver's-door window when he turned to her. "Is that their usual MO? Standing on the porch, shouting and whistling at you as if you were a dog?"

"Yes." Nicole sighed. Tense muscles started relaxing again. It was almost impossible to feel afraid inside the big, safe, locked car with Sam Reston at the wheel. "I think that they have a very narrow behavioral repertoire."

His dark serious gaze met hers. "Are they escalating? Becoming more forward? Because that's what punks like them do. Feel for the boundaries, then push until you push back. You're not going to pull a gun on them. If you were, you would have already. So they take one step forward. Then another."

Were they escalating? They'd moved in a month ago. Or maybe not moved in. They just appeared, like mold, out of nowhere. The first week they'd stared out of the front window at her. Then they came out on the porch and stared. It was unnerving, but she dealt with it. By the time she got to the corner, she'd forgotten they existed. The second week the whistles and cat calls started, together with rude gestures. It took her the entire drive downtown to shake the disgust from her system. The other day, when Creepy knocked on the car window, well, that had been truly frightening.

"I think—I think they might be escalating," she said quietly. There. She'd put it into words, that vague sense of unease hanging like a gray cloud in the back of her mind. "One of them knocked on the window as I took off the other day. I remember thinking that I could have been in trouble if the car hadn't started."

He nodded. "I was afraid of that. There are things you can do to block the escalation. Even better, there are things I can do . . ."

He left it hanging in the air.

Nicole closed her eyes in relief. Oh God, *yes*.

Let the Dreaded Dreadlocks problem go. Just tip it into those broad, tanned, very capable-looking hands. There was no doubt that Sam could deal with the punks with almost embarrassing ease, much much more easily than she could ever hope to. He'd frozen them literally with a look.

The temptation to let him handle the two punks was so strong she had to dig her nails into the palms of her hands to bring herself back to reality.

Having him take care of this problem for her was a huge temptation. But—she didn't know Sam Reston at all. He wasn't her partner in any way. If he warned off the Creeps by acting as her proxy, and she never saw him again, they'd notice and double the harassment.

"No," she said reluctantly. "I think I'd better handle it. Or try to."

He nodded, but didn't switch on the engine yet. He sat, big hands curved around the steering wheel, looking at her.

"Tell you what." His gaze went past her to where two thuggish faces looked out the porch window. He gave a sharp punch to the horn and the faces disappeared, the dingy beige curtain fluttering back into place. "My brother Mike is a cop. I can have him drive by a couple of times in a patrol car. Stop in front of your house and say hello. That way they know you have the cops at your back."

"That would be wonderful. Thank you." Nicole tried to keep the relief out of her voice. It was a perfect solution. Enough of a deterrent to keep the two thugs off her case, without it being directly linked to Sam Reston. It was an elegant solution. "That sounds great. I'm very grateful."

"His name's Mike Keillor and he'll stop by tomorrow. I'll give you his number."

"Perfect. I'll—" She stopped. "Keillor? I thought you said he was your brother."

"He is, in every way that counts." Well, that was intriguing. Sam didn't elaborate.

"Okay. Having him stop by a couple of times would be a big help. I think those two are dumber than they are nasty, but—"

"You can be stupid and dangerous at the same time." Sam's mouth tightened. "The world's full of very stupid and very dangerous ass—men."

"I grew up all over the world," she answered. "I know that deep in my bones."

She smiled at him. He was still turned toward her, a set expression on his face. However grim he looked, he'd actually been very kind, finding a good solution to a thorny problem while allowing her to save face.

Instead of putting the car in motion, as she expected him to, he leaned forward and gave her a kiss. A peck, really. But Nicole somehow found it hard to breathe. She huffed out a little breath of air, opened her mouth—and nothing came out.

She could object, of course. It was beyond forward to assume that he could simply up and . . . and kiss her. Just like that. But Nicole knew herself and knew that pretending to be outraged wouldn't work, because it would be a lie. The brief kiss had been far from unpleasant. Unsettling and unnerving, but not unpleasant.

It had been like coming into fleeting contact with something immensely powerful, something that could burn if the contact was too close. She could almost hear the hum of power coming from him.

He started up the engine and was pulling out before she could react. He was staring straight ahead but she felt he was aware of her every move. Soldiers developed good situational awareness, as they called it.

"I've been wanting to do that since I first saw you moving in." The deep voice was matter-of-fact, stating something obvious. He slanted a quick glance at her, not grinning like a male who'd made an advance. No, he was deadly serious, as if stating a military objective. "It was better than I imagined."

Nicole huffed out a breath from a suddenly tight chest. She had no comeback, none at all.

New York
June 28

He was tall, blond and blue-eyed. Very fair, prone to freckling in the sun. Courtesy, no doubt, of a Crusader who had raped one of his ancestors in Acre, bequeathing the cowardly genes of the West. The cowardice had been bred out of him by centuries of Arab warriors, but the coloring remained.

He didn't mind. It was a gift from Allah. His weapon against the infidels, to be used to the fullest, *imshallah*. He'd been born for this. Born to fit in with the unclean. Born for revenge.

Muhammed Wahed, aka Paul Preston, had the perfect cover. A Manhattan stockbroker, one of the tens of thousands toiling in the money mills on Wall Street. It was a genuine cover. He'd studied economics at Stanford and had made more than $10 million in the past five years investing in futures. He was one of few traders to profit in the recession.

Most of the money had gone to "the Cause." Freedom for Palestine. The destruction of the Jews. And where better to make the money for that destruction than in the belly of the beast, Manhattan?

His brethren in Hamas had worked hard on this. Twenty years training him to blend in, and three years of planning, of procurement, evading the sensors of the NSA and the spies who were everywhere.

Muhammed had worked a lifetime for what would happen over a few hours in five days' time. The day before the celebration of the Fourth of July. An apt moment to bring America down. By the Fourth of July, Manhattan would be a wasteland and America brought to her knees.

The plan was perfect. Forty martyrs in a secret hold of a ship. Several canisters of cesium 137, to be apportioned in equal parts to the martyrs. Forty martyrs wearing *shaheed* explosive belts laced with radioactive cesium, detonating at the same moment on July 3 throughout Manhattan.

Muhammed knew Manhattan, knew exactly where the financial nerve points were. He'd pinpointed forty buildings, the very nerve centers of the American and the world economy. Banks, brokerage houses, hedge funds. The SEC. The Federal Reserve Bank of New York.

The martyrs didn't have to go up to the offices,

necessarily, though Muhammed had made appointments under false names with the CEOs and directors and presidents for all of them. But if they couldn't make it to the heart of the buildings, it would be enough to enter the lobbies and blow themselves up to make the buildings uninhabitable. The tens of thousands of workers in the buildings would have to exit from the irradiated lobbies and would never go back to work again. Only hazmat teams would ever enter the buildings. By the next day, all of Manhattan would be evacuated.

All the paperwork, the computers holding the economy together—gone. Completely unusable. All the drones working in the financial mills—dying of radiation poisoning.

Perfect.

Finishing the work begun on September 11 and making the entire island a radioactive desert for thirty years, the way the West had made his homeland a desert.

Western capitalism would be no more.

Bringing the West to its knees had been his dream since he had been recruited into the organization at the age of ten.

They'd found him in the camps, a homeless orphan, scrounging scraps from the destitute, dressed in rags, this blond, blue-eyed, light-skinned freak.

They had taken him in, given him a family and a purpose. He was like an arrow, aimed straight at the heart of the corrupt and licentious West. Hamas had brought in tutors, instructing him not only in the language of the West, English, but in its ways.

At times, he had sensed that they were afraid that he would succumb to its lures, but there was no risk of that. None. There was no honor and no solidarity to be found among the infidels. Muhammed's heart and soul belonged forever to Hamas and to his people, to the day of his death.

They'd fought, his handlers and him. He wanted to become a warrior, *shaheed*, a martyr. It was the purest life he could imagine, exacting vengeance against the countries who were trying to crush Islam. Giving his life up seemed like the noblest purpose he could imagine.

But it was felt that the gift of his coloring, his looks, was too precious to waste. So Muhammed watched with sullen jealousy as other young men in the secret training camps were dispatched to meet a noble warrior's death while he spent his days and nights with tutor after tutor, instilling in him the ability to infiltrate the enemy with ease, the better to destroy him.

English, French, literature, music, math, science. And the terrible pop culture of the West, filled with shameless movies and music, whoreish women and soulless men. His head was filled with the useless knowledge necessary to pass as one of them. It turned out that he even had an aptitude for studies, which in his secret heart filled him with as much shame as his appearance. His young heart had ached to be just like his brethren, to move and live with them as one. But he'd been told over and over again that Allah had singled him out for a special mission.

That which had singled him out as a homeless boy in the camps, made everyone look at him with loathing and suspicion, was to be used in the name of Allah to slay their enemies.

So Muhammed studied hard, becoming well versed in the ways of the West. An identity was created: Paul Preston.

One entire edge of the Strip borders the Mediterranean. It was easy enough to smuggle him out and get him into Italy, where he emerged in Rome with a new US passport and a business-class ticket to California.

He was sent to Stanford to study economics, where he excelled. It was his way of combating the enemy, by studying its face, understanding its corrupt black soul.

He *became* Paul Preston, born of an American father and an English mother. He graduated summa cum laude in economics, with a network of future movers and shakers to use.

He was set up in Manhattan with a million dollars and orders to join a brokerage firm. Hamas's backers had plenty of money, and had been willing to write the sum off.

But it turned out that Muhammed was clever in the ways of the Great Satan. The million soon grew to five, then ten. He developed a solid reputation as a very good, very careful steward of money.

They bought him an apartment on the Upper

East Side that was perfect for someone of his so-
cioeconomic status. Muhammed—now Paul—
had a season ticket to the Met, wintered at Vail
and summered at Martha's Vineyard.

And all this time, his brethren's plans were
developing, all the pieces being put in place.
Equipment bought or stolen, martyrs recruited.
Radioactive material slowly acquired.

Finally, finally, the time had come. Muhammed
had begun despairing of ever being of use to the
Cause, when suddenly a message arrived. An encrypted DVD in his mailbox, with instructions on
how to destroy it once he had absorbed its message.

How his heart had pounded, how proud he had
been of his brothers, of the plan a hooded brother
had laid out on the disk. It was sheer genius.

Forty men, walking dirty bombs.

All those years of study and work would finally
pay off. The Brotherhood needed Muhammed's
help in knowing where to aim these human dag-
gers. They needed names and places. Names and
places only someone on the inside of the finance
industry could know.

Muhammed knew them, oh yes. Knew exactly
where the dagger's point should thrust. Which
businesses to destroy—a surgical strike at the very
beating heart of the economy.

The entire financial district, gone, destroyed,
rendered a wasteland. Manhattan emptied, its in-
habitants rendered radioactive lepers, condemned
to die a slow and painful death.

Perfect. A plan that would bring the West to its knees, in submission to the Prophet's will.

It was all in place, all perfect. And now this. Muhammed frowned at the printout of the decrypted e-mail he'd just received.

Trouble.

A crew member of the *Marie Claire*, the ship carrying the martyrs, reported that a member of the Marseille Port Authority saw the secret hold, had seen the men, the *shaheed* belts and the canister with its universally understood biohazard symbol and had grasped the significance. Luckily, the man had been terminated but had been alone in his office with his computer for a good five minutes.

Checking the server log, one message with attachment had been sent to pearce@wordsmith. com in the time frame between the clerk's arrival at his office and his death.

Close examination of the attachment showed merely a technical text pertaining to plans to expand the harbor, but the message and its recipient had to be destroyed.

Google told him that www.wordsmith.com was a translation agency based in San Diego. Its owner's name was Nicole Pearce.

Something had to be done fast. The *Marie Claire* was on its way. It would stop a hundred miles from the port of New York. The martyrs would be offloaded at night to four fast boats that would land in New Jersey, and from there would be bused to Manhattan. The *Marie Claire* would land briefly in port and be on its way to Panama by the time the bombs exploded. No one would ever suspect her.

It was all in place except for the wild card of Nicole Pearce, potential trouble.

Twenty years of planning was coming to fruition. It was unthinkable that they fail. Even more unthinkable that they fail because of a Western woman.

They wouldn't fail. Muhammed had a plan.

At the topmost levels of American finance, in the heart of America's softness, Muhammed had been astonished to learn that there were hard men. Money was defended as fiercely as land in this arcane world, by the iron laws of warfare, if necessary. Like all overlords, the kings of finance required warriors to deal with problems. A whistle-blower threatening to bring down a lucrative deal, a divorcing wife threatening to report hidden assets to the IRS, the head of a rival company whose plane had to go down . . . these required warriors to deal with them. And the men of money knew where to go.

Several times, late at night, after a luxurious meal and over the thousand-dollar bottle of cognac or brandy Paul had learned to consume, a man was mentioned. He had many names and no one knew his background, save that he had been trained to be a ruthless but efficient killer by the US Army. It didn't matter what his name was, what was important was what he could do.

Anything.

He could do anything at all for you, if the price

was right. He also commanded vast resources and highly trained men. No matter what the mission, he could deal with it.

The world of high finance guarded its wealth ferociously when threatened and it had its enforcer—shadowy, fast, smart. Paul only knew his code name: Outlaw. He knew nothing else, except that there was a cell phone number.

He did not have it but he knew who did.

Muhammed picked up his phone and began the long process of arranging a meeting with one of the most powerful men in the world.

It was a humiliating process but Muhammed swallowed his pride.

Soon enough, the world of dishonor would be wiped out, and Umma would rise from the ashes of the West.

Chapter 4

San Diego

To Nicole's surprise, Sam Reston hadn't booked at one of the top ten most expensive restaurants in San Diego, or one listed in the food guides, preferably one that had been recently reviewed by Lauren Spitz, the trendiest San Diego food guru, whose word was more authoritative than that of God.

Men have very simple thought patterns. Nicole had learned that fact through long exposure to the gender.

Sam Reston knew perfectly well that she had thought he was some kind of a low-level hired hand, one step up from a bum, where instead he was the proprietor of a successful company and probably earned ten or twenty times what she did.

A normal guy would go all out to prove just how wrong she'd been about him and just how successful he was, how powerful. Rub it in. Make her suffer a little remorse for thinking badly of him.

The easiest way to do that was to spend a lot of money on dinner, the more exclusive and expensive the restaurant, the better.

But it looked like Sam Reston had hidden depths.

The light kiss had shut her right up. She had no idea what to say. So she spent the car trip gratefully mulling over the fact that maybe Sam had engineered her an escape from Creepy and Creepier.

There was silence in the car as they drove south, to an outlying part of town she'd never been to before. She looked around as Sam started slowing down. This was definitely not expensive restaurant territory.

It was, however, a lively area, with a great deal of ethnic diversity, mostly Hispanic but with strong Asian flavors. Sam drove by taperìas and taquerìas and Vietnamese and Thai restaurants, finally pulling into the parking lot of a low, sprawling building surrounded by gardens. BALADI, announced a big billboard, and if that wasn't enough, there was a beautifully rendered cedar tree covering half the billboard.

Nicole gave a delighted laugh. She turned to Sam as he parked the car in an overflowing lot. "Oh my God! A Lebanese restaurant! How on earth could you know I love Lebanese cooking?"

His hard mouth turned up at her excitement. "I confess I checked your website. It said you spent some time in Beirut. No one can live in Lebanon and not love the food. I love it, too. This is one of the best Lebanese restaurants I've ever eaten at, so I hope you enjoy it."

He was a miracle worker. Already, her muscles were relaxing. However the night ended, she'd have had a fantastic meal and a rare evening dining out.

It occurred to her that she really needed this evening. She hadn't eaten out in, what? Six months, maybe? No, more like seven months. And then it had been to an extremely boring restaurant with bland, forgettable food. She'd ignored her instincts and accepted a client's dinner invitation. His conversation had been blander and more tasteless even than the food. He'd been appalled at how ill her father was, though Pops hadn't even been fully confined to a wheelchair yet. It had been a disastrous evening and she hadn't been out since.

No time. No money.

Whatever company Sam Reston turned out to be, she was really looking forward to the meal.

There was a long gravel walkway and he put a hand to her back as they walked up. She was actually grateful for that hand as her sandals had been chosen more for looks than function. The heat of his touch penetrated the material of her jacket and the dress.

She looked around as they approached the entrance. The building wasn't luxurious, but looked well tended and friendly. The big picture windows showing happy-looking diners inside sparkled in the evening light. The décor was simple and functional, waiters bustling to and fro.

The grounds were extensive. Off to the right she could see—

"Oh my gosh. Are those tomato plants?" Row after row of perfectly spaced stakes with small green knobs hanging off the plants. And now that she looked more closely, she could see tiny, tender tufts of baby lettuce, brightly colored peppers, zucchini.

Sam looked down at her. "The proprietor grows most of his own produce. He says that way he knows what he's getting. And it's delicious, which is an added advantage."

She smiled. "It reminds me of the hillsides outside Beirut. All those truck garden allotments." You could always count on seeing an elderly member of the family, carefully weeding and watering, a kerchief on his head to protect against the hot Mediterranean sun.

"Yeah." Sam smiled. "We used to go up into the hills and picnic with the guys we were training. Picked figs off the trees, it was great."

Sam was known here.

When he opened the door for her, a handsome olive-skinned man wearing a long apron came out of the kitchen and rushed toward him. They gave each other one of those manly thumps on the back where women would have kissed, and the man turned dark, intelligent eyes to her.

Sam did the honors. "Nicole, meet the best chef

in the state, Bashir Fakhry. Bashir, this is Nicole Pearce. She lived in Beirut for a few years."

"Pleased to meet you." Nicole had that phrase in Arabic down pat, having used it thousands of times in Beirut.

"Welcome to my restaurant. I hope you enjoy the meal." The beautiful Arabic syllables flowed like water as he took her hand and bowed over it.

"Thank you, I'm looking forward to it. You have a very beautiful place here," Nicole answered carefully, now having to create an actual sentence. Arabic was not her strongest language and she was prone to grammatical mistakes.

Either she hadn't made a mistake, or Bashir Fakhry forgave her. He beamed at her.

"A beauty beyond compare and she speaks Arabic," he murmured, dark liquid eyes gleaming. He shot a sly look at Sam, then smiled back down at her. "Ditch this hobo and run away with me."

Nicole laughed. His English was excellent, with a to-die-for accent. Nicole was sure Bashir was a great hit with the ladies. She'd loved the extravagant personalities of the Lebanese, who had managed to retain their humanity even as their country was being torn apart.

Nicole had been lucky enough to be in Lebanon in the halcyon years after the civil war had ended and before the new war started. Her father had been Deputy Chief of Mission of the Beirut Embassy for two years. She'd just started her studies in Geneva, but she spent her summers in Lebanon, enjoying her parents' company, desultorily studying Arabic and flirting with the cultural attaché she suspected was CIA.

Bashir led them through room after room of loud, happy diners to a quiet, small room in the back where a plate-glass wall gave out onto lush-looking fields.

The room was delightful—intimate and glowing with the evening light. He seated them at a corner table, at right angles to each other. Nicole was amused to note that Sam immediately took the seat with his back to the wall, which meant he had to turn his head to look out at the beautiful view.

Bashir disappeared without taking any orders, but within a minute, a beautiful young girl who looked like him started ferrying out bowl after bowl of food. A full array of *mezze* that smelled and looked delicious.

A young man who shared the family resemblance uncorked a bottle of Syrah from Baalbek and poured a finger in Sam's glass. He stood at attention as Sam sipped and nodded. Sam waved a long finger at Nicole's glass.

"I won't say anything until the lady has tasted."

Nicole sipped and narrowed her eyes at the explosion of taste in her mouth. Sunshine, cherries, oak . . . "Wow."

Sam nodded. "I think that will be fine, then, Maroun. Thank you."

The young man disappeared. Nicole looked around, pleased with everything. The room, the view, the food, the wine.

The man.

It was already the nicest time she'd had in, oh, at least a year, and she hadn't even eaten yet.

So far, Sam Reston hadn't said or done anything obnoxious, which put him in the tenth percentile of dates. The food smelled glorious, the wine was magnificent.

Her father was in good hands this evening. She'd landed the contract with the Wall Street Master of the Universe, inching her way slightly closer to, if not wealth, then at least solvency. Maybe.

The evening reminded her of happier days with her family and carefree summers with friends. It reminded her of another, lost, life.

Sam dipped a crispy lettuce leaf into the hummus in an enameled bowl decorated with swirling earth colors.

"If you're already smiling, then I want to see you after you put this in your mouth." He held it out to her. Her fingers brushed his as she accepted it.

It was like a little electric shock. Nicole paused, the leaf trembling in her hand and looked at him, dismayed.

Oh no.

No no *no*.

Just when she was settling into an enjoyable evening, too.

When her fingers met his, a powerful burst of heat had coursed through her system, head to toe, as if she'd stepped in front of an open furnace. Classic hot flush, only she wasn't menopausal.

Oh God, no. She was attracted to Sam Reston. Massively. It had been hidden by his little trip through Grungeville, but apparently underneath, humming like a powerful engine, there'd been attraction.

Sexual attraction. *Wild* sexual attraction, of a pitch and intensity she'd never experienced before.

She'd been pleased to think that she might be making a friend of him. It would be nice to have someone to go out with occasionally, spiced by a little tug of sexual attraction, just to keep her hormones ticking over. He spent most of his working days across the hallway from her, which meant maybe she could have company sometimes at her noonday meals, which up until now had basically been yogurt and a packed sandwich alone at her desk.

She needed friendship. She did not need this red-hot connection to every erogenous zone in her body.

Dismayed, she looked down at the uneaten hummus-laden leaf of lettuce, out the window at the neatly tended gardens below, then back at Sam Reston.

She winced at the heat in his eyes.

He saw her trembling hand and steadied it with his own. He removed the lettuce from her fingers, curled his big, rough hand around hers and brought her hand to his mouth.

His breath was a hot wash over her skin. Goose pimples broke out when he kissed her hand.

He understood exactly what was going on inside her. His dark eyes were so intelligent and so heat-filled she didn't know where to look.

If he had had that annoyingly smug male look of someone who'd hooked a live one, this would have been easy. Put up a wall, eat the nice food, make light conversation, be distant when saying good night, avoid the kiss.

But he didn't look smug. He looked serious, stern, as if wild sexual attraction were the most dangerous thing on earth.

And it was. A loaded grenade, in fact.

Oh God, she had to nip this in the bud, and fast.

"Look, I—" Nicole's eyes widened in dismay. The words didn't come out. This was terrifying. All that came out was a huff of air as her throat tightened. She had to stop and try again.

"Look." Through sheer willpower she steadied her voice, tugging her hand from his. Trying to, anyway. His hold was painless but unbreakable. "There's something I need to say to you, right up front, Sam. And I need you to listen to me carefully."

He bowed his head, eyes always on hers. "Fine." He tightened his warm grasp slightly. "But I want to be touching you while I listen."

Well, hell. Him not touching her was part of what she wanted to say. But her hand felt . . . wonderful in his. Warm, surrounded by hard male flesh, somehow safe.

She took a deep breath because this wasn't going to be easy.

For a moment she simply looked at him, at this

very large, very strong, utterly male man who had most improbably woken up her dormant libido at exactly the wrong time in her life. She had an enormous pang of regret for what she had to say to him, but there was no evading it. It had to be done.

From the moment she'd gone to pick up her sick father in Dushanbe and had been told by the doctors what condition he was in, she'd known that her old life was over and that everything but caring for her father was going to have to be tossed overboard. Her carefree single life in Geneva, friends, a love life. Everything had to go. She'd seen it all in one moment of brutal clarity.

The only other thing she could allow into her life was work, and that was purely out of necessity.

She hadn't been even remotely tempted to allow anything else into her life before now, but somehow Sam Reston made her yearn, yearn for the affair they might have had if things had been different.

But they weren't.

"This . . . this thing between us—" she waved her free hand between them, "and you'll notice I'm not denying that there's something. But whatever it is, it has to stop here. Much as I'd like to explore it, I can't."

His face was utterly impassive and he held himself still. He didn't even appear to be breathing. He was completely concentrated on her, all that male power, tightly focused on her.

She'd asked him to listen carefully because she

thought he wouldn't want to hear what she was saying. He didn't show any trace of denial, though, as most men would have. Maybe that was a soldier's gift—to see what was. If you couldn't see reality, no matter how unpalatable, you were dead.

"Explain, please." The deep voice sounded thoughtful, not angry or defensive.

"Okay. I need to tell you where my life is right now." *Deep breath. Let it out in one controlled stream.* Just like her yoga teacher had taught her. "A little over a year ago I was living in Geneva, where I'd gone to university. I was working for the UN as a translator. I loved my job and I had a wide circle of friends and an active social life."

She looked out the window for a second, allowing herself the sharp pang of pain at what had been lost.

How incredibly happy she'd been. Young, single, earning well. She'd loved translating, her colleagues, her friends, her life. The UN paid very well, in Swiss francs and tax free. Geneva was a dream city—pretty and green and safe, surrounded by gorgeous mountains with the best skiing in the world. A short train ride away from southern France and northern Italy.

The world had been her oyster. She suppressed a sigh. Those days were gone, forever.

She looked back at Sam, watching her steadily. "Well," she said briskly, "I imagine you know all that if you checked my website. Or at least you'd know the basics."

"Yeah." The deep voice was quiet. "I know you

lived in Geneva and worked for the UN. Sounds interesting."

A sharp little stab to the heart. "Yes, yes it was interesting. I loved it." Nicole sat up straighter, stiffening her spine. It had been good. It was now over. Deal. "But now I have other priorities. I've always been close to my parents. My mother died in a car accident in 2004 and it was a huge blow to my father and me. We just had each other. When I graduated and started my new job, he was appointed ambassador to Tajikistan, with special plenipotentiary powers. He seemed as happy in his new life as I was in mine. So I had no inkling of trouble when the call came. Midnight, on the fourteenth of May, a little over a year ago. The call was to say that Dad was in the hospital."

Nicole's mouth tightened. She remembered the scene so vividly. The call had come on a Friday evening. She'd been packing for a ski holiday on the glaciers, happily thinking of snow and schnaps and schnitzli. Then her world fell apart. The caller was an embassy secretary, to say that her father was in the ICU. An hour later, Nicole had been at the Geneva airport, waiting for the first of four connections for the 24-hour trip to get to her father's side.

"The Embassy said that my—my father was very ill, in a coma. I left immediately and when I arrived in Dushanbe, Dad was just coming out of it. In carrying out a CAT scan to exclude a stroke, they discovered that—"

Oh God. This was so hard to say. Her hand in his started trembling and his hold tightened slightly.

Just say it.

"They discovered that he has brain cancer. Not one big tumor, which would be serious but perhaps treatable. His brain is riddled with them, almost too numerous to count, the doctors said. Inoperable. The only thing they could do for him was radiotherapy to extend his lifespan a little, and some chemotherapy. I was making arrangements to fly him back with me on a medevac flight to Geneva, when he started waking up. I knew I could cope in Geneva. I could find a larger house to rent; medical care there is excellent; the UN has a very generous health plan that includes relatives; I was phoning people, working it all out. When he was fully awake, Dad was told his condition. And—and he told me he'd served his country abroad all his adult life, and that now he wanted to go home, back to the States to—"

Nicole's throat seized up, simply wouldn't work. Her eyes prickled and she had to look away for a second. She swallowed. Sam didn't show any impatience at all. He simply sat, looking at her, holding her hand. Quiet and still and focused.

A minute, two. She stared blindly out the window until she could get her voice back. She drew in a shuddering breath and looked back at him.

"To die. He wanted to come back home to die," she finally whispered. A single tear spilled from her eye and plopped onto the table. And here she thought she had no tears left.

Sam dried the track it had left with his thumb. The skin of his finger was rough, like a cat's tongue, the touch delicate.

"Sorry," she said, bowing her head. A weeping dinner date was no fun.

"Sorry?" He frowned. "For what?"

She was sorry about everything. Sorry that she was soon going to lose her father, sorry about her reduced life, sorry that this attraction couldn't go anywhere.

Okay, the next bit just had to be said.

"From that moment, from the moment I learned that my father was very ill and that he wanted to come home, my life changed on a dime. I quit my job and we moved here, to the house my grandmother left me." Nicole tried to make her voice brisk. "So, Sam. Like it or not, this is my life. My father is dying and we have no money. While closing up Dad's affairs, I discovered that Dad had invested his life savings in a mutual fund run by Lawrence Karloff."

She nodded when he winced. The tangled lawsuits of the thousands of people who'd lost every cent of their savings in the giant Ponzi scheme run by the Wall Street legend were still making headlines.

"Yes, indeed. Dad lost every penny he'd ever put aside to that bastard Karloff. He is essentially penniless. That SOB took everything. And since Dad had to retire from the State Department early for reasons of health, he has a reduced pension. Basically, the pension pays for the utilities, food, taxes and that's about it. The State Department covers hospitalization. But the costs for his nursing care, our housekeeper, his physical rehab, the drugs . . . they're all astronomical and they're all on me. I don't think we could have afforded to actually move back to the States if my grandmother hadn't left me our house. Luckily, we don't have to pay rent or a mortgage. Otherwise I don't think it would have worked and Dad wouldn't have gotten his—his wish.

"So we came back to the States. I founded Wordsmith with my contacts from university and from my UN job. I tried to work out of the house all last year, but it wasn't ideal. Dad, bless him, interrupted a thousand times a day, and I do need to meet with clients, so that's when I decided to get an office downtown. At Wordsmith we're good at what we do, but it's a typical small company that is growing steadily but not always fast enough. With what I earn from it, I can barely keep up with the medical bills."

She looked him straight in the eye. Recounting her life like this was painful and depressing. And, unfortunately, necessary.

"I'm not saying any of this to make you feel sorry for me. Please don't. I'm doing exactly what I want to do and right now, I wouldn't have my life any other way. But I do need you to know that this *is* my life and there's no reason why any of my problems should be a part of yours. It's no fun dating someone who has no money for anything. And it's not just money I lack. Every second of my day is dedicated to my father or to work. That's it, that's what I do. I take care of Dad and I work. I don't go out, I don't go to the movies or to plays or concerts. I can't even think of a vacation—not even just a couple of days away. I won't leave my father alone and I couldn't afford it anyway. This is the situation as long as my dad is alive, which I hope with all my heart will be as long as possible. So you see, I am not free to just . . . come out and play with you. There's nothing lighthearted or easy about my life right now, Sam. I am, in all senses, a burden. I'm saying this to you because you—well, your body language is pretty clear. You seem to be, for want of a better word, attracted. Am I right?"

He nodded, eyes never leaving hers. "Jesus. Absolutely. From the first second I saw you."

She sighed. He wasn't making it any easier. The attraction was mutual. Except she'd been able to explain away the sharp awareness of him, the accelerated heartbeat, the slight trembling when she saw him as fear of a dangerous-looking man.

He was still dangerous-looking, but it wasn't fear she felt. Oh God, no.

He wasn't handsome but he had sharp, clean features, the strong features of a man used to wielding authority. The whole package—the outsize body, the big rough hands, the penetrating dark eyes, the no-nonsense air, the deep voice—was delectable and made her tremble deep inside.

She'd been so caught up in what she was telling him that she had had no sense of herself, but now sensations came rushing back in.

She was aroused by him, it was absolutely unmistakeable. Right now, in a perfectly nice Lebanese restaurant, blood was rushing to her sex and her breasts, her breathing was speeding up, her head filled with heated images of her crawling onto his lap and simply licking him all over.

Nicole hated machos. She'd grown up in third-world countries where the most idiotic male felt he was superior to all women because he had a Y chromosome and a piece of flesh dangling between his legs.

She was immune to their posturing, to their torrid glances and boasts of sexual prowess.

But Sam Reston was the real deal. He didn't flaunt his maleness, it just . . . was. As much a part of him as his hands or feet. Male strength, not just of his muscles, but of his will, exuded from him, together with a godzillion male pheromones that had her heart racing.

He was still holding her hand and the connection felt electric, the heat running all the way up her arm. Even his smell was delicious. Not a cologne, just clean male skin, the starch in his blindingly white shirt, and a faint scent of soap. Not Armani or Boss, but still guaranteed to make female hearts trip up. He simply exuded power and sex.

Hormone city.

She was as turned on as she'd ever been in her

life, yet they were simply sitting in a restaurant, hand in hand. Though nothing overt was happening at all, her chest felt tight and it was hard to breathe. She was hot all over, like she had a fever.

She had never felt this before, and it wasn't . . . unpleasant. How sad to have to give it up without even having a chance to taste it first.

With a sigh, she tugged and he allowed her to slip her hand from his. She dipped into the hummus with a slice of homemade bread and hummed with pleasure. Delicious.

Nicole had learned the hard way the lesson of living moment by moment, being grateful for even the smallest of pleasures. This was a fabulous meal in the company of an amazingly sexy man. She had to put her feelings aside and enjoy it. She hadn't had this nice an evening since she'd learned her father was sick. God knew when she'd have another evening like it.

"This is fabulous." Nicole refrained from rolling her eyes with delight, and spooned some tabbouleh onto a torn-off chunk of fried bread.

Sam nodded gravely. "Yes, it is. Bashir and his mother are fantastic cooks." He pushed a terracotta bowl of *fatteh* toward her. "Are you finished?"

She stopped, another bite halfway to her mouth. They had to leave already? A pang of sadness shot through her. Wow. That was quick. She'd said she wasn't available for an affair and he wanted to end the evening as fast as he could.

Nicole tucked the disappointment away. "Finished? With the meal?"

"No. With what you wanted to say to me. Said all you wanted to say?"

Not really. She'd only lived in San Diego for a little over a year and between Wordsmith and her dad, there'd been no time to make any friends. This was the closest she'd come to a heart-to-heart talk since her lost carefree life in Geneva.

She hadn't told him how her heart broke at watching her father die, day by day, piece by piece. How hard she tried to hold on to him, how horrible it was to feel him slipping from her grasp.

She hadn't told Sam how tired she was between caring for her father at home and the fouteen hours a day and more she put in at work.

She hadn't told him how lonely she felt, sometimes, without a friend to help relieve the relentless pressure. Or how worried she was about money, wondering whether her money would hold out to help ease his end.

But he wouldn't want to hear that. Her story was pathetic enough as it was. "Yes. I think I more or less said what I had to say."

Those dark eyes bored into hers. He raised his hand and brought it to her face. The fine hairs on the nape of her neck lifted as he ran the back of a long index finger down her cheek.

"I've never felt skin this soft before." The finger ran lower, over her jaw and rested on a vein in her neck. Surely he had to feel how her heart pounded?

She was finding it hard to breathe as he ran his finger up and down the pulse point. He could read her every reaction there, as if her neck were some kind of lie detector.

He wasn't reacting at all, simply looking at her, touching her. "Did you even listen to a word I said?"

His mouth tightened. "Oh yeah. Every word. So. Let me get this straight. You're caring for a sick father, while trying to start up a new business and keep your head above water financially. Is that about it?"

"*Very* sick father." How it hurt, every time she said it. "But yes, that's about it. And what it means is that I don't have the time or the energy for an affair." She finally found the strength to move her head away from his touch and sopped up some *muhummarrah* with a pita triangle and put the whole mess in her mouth. Hot, spicy, delicious. Pure heaven, tinged with regret. Well, the bitter taste of regret was one she was used to by now.

Man up, she told herself.

"I'm sorry." Nicole studied the grain of the wooden table for a moment, then met Sam's eyes again. "I'm trying to be as clear and honest here as possible, Sam."

"Yeah, I can see that." His jaw muscles clenched. "And I appreciate your honesty. What I don't get at all is why should any of this should make me desire you any less?"

She blinked in surprise. "Well, I told you. I don't have time for an affair. Time or energy. My father is my top priority, and after that comes trying to make a living. There just isn't anything else in my life. There can't be. So . . . anything you might want from me, I can't give you. You'd be better off with someone else, someone who isn't so wrapped up in problems. Actually, frankly, right now you'd be crazy to want me."

He was silent a long moment, then picked up his fork. "I think we'd better eat some more of this meal, otherwise Bashir will have my head."

Nicole put on a wobbly smile. He was right. The food was fabulous, it would be a huge pity to let it go to waste. Live in the moment, and all that. A sigh was in her chest but she refused to let it out. What good would it do?

It felt good to have spelled out the situation to Sam, clearly and coolly. She'd definitely done the right thing. And if it felt like she'd stabbed herself in the heart, well, her heart had been taking a pounding for quite some time now.

Her appetite had gone, but she made a real effort to do justice to the magnificent meal. She was a diplomat's daughter and had attended 17-course state dinners even when she was ill and had to choke down the food. She knew how to do this.

Sam was quiet, and so was she. Maybe he was feeling the regrets, too. But life was like that—good things happened at the wrong time. It was simply fate.

Kismet, Bashir would call it.

The sun was starting to set over the pretty gardens by the time the waiter came with a small bronze coffeepot with a long wooden handle, the *dallah*, that had always somehow reminded her of Aladdin's lamp, and poured a fragrant brew. The cups were without handles. Smiling, Nicole brought the warm cup to her nose and sniffed appreciatively. The coffee had been brewed with cardamom and was dense, sugary, delicious. It set off perfectly the tiny bite-sized pieces of baklava the waiter slipped on the table. She loved the Lebanese version, made with rosewater syrup instead of honey.

The room was dramatically lit by the intense glow of the setting sun, turning everything golden; even Sam Reston's dark, deeply-tanned skin turned bronze. Right at this moment, he looked almost sinfully attractive. And utterly beyond reach.

Sam put down his coffee cup, crossed his arms on the table and leaned forward, face deadly serious. Deep grooves bracketed his strong mouth and his nostrils were white and pinched, as if from some strong emotion. "Now I have something to say to you."

Nicole put down her cup, leaning a little forward, too. He'd done her the courtesy of listening carefully to what she had to say. Now she'd return the favor.

Whatever he had to say wouldn't change the situation, but he deserved a hearing. Whatever it was he wanted to say wasn't pleasant, though. His face had taken on such a grave cast.

"Here's the deal. I never talk about my past. It's no one's goddamned business but my own. But I think there are a few things about me you need to understand. You know I talked about my brother Mike, and that though we don't share any blood, we're closer than most brothers?"

Nicole nodded. The cop. The cop who was going to be driving by and deterring Creepy and Creepier.

"There's a third brother, Harry. He's not in good shape right now. He was shot up pretty bad in Afghanistan. He's working with me. I'm going to make him a partner as soon as he's better. Right now he's barely on his feet. That's the three of us. The reason Harry and Mike and I are so tight is that we spent part of our growing-up years in the same foster home, run by a brutally cruel couple. We had each other's back, always, otherwise I don't think we'd have survived. We've been looking out for each other ever since."

He stared down at his clasped hands. They were clean, the nails short, but they looked like they'd been used a lot, and hard. There were scars and nicks and calluses, the hands of a man who, though a businessman, didn't shy from manual labor. Completely unlike the hands of any other man she'd ever been out to dinner with.

Nicole couldn't help herself. She reached out, one hand hovering over his clasped ones. She hesitated for just a second, then covered his hands with her own. She wanted him to feel the human connection. He'd known hard times, too.

His hands were warm, radiating heat and strength.

He spoke, looking at their joined hands.

"My mother abandoned me in a Dumpster. Just threw me away, like garbage." He looked up at her shocked gasp, opened his hands and sandwiched her hand between his. A wry smile lifted his mouth. "It's okay, honey. The story has a happy ending. Eventually. I'm here, aren't I?"

"Yes, you are," she murmured. He *was* here. And how. Huge and strong and utterly unlike any other man she'd ever met. She tried to suppress the sharp punch she'd felt when he called her "honey." *Stop that*, she told herself sternly. This wasn't going anywhere. Getting her heart involved wasn't going to help anyone, least of all her.

"Someone had seen her doing it and fished me out. They took me to the hospital immediately and I was put in an incubator stat. Apparently I was about a month old and seriously underweight. Hard to believe, isn't it?"

"Yes, it is." Nicole looked him over. Immensely broad and tall, with hard-packed dense muscles. It was impossible to connect him with an undernourished baby. This tragic story definitely had a happy ending.

"This woman—my mother—was a drunk and a prostitute. She was known in the area. I have no idea who my father was. I don't think she did, either. The police tracked her down and she was tried and convicted for attempted homicide and was sentenced to ten years in jail. She served eight years, then was paroled. She went looking for me at the orphanage, spouting nonsense about wanting to atone and start over." He rolled his eyes. "Some nutcase of a social worker believed her and they simply gave me to her. I was eight years old and I'd never seen the woman who claimed to be my mother before."

"Oh no," Nicole breathed. The story might have a happy ending but it sounded like there was to be tragedy before they got there.

"Yeah." His hands tightened on hers. "Her name was Darlene Reston. I can't think of her as my mother, she was just this . . . woman I had to live with for a few years. She drank away the welfare checks and there were drugs going on, too. One thing I do know is that she sure wasn't buying food and milk and clothes with what the State sent her. Once I got a bad ear infection that went untreated and I was left with a weakened eardrum. I squeaked by the physical to get into the Navy but then a mortar round finished the eardrum off. I was almost deaf in one ear, had to leave the Navy on a medical discharge. I had an operation that restored some of my hearing. But I can't dive to any depth." He shook his head. "Can't be a SEAL if you can't dive."

Nicole had a flash of a young, skinny, vulnerable Sam, trapped in the care of a woman who drank away his food money, who wouldn't get him medical care when he needed it.

"There were men around, too, lots of them." Sam's deep voice was low and dispassionate. "Most of them were high and stayed high for days. They barely noticed me but when they did, I got the shit kicked out of me. For most of my childhood, I was badly undernourished and weak." His mouth tightened. "The kind of kid a bully loves to kick around. Makes them feel strong. When I was around twelve, a teacher finally noticed that something was deeply wrong. So the State took me out of Darlene's care and put me in a foster home."

"Thank God." Nicole blinked the tears back. The strong, successful man in front of her was light-years away from the small, abused boy and he wouldn't want her tears. But her heart ached.

"Not really. The foster home wasn't any better. Old Man Hughes and his wife took in older, unadoptable kids because they got paid more. The wife gave us watered-down canned soup and crackers bought in bulk, slapped us upside the head when the spirit took her, and locked herself in her room when her husband had his little spells of rage. He could go beserk on a dime. Anything could set him off. An unmade bed. Cracker crumbs on the table. A look, even. We learned never to say anything, ever. He hated a lot of things, but mostly he hated what he called 'mouthy' women and kids. He was a big, mean son of a bitch and he loved using his fists on us."

There was a huge boulder on Nicole's chest, making it hard to breathe. Her battle against her tears was a losing one. He reached out once more to dry a tear against her cheek.

How terrible life could be. She'd wept for her dying father and now she wept for a child who'd never known love, only neglect and violence. She met his impassive gaze. "Tell me something good happened. Please. Tell me they took you out of that foster home and put you in another one."

He shook his head. "Nope. Stayed there until I was old enough to enlist. But a couple of good things did happen. There was a nice elderly lady lived next door. Mrs. Colley. Strange old coot, but kind-hearted. She was scared to death of Old Man Hughes but when he wasn't around, she invited me over and stuffed me full of food. I grew six inches and put on forty pounds in one year. I made sure they were forty pounds of muscle. The old man started thinking twice about using his fists on me."

"Good for you," Nicole said fiercely. Sam Reston had grown up to be the kind of man no one beat up on, not without serious consequences.

"Another good thing happened when I was twelve. My brother Harry Bolt arrived and then three months later my other brother Mike Keillor. Harry had tried to defend his baby sister and his mother against his mom's meth-head boyfriend. The fucker—pardon my language."

Nicole nodded and waved the expletive away with her free hand. *Fucker* sounded about right for a man who hurt little girls.

"Fucker beat Harry's little sister and mom to death. Harry went wild. Put the guy in the hospital but not before he got both legs broken. He was fostered out to the Hughes. I saw Old Man Hughes smile as Harry walked through the door on crutches and I knew exactly what he was thinking. I wasn't an easy target for his rage any more. He needed an outlet and here comes Harry, crippled, fresh meat. That night I took a knife to Old Man Hughes and I told him that if he so much as touched the new guy, I'd cut his miserable hide to ribbons, starting with his balls. I meant every word, too, and I think he knew it. By that time I was as tall as Hughes, though he had a lot of weight on me. But it wasn't muscle, it was all gut. Harry healed and Mrs. Colley shoved as much food down his throat as he could eat and by the end of that year, he was as big as I was. Harry and I were really tight. And then Mike came. It was his eighth foster home. The three of us banded together, looked after each other and we all shipped out as soon as we could. Me to the Navy, Harry to the Army and Mike to the Marines."

Nicole opened her mouth to say something but he hadn't finished. He brought her hand to his mouth and kissed it, lips warm against her cold skin. Sam's story had chilled her to the bone.

"Now, the reason I told you all of that is so that you can understand something. Me and my brothers came out okay because we looked after each other, no matter what. All three of us know, up close and personal, what it means when no one looks out for you. When no one cares. And we know, deep down in our bones, what it means when someone cares and does the right thing. We all have jobs where we see, daily, the effects of not caring for your kid or your wife or your parents or your friends."

His face suddenly sharpened, the skin over those high cheekbones tightening, eyes boring into hers.

"So, Nicole, you will forgive me if I don't find it a turnoff that you love your father so much. That you're sacrificing important things to make sure he has a dignified death and you're making sure that he's right where he wants and needs to be. You're doing the hard thing, the right thing, and I admire you for it. I was blown away by you the first time I saw you, but by God, it's worse now that I know what's behind that gorgeous face."

Sam took her hand and, shockingly, brought it under the table, between his legs. He folded her hand over his penis. His huge, rock-hard penis. At her touch, she could feel the blood coursing through him, turning his penis even harder, thicker.

The feel of him beneath her hand brought a rush of blood to her own sex, which clenched involuntarily, once, twice.

She was utterly incapable of movement, of thought.

"Not want you?" Sam's voice was raspy now, as if he found it difficult to get the words out. He breathed out hard. His jaw muscles bunched and his nostrils flared. "I've wanted you since the first second I saw you. I couldn't do anything about it because I was on an undercover job but I sure as hell thought about it, night and day. Christ, Nicole, I want you so much I can hardly breathe. I want you so much I can't think. Say you'll come back home with me. Now."

She couldn't remove her hand because his big

one was curled around it, keeping it over his penis. This was utterly insane. Nothing like this had ever happened to her before.

There was no air in the room.

No, the answer was no, of course. She had to say no. How could she go home with him, just like that? This was crazy, she'd never done anything like that in her life.

She'd had her share of lovers but she was incredibly picky. It took several evenings out and if there was a false note, if she was uncomfortable in any way with the idea, she just said no. She was good-looking, she got asked out a lot, but then a lot of men were jerks. She'd said no a lot since puberty. There were tons of reasons to say no right now to Sam, if only she could get her brain working again to think of them. Like her hand, like her breasts and between her thighs, it was hot, melting in a sudden surge of pulsing desire.

No, of course not, are you crazy? she said, only the words didn't quite come out that way.

Somehow, what came out was, "Yes."

Chapter 5

Yes!

Sam stood up abruptly, tilting his chair over. He barely heard the clatter as he reached into his pocket and pulled out a hundred-dollar bill. He threw it onto the table—it was more than enough, but even if it wasn't, Bashir knew he'd be good for it later—and grabbed her hand.

Nicole was looking utterly shocked at what she'd said, big blue eyes wide in dismay, that luscious mouth a shocked *O*.

Sam couldn't stop to think about that. He couldn't think about anything, actually, except getting her into his bed. Or wherever. It didn't have to be a bed. Against the door or the wall or on the floor or the couch would do just fine. He didn't give a shit.

The important thing was to get into her as fast as possible and stay there as long as possible. Till next year, if what he was feeling was any indication.

It was as if he'd never had sex before, ever. He was so excited he could barely feel his hands and feet as he walked to his car, moving fast. Luckily, he had his arm around her waist when Nicole stumbled on the gravel.

Sam held her fast. She'd never fall when she was with him, but he was ashamed that he'd been half dragging her along.

"Sorry," he mumbled and slowed his stride. He was a runner, and he was used to getting from A to B fast. He moved fast on principle and when he was aiming toward something he wanted, he picked up speed.

Had he been running? God only knew. His senses were so blasted he wasn't getting any input except from his dick, which was communicating what it wanted loud and clear.

He tried to slow down, even out his stride, but damn, it was hard.

Later, he'd reflect on what it meant for him to be out of control of his body. It was unthinkable. He'd learned self-control in the hardest school possible—his early years. And then the Navy and SEAL training had taken those skills and honed them to machine-like perfection.

He was in charge of himself—always. Aware of his surroundings and his place in any given setting. He was rock steady. For a while he'd been a fucking *sniper*, for God's sake. Snipers could control their own heartbeats, certainly their breathing. And their hands never trembled.

Right now, he was barely aware of the outside

world, only of the beautiful woman by his side. Everything else was fog. He was tunnel visioning, like untrained soldiers in battle, hands trembling.

Ten feet from his car, he took out his key fob and unlocked the doors. It took an effort not to simply throw Nicole into the passenger seat. A couple of seconds later, he was in the driver's seat, hands curled whitely around the steering wheel. He was so excited, he was almost panting.

Sam looked over at Nicole and winced.

She was pale, eyes wide with what he recognized as dismay and not desire, hands in her lap clutching each other so hard she was white-knuckled. A vein pulsed in her neck.

Fuck.

She was scared of him.

He had an idea of what she was seeing. A large, very strong, very fit man with clenched jaws and narrowed eyes, emanating aggression.

Fighting and fucking are closely related, certainly for a man like him. He was dominant on the battlefield and dominant in the bedroom. That was his nature and he'd long since grown used to it.

But he did *not* want Nicole Pearce scared of him. Shit, no. She was the classiest lady he'd ever gone out with, bar none, and the most beautiful, too. And by some miracle, it turned out she was kindhearted. Women like that didn't grow on trees. They were so rare, in fact, that he'd never met anyone even remotely like her.

She needed to be treated gently, like a lady, but goddamned if his blood wasn't up. He recognized it, oh yeah. Now that he was in the car, ready to make it to his house and to his bed as fast as the law would allow, he realized he'd somehow gone into combat mode.

The slight panting was to pull in oxygen for a major effort. His body was preparing itself for something big—fighting or fucking, it didn't care. It just knew that it had to be ready and that it was going to be rough.

At every level, Nicole was perceiving this, perceiving that he was a male with a broad streak of violence to him and a major case of almost out-of-control lust focused tightly on her.

She'd have to be crazy to go home with him in this state. But if she said no right now, he'd simply howl at the moon.

Sam knew he had to do something, and fast.

First, relax. He uncurled his hands from the wheel, sat back and consciously unclenched his muscles. Forced himself to breathe slowly. Forced his face muscles to relax. Closed his eyes and took a deep breath.

Opened them.

For the brief time he'd been a sniper, he'd learned a lot. He didn't love the mechanics of sniping like Mike did. Mike loved his guns like children. For Sam they were tools, and not particularly interesting ones at that.

But still, sniper training included big chunks of bodily control. They'd taught him how to slow his heartbeat. They'd been taught to let their bodies go into a weird form of hibernation, where they could stay utterly still for days at a time, bodily functions set at minimum, turning over just enough to stay alive.

He reached deep inside and dialed himself down. Way down. Over the next minute, like the ticking of an engine cooling, he slowed his heart rate, his breathing, even stilled his thoughts.

No more fevered images of Nicole Pearce under him, deep blue eyes slitted in ecstasy, long slender legs open for him, soft cunt accepting him.

No no. Instead, he filled his head with quiet pools of emptiness and gray nothingness, willing his body to cool. The first time he'd been told that SEAL training taught you to do that, he'd laughed. It sounded too much like something beamed in from Woo-Woo Land. Sam had wanted into the SEALs more than anything else in the world because he wanted to be the hardest man in a world of hard men. When told part of that included becoming like Yoda, he'd scoffed.

But it had worked then and it was working now.

Nicole's hands were now still in her lap and a little color had come back to her face. She'd lost that shocked look, as if she'd suddenly found herself face to face with a wolf.

Their eyes met. Christ, her eyes were beautiful. Such a deep, intense blue, framed by ridiculously long lashes. How the hell could she keep her eyes open with lashes like that?

"I want you. A lot," he blurted out. Oh shit. He'd wanted to say something soothing, maybe even suave, not that he was known for his smoothness. Usually he was pretty blunt with women.

She looked like the kind of woman who'd appreciate a little suavity. It seemed that right now he didn't have any in him. Desire had fried his circuits. "Sorry." He winced. "I mean—"

Nicole huffed out a little breath. She wasn't smiling, but her face had lightened. "That's okay. I kind of got the message when you dragged me out to your car without stopping to ask for the check."

His back teeth clenched. "Sorry," he said again, then stopped. Quit while you're ahead.

"Yes, I can see that." Her voice was soft. They looked at each other, gauging each other, the cabin of the car utterly quiet. Sam controlled everything—his breathing, his movements. Stillness would have to be his gift to her, a sign that he could control himself later, in bed.

He hoped.

Nicole lifted her left hand from her lap. How could absolutely everything about her be so frigging beautiful? Her hands could figure in one of those soap commercials. Pale ivory skin, long, slender fingers. Some kind of complicated ring with several kinds of stones on the middle finger, not the ring finger, thank you, God.

Nails manicured but short without that white square-top craziness and not painted black or purple. That and black lipstick were real turnoffs for him, made him think of fucking a zombie. Gah.

There was nothing about Nicole that was a turnoff.

Nicole's hand was so gorgeous he had to freeze his muscles not to grab it.

Her hand was moving, floating in space. He didn't take his eyes from her face, though he could easily see her hand in his peripheral vision. Slowly, she placed her hand over his on the wheel. It felt cool, and soft.

The contrast between their two hands was amazingly erotic. His hands were large, tough, scarred. Hers were like some marble statue by the world's greatest artist.

He became, if possible, even more still for a breath, two. Something must have reassured her because she smiled, faintly. She squeezed his hand, a light caress that shot straight to his dick, then put her hand back in her lap.

"Are we going to do this?" she asked, her voice low.

Fuck yeah! Sam locked the words in his throat instead of yelling them out.

"Yes. I hope." His voice came out hoarse, as if he hadn't spoken in years. He cleared his throat, then locked his mouth shut. *Do not jinx this*, he told himself. Anything that came out right now would be wrong.

Her eyes dropped to his groin, where a blue steeler was trying to punch its way through the lightweight wool of his expensive suit pants. Unlike the jeans, the suit pants simply outlined him.

"I can see that."

Blood pulsed in his dick, and it moved in his pants. She couldn't miss it. It was like his dick was reaching out to her.

There wasn't anything he could do to hide the hard-on. Sometimes when an erection became inconvenient, he could think it back down, like slowing his heartbeat. Life was full of downer thoughts, images that could dampen desire.

Nothing like that could work now, though. There wasn't any thought in the world that could make his dick go down with Nicole Pearce a foot away from him, contemplating letting him fuck her. His dick actually hurt and his balls were curled right up tightly against him, waiting to blow.

She searched his eyes, looking for something. He imagined she was looking for signs of violence. There was violence in him, sure, always had been, but never toward women or children. He'd never hurt a woman or a child and was grateful that his military career had never forced him to, because he wouldn't have been able to.

But beyond that, he could never hurt Nicole Pearce. He'd rather shoot himself in the chest. He just hoped with all his heart that he could keep in control in bed with her, which was another matter.

Control.

He'd spent a lifetime in control of himself and had to grip himself tightly to keep it, because it felt like it was slipping away, like sand through a fist.

Finally her lips turned upward in a faint smile. "Okay," she said softly.

All right! It was like letting a greyhound out of the gate.

A second later, they were shooting down the road, Sam trying to make it to his apartment as fast as legally possible. He wished he had one of those James Bond cars that could fly.

After twenty minutes at top speed, they were driving along the waterfront, the sun starting to set in a bloom of red on the water. It was a beautiful evening.

With any other woman, he'd remark on that. He'd driven countless women to his house or their house, knowing they were going to fuck, and he'd always been capable of keeping up a light conversation.

He couldn't get any words out now, though. None. It was like his throat was seized up.

She didn't seem to have any problems with that. He liked that she was comfortable with silence. She looked out at the vastness of the Pacific, the lower edge of the boiling crimson sun lighting gently on the horizon.

"It's a lovely evening."

Sam made a strangled noise in his throat and she turned to look at him.

"Where do you live? Where are we going?"

An ordinary question, deserving of an answer. He was going to scare her again if he couldn't even fucking *talk*.

He wrestled with himself, grabbed at a little self-control.

"Coronado Shores. Bought an apartment there over a year ago." He had to actually think about driving. Red lights, green lights, brakes. He was a good driver, had a natural feel for it, but right now he had to work hard not to press the accelerator to the floor and the hell with everything. Probably drive them straight into a goddamned light pole. "I was essentially a Navy diver and when I moved back here, I knew I wanted to live close to the sea."

That was part of it, but he didn't say the whole truth—how he'd spent countless afternoons on the dunes a couple of miles down, spending as much time as possible away from Old Man Hughes's fists, watching Navy SEALs go through their brutal paces. He'd longed to be one of them, part of a team of men with all the skills to make the world safer. Over the years, watching the hard men become harder by the day, he knew what he wanted to do with his life.

And now, in his post-military life, living in Coronado Shores meant he could run along the beach down to the training area and watch the new recruits rolling in the freezing surf and know that there would always be a new generation of men to watch over his country.

Nicole was looking around her with interest as they drove into Coronado Shores, passing by the first of the big condominium complexes. His was the last, La Torre. "I've been meaning to explore this part of town but I never got around to it," she said softly.

"That so?" He was surprised. The area was a popular outing for San Diegans.

She looked at him with a faint smile. "We've only been here a year. Since we arrived I've been really busy with Dad and Wordsmith. I've barely explored San Diego, just poked around a little, mainly in our part of town and the downtown area near our building."

"I'll show the area to you," Sam offered. "Be happy to. I know the city like the back of my hand." *Afterwards. When we come up for air, whenever that will be.*

She looked at him, a sideways dark blue glance that held a slight note of sadness. It hit him like a sledgehammer that she wasn't really expecting to see him again after tonight.

Oh no, he wasn't buying that. No way.

That big song and dance about her not having room for a man in her life? Fuck that. Sam would fucking plant himself at her fucking feet if that was what it took to keep seeing her.

"We're here," he said, veering sharply into his condo's driveway, then plunging down into the underground garage. He drove into his slot and killed the engine.

His condo had 140 units and the garage was usually busy 24/7 with people coming and going. Oddly enough, though, right now it was deserted. The only sound was the ticking sound of his engine cooling.

They sat in silence for a moment, looking at each other. Nicole swallowed.

Do something, dickhead, he told himself.

Clutching the wheel tightly, because he didn't trust himself to touch her, he leaned over to her, slowly. She was still a moment, then moved her head to meet his, hands in her lap. Their lips met over the central console.

The first real taste of her was electric. He felt it down to his balls. The merest taste, a brush of the lips, then, heads tilting, a deeper taste.

Oh God, it was like drinking fine wine. His nose was against her cheek. Close up, she smelled even better. They should just bottle up that smell and call it Desirable Woman. Men would follow women wearing it over cliffs.

He opened his mouth and licked her tongue, feeling her indrawn breath from his mouth. Oh Jesus. One more second and he'd tilt her seat back, climb on top of her, lift her skirt, rip her panties open and drive into her.

He could barely breathe from the excitement. They had to take it inside. He didn't give a shit, but presumably Nicole would mind being caught humping in the front seat.

He lifted his head, watching her eyes slowly open, like huge dark blue headlights. She looked dazed, the skin over her cheekbones flushed. She was aroused. Not as much as he was—that would be impossible—but she was definitely turned on.

"Let's go up." He was whispering. Everything felt fragile, as if the moment were of glass and could shatter at too loud a sound.

"Okay," she whispered back.

There was no small talk in the elevator going up. Nicole couldn't utter a word, her throat was too tightly closed. What was there to say, anyway? She couldn't have made any small talk that wouldn't arrow right back to what they were about to do.

Sam Reston stood beside her, looking as if he were about ready to explode, with an enormous erection tenting his pants. Any possible comments she might make about the weather or the building or the food they'd just eaten would be inane.

The very air felt charged, as if something enormous, something dark, surely momentous, possibly dangerous, were coming closer with each second.

This hadn't actually happened to her before— going to a man's house on a date having already accepted the idea of sleeping with him. Ms. Cool always kept her options open, never promising anything. A number of men who thought going to bed with her was a done deal had been left hanging. She made no promises and always reserved the right to say no if she became uncomfortable with the idea.

She wasn't going to say no now. She couldn't. It was as if Sam were this . . . this dark wizard who'd somehow cast a spell. Cast a glittering net over her so she couldn't escape, couldn't go back, could only go forward. The way an arrow, once loosed from the bow and embedded in flesh, can only be pushed forward, never pulled back.

There was this huge, rushing stream of dark sensuality, flowing directly toward his apartment and his bed, and she was caught in it.

At the thought of being in Sam Reston's bed, her vagina tightened, hard. Oh God, she was so aroused, she could feel the lips of her sex rubbing together as she moved.

This was absolutely new territory for Nicole. Another country altogether. One so far away from her knowledge of herself she could have been on an alien planet.

She couldn't say anything. Her voice would betray her agitation. She was barely holding on to a semblance of control, trying to keep her breathing regular, but it was all but impossible when she realized they were minutes away from bed.

At the thought, at the heated images in her head of Sam Reston's broad, naked shoulders above her, dark eyes staring into hers, long legs twined with hers, her vagina clenched again, her stomach muscles pulling sharply.

Heavens, she was minutes from orgasm, just from riding in the car and walking beside this man! Her heart pounded, her knees were weak.

This was ridiculous. Insane. Nicole was not highly sexed. Even in Geneva, footloose and fancy free, with all the money in the world and a city of diplomats and bankers at her feet, she hadn't dated that much. Certainly hadn't slept around.

She was hard to please, easily bored. Cool and in control, always.

Not now. This rough former soldier had somehow shaken her so hard she'd come away from her moorings. She was so filled with nervous excitement she had to stop herself from drumming her fingers on her purse.

She looked up, once, then looked away. He was watching her, dark eyes fixed on her, unwavering in his attention. Most women wanted their dates to pay attention to them, but this was way beyond first-date vibes. He was a soldier, and he was fixed on her as if she were a mission.

She'd never been in an enclosed space where the silence had weight and density. The silence felt like a living thing in the cabin, alive and sinuous, thick, snaking around them like an invisible fog.

It robbed her of breath and, obviously, of all common sense because she found she wanted to jump Sam Reston's bones. It was hard to think of a more un–Nicole-like thought, but there it was.

He exerted a pull she'd never felt before, though it was true she'd never gone out with anyone like him before, either. Her dates up until now had been elegant metrosexuals. Certainly not big and tough like Sam, incapable of playing those sophisticated man-woman games she was so good at. Sam didn't hide his desire in any way. He wasn't playing in any way. It was as if his desire were a huge emery board, filing away a layer of her skin until she was rubbed raw.

She chanced another glance up at him then away again, fast. He was still focused on her, jaw muscles jumping, eyes narrowed into slits.

Her heart jumped and she had to remember to breathe.

Nicole stared blindly at the door panel because if she looked at him again, she'd move toward him or reach out to touch him and he looked like he was barely controlling himself. She barely had *herself* under control. When the doors swooshed open, Sam put a hand to her back and her knees nearly buckled.

A large well-lit expanse of highly-polished hardwood floor stretched out left to right. At each end of the corridor were huge plate-glass floor-to-ceiling windows filled with a crimson glow. One side of the building gave out over the ocean, the other side onto the bay.

Sam took her elbow and moved them right, walking them down to the end of the corridor.

Nicole's heart was pounding. There wasn't going to be an hour of sipping whiskey and listening to music while she leisurely decided whether she wanted to take the next step. Once inside his apartment, they were going straight to bed, she could feel it.

Sex pulsed around him like an almost visible aura. As they walked, their eyes met at the same time, then Nicole's gaze slid away. It was too intense. She was burning up.

She could feel everything, every inch of her body. She was as aroused as she had ever been in her life, after one kiss, the only physical contact his big hand on her elbow.

All she could hear were her own heels, clickety clacking over the hardwood floor, in time with her trip-hammering heart. Sam moved utterly silently, like a huge, dark wraith.

They reached a door on the left-hand side, the side that looked out over the ocean.

He swiped a card down a slot and put his hand on a panel by the side of the door. The panel flashed green and slid open to reveal a keypad. Sam punched in five numbers and with a soft whir-ring of precision machinery, the door slid into the wall.

Straight ahead was a corridor of broad light-colored maple planks opening onto a large living area. The back wall was glass panels giving out onto a balcony, the sea darkly purple in the distance.

Nicole stood on the threshold, suddenly unable to make a move. Sam stood beside her, waiting.

She looked up at him, dismayed, unable to step forward, unable to go back. Her knees shook. She was suddenly seized with an attack of nerves. Everything about this felt new and scary.

Somehow, he understood. He was so worked up he had an erection like a hammer in his pants, but he didn't push her over the threshold or take her elbow and walk her through.

He didn't move.

"Welcome." The deep voice was soft as he gestured with his arm at the open doorway. He said nothing more, simply waited for her. The unspoken message was very clear. Stepping into his home had to be her choice.

Trembling, feeling as if she were stepping through an invisible barrier into another life, Nicole entered.

The house smelled good—of clean textiles and lemon polish and the sea breeze coming in from an open window, white cotton curtains billowing with the wind coming off the ocean.

A hiss, a metallic *whump* behind her and the door was closed and locked.

She was in.

She was going to do this.

Oh yes.

The next second her back thumped against the door and Sam Reston's entire weight was against her as he kissed her wildly. Not the fragile, tentative kiss in his car. Oh no, this was as if he were trying to inhale her, while punching his skin through hers. A deep kiss, wild, going on forever.

Oh God, his taste! Like a fresh mountain stream pumped full of male hormones, calculated to drive any woman wild. His mouth ate at hers, coming at her from various angles, as if one weren't enough. And it wasn't.

Her bag plopped to the floor, followed by her jacket.

Nicole could now hold him to her heart's content, though "holding" was a bland term for what she really wanted to do—crawl into his skin, feel every inch of that hard, delectable body, not with her fingertips but with her whole being. She twined her arms around his neck and arched her back. His chest muscles were so cut, she could feel them through his jacket, shirt, and her dress and bra, hard, ropy ridges of muscle, moving against her. Nicole astonished herself by rubbing against him, for the sheer pleasure of it, and because she was burning up and he seemed to be the only thing that could extinguish the fire.

His penis was hot and hard and huge against her belly and she could feel the pulses running through it against her skin. She tightened her hips, rubbing herself against him, and heard him moan in her mouth. Sam crouched and lifted her with an arm across her bottom, aligning his penis with her mound. She ground against him and the answering pulse of his penis against her made every muscle in her body contract.

Sam growled and leaned into her even more heavily, mouth grinding against hers, hips grinding against hers . . .

It was unthinkable that there be anything separating them. It was as if they both came to that conclusion together, at the very same instant. She reached up, swept his jacket off those broad shoulders. Her shaking fingers tugged at his tie and before it floated to the ground, she was at his shirt buttons, freeing the round bits of plastic from the eyeholes, pulling the tails out from his pants. She couldn't take off his shirt because his hands were on her bottom, holding her up, so the shirt fell off his shoulders just enough for her to feel the curly chest hairs and hard muscles of his chest against her. It was maddening that she still had the barriers of her dress and bra between them. She ached to feel him, hard to soft. Absorb some of that strength and heat through her skin.

Sam's callused hands ran up her thighs, bringing the skirt of her dress up, until he touched her panties. Her very expensive, mauve silk panties which she expected he'd let slither down her legs, like in some perfume ad, once he let her feet touch the floor again.

What happened next happened so fast she couldn't follow the movements. A ripping sound, a zipping sound, rough fingers opening her up and—*oh my God!*—he was in her, impossibly hard, impossibly hot, deeper than anyone had ever been before.

They were both frozen, Sam embedded in her while she struggled to accommodate him. She wriggled a little and he surged inside her, so deep the sensitive tissues of her flesh could feel his wiry pubic hairs.

She was filled with sensory input. His penis, buried inside her, his two hard hands holding her bottom, skirt now up to her waist, ruched over his arms, his hard broad chest pinning her against the wall . . .

Thunk! Sam's forehead hit the wall beside her.

"Condom," he groaned, panting like a maddened bull. A muscle twitched in his cheek. He groaned again and she felt his body stiffen, start to pull out.

No!

"Pill," she gasped and his entire body jerked.

"Oh man," he breathed. "Bareback." He pulled out slowly, went back in, an exploratory stroke and groaned. "You feel like a glove."

"Mm." Nicole hardly had the breath to respond. He was hot inside her, her entire lower body glowed with heat, but he wasn't moving. She understood quite well what he was doing—giving her time to adjust to his size. No question, he had a champ of a member there, certainly the biggest she'd ever come across. But he needed to use it, the dummy, instead of simply waiting for her. What did he want? A sign? She'd give him a sign.

Nicole turned her head slightly, nose against his cheek. He smelled so delicious. He'd clearly shaved but there was a slight bite of growing beard against her face as she rubbed her cheek against his. Tentatively, she licked him. She'd been wanting to do that all evening, just to see what he tasted like.

Delicious.

At the touch of her tongue, Sam jerked, but he still held himself quietly inside her, breathing heavily. She wriggled a little and he jumped inside her, there was no other word for it.

She'd started taking the pill several months ago upon doctor's orders, when stress had caused her to miss several periods. She'd never taken it while sexually active. This was the first time she felt a man's penis inside her without a latex barrier and it was . . . wonderful. Intense, almost unbearably intimate.

She opened her mouth and bit him, a sharp nip along his jaw, and it galvanized him.

His big body jerked and he started pounding in her, hard deep strokes which were possible only because she was wet with excitement. The whole evening had been foreplay.

His entire heavy weight was pressed against her, mouth on hers, hips jackhammering. Not the polite, regular strokes of a first-time lover, sounding out what the woman liked. No, these were out of control movements of a man using his entire strength and . . . she loved it. He must have felt that because, impossibly, he picked up the tempo, moving in and out of her so fast it was a miracle she didn't go up in smoke from the friction.

It was amazing, and a degree of excitement impossible to sustain. Inside a few minutes, Nicole froze, every muscle in lockdown, as she felt her orgasm approaching, like a thunderstorm on the horizon. She stopped breathing, eyes closed, totally concentrated on where he was pounding into her with hard, heavy strokes. One particularly deep thrust and . . . oh! Her entire body convulsed, vagina tightening around him, arms and legs clinging tightly, wanting to feel him as close as possible.

Her breath came out in a low, ragged moan, stuttering in time to his sharp thrusts, faster now and harder, until he swelled inside her and exploded.

Oh my God! She could feel the jets of semen splashing against her supersensitive walls, a hot, rhythmic wash inside her, unlike anything she'd ever felt before, so exciting it prolonged her orgasm. She tightened around him in an erotic rhythm that matched the pulses of his own orgasm, the feeling so intense she nearly blacked out.

It had been like running a marathon. Nicole's head batted back against the wall because she didn't have the strength to keep it upright. Her arms dropped, unable to cling to those broad shoulders anymore. Her legs were still around his hips, but they were trembling.

Her entire groin area was wet and the smell of sex rose, sharp and earthy, from where they were joined.

"Oh," she breathed, unable to form anything more coherent.

"Yeah," Sam grunted. "I know. Hold on tight, honey."

What . . . ? Oh. Sam tightened his grip on her bottom, pulled them away from the wall and walked them through the house, still joined. He was still rock hard inside her, as if he hadn't climaxed at all, rubbing against her incredibly sensitive tissues as he carried her.

He was kissing her, carrying her as if she were weightless, straight into the bedroom. There was still a little light outside and she opened her eyes enough to get an impression of space and Spartan order, then he kissed her again and the outside world was gone.

She had no idea how he did it, but when he eased her down on the bed, they were both naked. He was still inside her, and now he was on top with his full weight bearing down on her. It was so delicious, feeling his hard muscles against hers, chest hairs rubbing against her breasts. He opened strong, hairy thighs, opening her own legs much wider, and slid even more deeply inside her.

He nuzzled her ear with his nose, dropped light kisses all over her face and neck. In between kisses he whispered to her.

"That was too fast, I'm really sorry. I want you to know that I do have some moves in me, just not right now."

She barely heard him, concentrated on where they were touching, on where he filled her. But at the word *moves*, her vagina contracted around him. His penis lengthened inside her.

"That's one of them, right there," she sighed.

He laughed, a charming low male rumble. "Oh yeah."

He wasn't moving, allowing her to come back a little to herself. She smoothed a hand over the ball of his shoulder. His skin was so hot and hard. Warm steel. She frowned as her fingers met thick, rough skin. A scar. A round scar.

Her eyes fluttered open, only to see his an inch away. Deep, dark eyes, staring into hers. He wasn't smiling anymore.

"Is that what I think it is?" she whispered.

He gave a short, brusque nod.

"Are there any others?"

"Low on my hip, missed vital organs by a hair. Right biceps, flesh wound, but it hurt like hell."

She touched each one as he mentioned them. The wound low down on his hip was big, ugly, with thick ridges of scar tissue. She frowned as he kissed her.

"You had a really lousy surgeon."

He shook his head, nipped her jaw. "Field dressing. We were way out to hell and gone. Took me a week to get back to a hospital. Navy offered plastic surgery, but frankly, I never want to see another needle again in my life."

Nicole stroked his sides. He hadn't led a charmed life, this man. He'd walked into danger, probably more times than he could ever tell her. A few inches to the left or right, and he'd have bled out. She'd never have met him, never have realized what her body was capable of feeling.

Lifting her head a little, she kissed him, gently. As if he were still hurting from his wounds. Sam took control of the kiss immediately, mouth open over hers, tongue stroking hers in time with the strokes of his hips.

He began moving heavily in her, faster and faster, and she curled her hands under his arms, holding on to his shoulders for dear life. Sam wrenched his mouth away from hers with a gasp and buried his face in her hair and she closed her eyes and arched her neck.

He was right. They couldn't kiss right now. It was too much.

Sam lifted her knees, moving impossibly deeper, touching something . . . Nicole came with a wild cry, clenching tightly around him, shaking and shuddering, sweating, tears leaking out of her eyes, the climax so intense she lost herself for long moments, spinning way out in space, coming back to herself only when Sam grunted and started coming inside her, long, hot spurts of semen bathing her sheath.

He was moving inside her with enormous ease now. She was incredibly wet, full of his juices and hers. Time stretched, became meaningless.

He stilled finally while Nicole drifted lazily on waves of pleasure. She was incredibly sweaty, but it was more his sweat than hers. Their chests were stuck together, she discovered as she pushed at his shoulders. Her entire groin area was sopping wet, including her thighs. Her vagina was sore, super-sensitized. She could feel every inch of his penis, still hard inside her. Her muscles felt lax, unable to work.

She felt . . . wonderful. She'd be floating if she didn't have his enormous weight on top of her. She pushed at his shoulders again and with an aggrieved sigh, he lifted himself up on his forearms and smiled down at her.

A tiny forelock of dark hair had fallen over his forehead and she reached up a hand to smooth it back.

"Are you hungry?" he asked and she was about

ready to answer, *No, of course not, we just ate,* when her stomach rumbled, loudly.

"Apparently, I am." This was amazing. They'd had a full meal and yet, consulting her stomach, she realized she was famished.

Sam dropped a kiss on her nose and pulled out of her. So slowly it was arousing. If that hadn't done the trick, seeing him standing by the side of the bed naked would have been enough to turn her on.

Though he was huge, he was lean with it, perfectly proportioned, graceful and strong. And— whew!—hung.

For the first time, Nicole was able to appreciate his, um, attributes. Amazingly, after coming twice, he was still aroused. His penis, glistening with their juices, a dark suede color, with big veins running up it, nearly reached his navel.

Sam reached down to encircle her ankle for a second. "I'll bring you something out on the terrace. We're going to need some fuel for round two."

Sam nearly laughed at her expression. She was ready to call it quits, but he wasn't. Not even close. He was as revved as he'd ever been in his life.

Man, just looking at her, there on his bed . . . like some seventeenth-century painting. Just the colors of her would be enough to wake a dead man. Midnight black hair; porcelain skin; red, red lips, slightly swollen from his kisses. Cherry red nipples, cloud of soft black hair between her thighs.

She glistened, from her sweat and his. From his come, from her girl juices. She hadn't moved an inch after he'd pulled out. She looked as if she were fucking some phantom lover—legs bent and apart, so wide open to him he could see the puffy, deep pink tissues of her cunt, arms still outstretched, eyes half closed as if still kissing him. He wanted to climb back onto her, slide right back into her. He wanted that so hard he clenched his fists.

But she needed food. Sam was used to pushing himself, but she wouldn't be.

He watched her as her eyelids slowly lowered until there was only a sliver of that amazing blue, watched as her breathing slowed, watched as the wild heartbeat over her left breast beat less frantically.

Shit, even looking at her was better than fucking anyone else.

That was a scary thought. He left it behind and went to the kitchen to scrabble for food. He didn't cook much but his housekeeper sometimes left him things and there was always fruit.

Five minutes later, he was carrying a big tray out onto the balcony, pleased with what he was able to scrounge up. A big plate of grapes, a couple of slices of cheese that, miraculously, had no mold on them. Half a loaf of frozen whole wheat bread he nuked in the microwave.

Two stem glasses and a bottle of really good Chilean sauvignon blanc. She'd know how to pronounce it. He placed the tray on the wrought-iron-and-glass table outside and debated whether to turn on the outside terrace lights. It was dark outside, maybe around midnight. They'd been fucking for three hours straight. He switched on one of the halogen lights, just enough for them to see the food by, not enough for a boat out on the ocean to see what they were doing.

Sam looked out over the dark ocean, then down at himself, at his boner that simply wouldn't quit. He had plenty of stamina but after a couple of hours, he was ordinarily ready to call it quits. Drive the lady home. Relax.

He wasn't anywhere near that point with Nicole. Couldn't even imagine it.

He was in deepest shit, he reflected, as he went back into the bedroom to carry her out to the terrace.

Chapter 6

The sky had turned pewter, a shade lighter than the ocean that still carried the darkness of the night.

Nicole opened one eye, then closed it quickly.

Eyes closed, she tried to process what she'd seen.

A train wreck, that's what she'd seen.

She opened her eyes each morning to her calm, orderly bedroom, with the four-poster that she'd slept in in seven countries, with its French lace canopy and Frette sheets. The seventeenth-century armoire and eighteenth-century Italian *madia*. The vases with fresh flowers, the ceramic bowls of potpourri, the big Baccarat crystal vase full of multi-colored sand. Her mother's lovely watercolors and a collection of photographs taken by an old school friend who was now one of the top fashion photographers in the world.

Everything in its place. Cool and quiet and neat, exactly as she liked it.

This room looked like it had been at war, particularly the bed. She looked down at herself, naked, one leg trapped by the powerful, hairy leg of an equally naked man. A man with hormones instead of blood, she'd swear.

Sam Reston did not have an "off" button. He'd finally stopped a few hours ago because she was ready to go into a coma, after too many orgasms to count.

Time out, she'd gasped, and he'd laughed and slowly pulled out of her, the act so sexy she'd mourned the absence of his penis immediately, though she'd been the one to call a halt. He'd disappeared for a moment and come back with two glasses of chilled white wine and a plate of ripe grapes.

Even after dinner, even after the impromptu midnight picnic on the terrace, she'd been ravenous. Nonstop sex, it appeared, was an appetite stimulant, in more ways than one.

As she sipped the wine, she couldn't help but give an admiring look at him sitting beside her, muscles bulging as he fed her grapes, big, thick, erect penis dark, engorged with blood, twitching when she looked at it.

She'd glanced at his lap then looked away again, but she could feel the flush rising from her breasts to her face. She thought she'd stopped blushing in her teens, but apparently not. Close proximity to Sam Reston made the blood pound through her body, rise to her face, color her nipples deep pink.

He'd looked at her, *really* looked at her, from her flushed breasts, the left one moving slightly with the hard pulses of her heart, the vein beating in her neck, the pearls of moisture in her pubic hair, a mixture of his semen and her excitement.

His eyes had lifted to hers and her entire body thrummed. But it was like asking a car to start on fumes, after having been pedal-to-the-metal running straight through every molecule of gas in the tank. She was sore all over, particularly her sex, and the desire she felt was only a faint echo of the all-consuming drive to have him in her she'd felt all night in his bed.

There it was. She'd hit her own personal wall. Finally. It had been a night of excess that had astonished her, but she had her limits and she'd reached them.

Sam had moved his free hand to her knee, cupping it, narrowed dark eyes burning into hers. He'd brought his mouth to her ear.

"Nicole?" The deep voice had been like a caress. How incredibly sexy it had sounded in her ear while he'd been moving heavily inside her. Her stomach clenched at the memory.

Oh God, he was ready for another round. How could he? With a sigh, Nicole realized she wasn't being fair. She'd nearly crawled into his skin up until now, matching him heat for heat. If she'd reached the end of her rope, and he hadn't, it wasn't his fault.

"Lie down," he'd said softly.

Heart pounding, she let her back settle on the mattress. How to do this? Maybe she could psych herself up for another round.

He shifted on the mattress and she controlled a wince. But instead of climbing on top of her, as she expected, he smiled and positioned his glass of wine over her belly and slowly, slowly, poured a thin, cold stream of the fragrant Chardonnay over her.

It felt good on her overheated skin, the fragrant fruity notes rising to her nose.

And then Sam had bent to lick the wine off her stomach, slowly, like a cat lapping cream. She'd tried to rise on her elbows, but he'd simply put a big hand on her chest and gently pushed her back down.

He lifted his head and smiled at her. "No, honey," he said, his voice a deep, dark whisper. "You don't do anything at all. You just lie back and let me pleasure you."

That was good, because her muscles felt like water, incapable of holding her up.

Sam's tongue moved lower, lower and she gasped as he licked around her sex, gently, as if aware of the fact that she was sore.

"Close your eyes." The deep voice came from far away.

"Okay." She closed her eyes, heard the faint click

as he turned the bedside lamp off. Her eyelids turned from pink to black.

Sam nuzzled her sex, nose against her clitoris, tongue gently swirling, dipping into her, where his penis had just been. Her breath came out on a sigh, his own murmur of satisfaction echoing hers.

Soft plashing sounds came through the open French windows, gentle and regular, as if the sea were breathing. There were soft gentle sounds coming from down her body as Sam worked her with his mouth.

Such a strange sensation, slowly becoming aroused while the mantle of sleep bore down on her, as she drifted further and further away, to a land of pleasure that grew ever darker . . .

Unlike the other contractions of orgasm, so sharp at times they poised on the knife-edge of pain, this climax was gentle, dreamy, her body a boat rocking on the soft waves of the sea, rocking, rocking . . .

It was the last thing she remembered.

The sky was growing lighter by the minute. Soon it would be dawn.

Nicole rose slowly from the bed, wincing at all the sore muscles, making her halting way to the bathroom. She passed a mirror and winced at the sight of the unknown woman in the mirror, clearer by the minute as the world outside lightened, like an image emerging from the fog. Wild, dark hair tangling around her head, huge eyes, swollen lips.

She looked back at the bed, at him. He was so long, his feet hung off the bed. Even his feet were gorgeous, long, lean, high-arched. One thick arm was over his eyes, the other outstretched to her side of the bed. Deeply asleep, completely still except for the expansion of his broad chest with each breath.

Well . . . he'd made love all night. Literally. She'd had no idea that any male over the age of fifteen would have been capable of that, capable of coming so many times she'd lost count. Even now, in complete repose, in a sleep so deep it could have been a coma, his penis looked full, veins visible, semi-erect on his thigh.

If Sam's eyes were to open right now, and if he were to see her naked, that penis would swell fully erect in an instant. She'd bet the bank on it.

Something in her seemed to set him off. Certainly, something in him set *her* off. She looked like she was making love right now. Her breasts were swollen, nipples red and hard. And oh God, just *looking* at him, like some Greek statue come to life, her thighs trembled.

She had to get out of here. Fast.

For a second, she looked with longing at the bathroom door. A shower. A shower would go a long way toward making her feel like herself again, washing away the smell of him permeating her skin. He'd touched every inch of her last night, marked her irrevocably, inside and out. She wasn't used to not feeling fresh and she definitely wasn't used to smelling of someone else.

She stared at herself in the mirror, this face she'd never seen before, eyes wide, pupils dilated.

And then she was aware of something else. Wetness between her legs, running down her thighs. For a moment, she thought she'd unexpectedly got her period, that her body had simply disobeyed the pill and gone ahead and had a period, breaking the hormonal schedule. An entire night of wild sex surely would be enough to knock her for a loop, hormonally speaking.

She looked down at herself, expecting to see drops of blood, but all she saw was a gleaming wetness.

His semen.

Sam had shot a small lake into her during the night. At the memory, her knees wobbled. She gasped for air, the sound loud in the quiet room. Nicole's head whipped around to see if she'd somehow woken Sam up, but he was out like a light.

The thought of that—of Sam waking up and finding her here, of having to face him after last night's excesses . . . Oh no.

It wasn't that she wasn't still attracted to him, it was that she was attracted too *much*. The Nicole Pearce of last night—the woman who had wallowed in sex, who had tuned out the world to focus narrowly on Sam Reston and his luscious, utterly male body—she had to simply put that woman away. That Nicole was an aberration and she had to disappear, right now.

Speaking of disappearing . . .

She looked around wildly. Her dress was on

the floor, crumpled, bra on top. Jacket on the back
of a chair. One sandal was toppled on its side next
to a big, sleek chest of drawers, and its mate . . .
where the *hell* was its mate? Walking barefoot out
of Sam's house was too awful to contemplate, but
the other sandal was nowhere to be found. Two
sweeps of the room and no shoe. Just one place
left to look. She crouched and yes, there it was.
Under the bed. Under Sam's very large, very low
bed. It took a full minute, but she finally got it.

She couldn't possibly walk out looking like
this, but on the other hand, there was a drumbeat
inside her, insistent and loud. *Get out now. Get out
now.* Before he woke up, because she had no clue
what she could possibly say to him.

Dress and go, now.

She slipped into the bathroom, leaving the
door open, so that a little of the faint morning
light could seep in. If she turned the lights on in
the white-tiled bathroom, the glare could wake
Sam up.

A splash of cold water on her face, a quick wash
between her legs—and oh my god, the nap of the
washcloth felt incredibly rough against her super-
sensitized flesh—a comb hastily pulled through
her hair was all she allowed herself time for. Bra
and dress went on in under a minute.

Holding her sandals by the straps, she tiptoed
her way to the front door. On the floor was a silky
mauve slash of material. Her panties. Her beautiful La Perla panties, ripped apart. And how she'd
reveled in Sam tearing them off her, because

they'd been this unacceptable barrier between her and Sam's hard flesh.

She closed her eyes for a second, then opened them, intent more than ever on getting out as fast as she could, like someone fleeing from the scene of the crime.

The door. She eyed it warily. Last night, getting in had been like getting into some secret room at the Pentagon. Palm print, keypad, five-digit code. She had no idea what the numbers were. Her mind had been utterly lost in mists of lust.

If she needed a secret code to get out, she was in trouble.

The idea of having to walk back into the bedroom, wake Sam up and ask for a code made her focus, concentrate. She studied the door, narrow eyed. A door had to work both ways, didn't it? You have to be able to get out, not just in.

There was no security panel. No door handle, either, for that matter. She stared at the door, willing it to yield up its secrets.

Did it open by remote control? Did she have to go back into the bedroom and root through Sam's pants? That would be the last straw.

There was one button on the wall next to the featureless door. She held out a hesitant finger, hovered over it, then gathered her courage and pressed it, hoping it wasn't connected to something dangerous, like a siren. Or a bomb.

A crisp *click* and the lock disengaged, the door sliding open.

Yes!

Nicole tiptoed through, then quietly slid the door closed behind her.

She stood in the hallway, breathing heavily, as if she'd just engineered a jailbreak. Her heart was pounding so hard it was a miracle the sound didn't echo in the quiet corridor.

It was utterly ridiculous, but she couldn't do anything about the way she felt—panicky and broken, as if running away from something dangerous.

Mindful of the clickety-clack of her heels on the shiny hardwood floor of the corridor last night, she walked barefoot to the elevator and called it up, wincing at the little ping as it reached Sam's floor. It sounded so loud in the silence.

In the elevator, she clutched her pochette tightly, like a shield, and stared mindlessly at the elevator doors.

When they opened, she stepped out into the huge, glass-encased lobby. The sky was now a dark pearly gray and she could see the beach not fifty feet away, the small waves curling like lace on the sand.

"Miss?"

Nicole jumped and barely managed to suppress a scream.

"Miss? Can I help you?" The tone more pointed, with a slight Hispanic accent.

A security guard, dressed in some security company's livery, surrounded by a circular polished-wood barrier with lots of video screens showing empty hallways, looking at her with a frown.

Nicole heroically refrained from looking down

at herself in dismay but she knew exactly what he was seeing. A disheveled woman who had obviously been up to no good, tiptoeing away shoeless from a night of excess in one of the apartments.

This was just so *unfair*. Nicole was the epitome of a proper lady. Even in the midst of a hot affair, she always kept her decorum; it had been drummed into her. She prided herself on the fact that a casual observer would never know what she was thinking, what she was feeling.

Right now, she might as well have had *babe after a hot night* tattooed on her forehead.

The only thing to do was brazen it out. She straightened, put on her best ambassador's-daughter polite smile and lifted her head.

"Good morning," she said evenly. "I wonder if you could call me a taxi?"

"Sure thing, ma'am," the guard said, punching out a number on the phone keypad without taking his eyes off her. Presumably in case she made off with one of the stone planters that must have weighed three hundred pounds each.

"Thank you," Nicole said primly, and walked to the front of the lobby, sitting down on one of the long, gleaming oak benches. She carefully put on her sandals and stared out the two-story windows at the beach. The sky was cloudless, pale blue, the ocean light gray. It was going to be a glorious day, as so many days were in San Diego.

She stared out at the ocean, thinking of absolutely nothing, until she heard the guard call out. "Taxi's here, ma'am."

She turned her head and sure enough, a cab was coming around the circular driveway. Nicole nodded to the guard and got into the cab. She gave her address to the driver and stared blindly out the window as he took off.

This part of San Diego was beautiful, but she barely noticed the white sand beaches, lush vegetation, the light dancing on wavelets over the ocean, the runners on the beach.

All she could think about was Sam Reston on top of her, nose an inch from hers, staring at her fiercely as he moved in and out of her. And the fact that all last night, she hadn't thought once about her father.

New York

"Paul Preston for Mr. Mold. I have a ten o'clock appointment."

Ah. Finally. The last secretary in the gauntlet. She lifted her gaze and gave him a small smile, just a slight baring of beautiful white-capped teeth as large as Chiclets, then her gloss-covered mouth closed tightly. Muhammed had learned that the more powerful the man, the less friendly the secretary.

He'd cycled through three secretaries already,

offering smiles in decreasing increments, as he neared the "Holy Presence." This secretary was the one who held her boss's schedule. She was powerful beyond measure and she knew it.

Muhammed had asked for this appointment, desperate to get to top financier Richard Mold as fast as possible, knowing that time was vital, yet trying not to press too hard, because Mold would see it as a sign of vulnerability.

These men could smell desperation at a hundred paces, like hyenas can smell blood from miles away. Muhammed *was* desperate, but not for money. Though he lived in a world that would do anything for money—live for it, die for it, even kill for it—he was indifferent to its lure.

Particularly now, when he—Muhammed Wahed, a child of the camps—was going to change the course of human history. Men would weave stories of his actions for a thousand years. More.

So it was hard for him to keep calm in front of the secretary's cool gaze as she pressed a button and quietly said, "Mr. Paul Preston to see you, sir. Your ten-o'clock appointment."

Did she notice the slight sheen of sweat on his forehead? See that he had to work to keep from wringing his hands?

Maybe she did. Maybe that was for the best. Maybe if he were too cool, it would be noted, commented on. Richard Mold commanded an empire and his methods were harsh. In his own world, he was a caliph, a sultan. Anyone asking a favor was meant to be a sweaty, trembling supplicant.

There was a low, calm, deep murmur from the intercom—the tone of command very clear—and the big mahogany and brass door to the right of the desk issued a faint click and slid smoothly into the wall.

The secretary looked at him coolly. "You have until ten fifteen, sir."

The subtext was that at 10:15, security would be called in.

Well, by 10:15 he'd either have a name, or not. It was in Allah's hands at this point.

He walked through the door.

Over the past years, Muhammed had been in countless offices of the rich and powerful. Some preferred the English Lord look. Paneled walls, deep leather armchairs, crystal decanters, as if an office on the fortieth floor of a Manhattan sky-scraper had been in existence for three hundred years, bequeathed down through the generations, from earl to earl.

Some had offices that looked like they'd time-traveled back from the twenty-second century.

But all of them, *all* of them exuded a specific aura—*look at me. Look at what I've accomplished. Look at how powerful I am. Do not mess with me because I will crush you.*

Muhammed had been in this office once before, when Mold had just taken over the big hedge fund. It had looked like Versailles then. Now it was all sleek black marble and Lucite.

They said that Mold had spent three million dollars redecorating his office.

And there he was, behind a twelve-foot-long slab of ebony with transparent legs, the desk empty and bare and highly polished, as befitted a Master of the Universe.

Mold stood but didn't offer his hand. "Preston," he said. The deep voice wasn't particularly warm or welcoming. "What can I do for you?"

That was a loaded question, if ever there was one. Muhammed was here only because Mold hoped Muhammed could do something for him. If it was only a favor being asked, Muhammed would be marched out by security the instant Mold pressed the red button that was undoubtedly on the underside of the desk.

All nervousness had gone, sucked away like the stale air into the invisible conditioners.

Muhammed had seen the future.

Mold's office building was one of the top ones of the list. The instant his martyr brothers could fan out, this building was to be one of the first to be irradiated. The brothers would be freshly barbered, dressed in the uniforms of Wall Street—suits by Armani, Boss, Jil Sanders. They would have ID that would bear up to a security guard's scrutiny. Muhammed would give the order that one martyr stay in the lobby and another martyr brother come up here, to the fifty-fifth floor, and blow himself up right in front of the snotty secretary's desk. Mold would die instantly. His company, everything he stood for, would be gone in an instant, everything untouchable for decades.

It calmed Muhammed right down. Mold was

giving off the waves of aggression typical of a Wall-Street trader turned hedge fund manager. His temper tantrums were famous. He was used to screaming, intimidating underlings to get his way.

Muhammed looked at Mold calmly, at this dead man walking.

Only a few days to go.

He looked around, then chose a chair and sat down just as Mold said, "Have a seat."

The chair was by a hot new designer and was made of paper. Muhammed had read that it sold for $10,000, enough to feed hundreds of people in the camps for a year.

Richard Mold deserved to burn. They all did.

Muhammed hitched his trousers so as not to ruin the excellent crease, and crossed his legs.

Silence.

It irritated Mold. His deeply tanned face turned tight, his eyes narrowed. "So, Preston, what's this about?" he asked coldly.

Muhammed waited a beat, then spoke. "I have a piece of information you might find interesting, and in exchange, I want a name and a phone number."

Mold's thick gray eyebrows drew together. "What's the info and what name?"

Muhammed plucked at the crease of his trousers, enjoying the feel of the fine linen. He let a minute go by, two. Oh, he'd learned the subtle ways of power of the West. Mold watched him, face growing even tighter.

Finally, Muhammed gave a small sigh. "A company you invest in, a very well known corporation, has just announced one of its best quarters ever. A double-digit increase in sales. Its stock has risen by almost fifteen percent on the strength of the report. But it's false. The CEO is hiding almost twenty billion dollars in losses and the FBI will arrest him in four days' time. If you short that stock, you can make millions. In four days."

Mold's face betrayed nothing but Muhammed knew the thoughts going through his mind. Over the past week, several corporations had announced big gains after almost two years of recession. Muhammed could be referring to any one of a number of companies. Guess wrong and you lose a bundle. Guess right, ah. Make millions in an instant. Add to your reputation as a miracle man. To someone like Mold, it was irresistible. He and his kind were born for this kind of challenge.

That tight slash of a mouth opened, cranked the words out. "And what would you want in return for that name?"

Yes! It was a done deal.

"Another name," Muhammed murmured. "All we both want is a name."

Mold wasn't one to utter unnecessary words. He simply stared.

Muhammed leaned forward slightly, lowered his voice. "Some time ago, I heard that there is a man the financial community . . . uses. When there are problems you can't buy your way out of. I want the name and contact details of the man who makes problems and people go away."

Silence. Utter silence.

They were so high no sounds could penetrate and one of the things the woman outside was there for was to prevent noises or distractions. There was no sound at all. Even the air-conditioning was utterly quiet.

Mold watched his eyes for a long moment, then took out a sheet of thick stock, clicked his Cross pen and wrote. The sound of the pen moving across the thick paper was loud in the morning silence. Mold folded the sheet once, twice, then slid it across his desk.

Muhammed had taken his own pen and written out the name of a company on the top of a page torn from the *Wall Street Journal*.

The name was that of the second-largest corporation in the US. It had just announced record sales after the long slump. As far as Muhammed knew, the figures were correct. Mold would sell short and lose a lot of money.

It wouldn't matter, because in four days, Mold, his company, the corporation and all of Wall Street would be gone.

Muhammed folded the newspaper page neatly in half and slid it across the half acre of Mold's desk, pocketing the paper Mold had written on without looking at it.

He rose, briefcase in hand. He didn't make the mistake of offering his hand. They stared at each other for a moment. Muhammed bowed his head soberly and walked out, feeling Mold's eyes boring into the back of his head and hearing the slight crinkle of the piece of paper in his pocket with the name of the man who would solve his problem and help him bring down the world.

Georgia

The name was Sean McInerney. He worked undercover often and had had numerous aliases, but Sean McInerney was the name he'd been born with.

It wouldn't be the name he'd die with.

After the military, starting his new profession, Sean had thought long and hard about his cover name. He wanted it short and snappy. One word, memorable, like Cher or Madonna, only instead of thinking good-looking chick, you had to think lethal.

He'd been listening to Outlaw by Whitesnake, and it came to him. *Of course.*

He'd had a number of aliases in his time, but "Outlaw" worked real well in his new profession. The name was corny, but his new employers loved it. Made them feel sexy, made them feel tough.

Life after SpecOps was good. Real good.

He'd lucked into a little cohort of bankers, CEOs, hedge fund managers, financiers and money managers who spent their time hunched over computer monitors, thinking they were dangerous dudes.

Outlaw had heard all the macho phrases: *Eat*

what you kill, Put wood behind the arrow, Drink the Kool-aid.

Men in finance liked to think of themselves as real tough dudes, but they were tough only because they had a wall of money behind them. When that wall threatened to fall, they crumbled and showed their true natures—that of pale clerks, not alpha males, as they so fondly imagined themselves.

The only attribute Outlaw recognized of himself in them was utter ruthlessness. Touch their money and they would hire the best to fight for them and give no quarter.

And so his post-military life began. The dishonorable discharge—thrown out of the Army for selling arms when there were fucking warehouses full of them rusting in the desert—stopped him from applying for a white-collar job, not that he had ever wanted one.

No, a freak connection between an old Army buddy and his brother in finance had set him up in his new profession.

The first job couldn't have been easier. A whistleblower, about ready to send a hot set of documents showing malfeasance to the SEC and blow a fifteen-million-dollar bonus out of the water. The CEO met with Outlaw in a luxury room at the top of a business skyscraper about five blocks from where he worked. The financier might have been a god in the world of finance but he was a fuckhead in real life.

The financier had given a false name and made sure that he employed euphemisms, but it was clear he wanted the whistleblower taken out. Outlaw had showed him the Barrett 95 in its carrying case and watched as the banker's eyes widened.

It was bullshit, all of it.

Outlaw knew perfectly well who the banker was. Lewis Munro, CEO of the tenth largest corporation in the US. Outlaw had his name, home address and address of the hideaway apartment on Lexington where Munro's mistress lived. Outlaw knew how much cocaine Munro consumed in a week and how much he paid for it. He knew what private schools the kids were in, how much Mrs. Munro dropped weekly at Hermés and even the amount of taxes Munro had evaded.

Even the Barrett was bullshit. A .50 cal bullet was guaranteed to rain down police attention like nothing else. For the Barrett he used an armor-piercing bullet, the Raufoss Mk.211, containing an incendiary, and very accurate in sniper rifles. He'd lifted three thousand boxes of the stuff from the base warehouse.

It was a military bullet, totally wasted on a civilian target unless you had to snipe at two grand out. Like a big, red fucking sign hung around the dead guy's neck that this was a hit. Sometimes that was necessary. Most of the time, it wasn't.

When it went down, it was a perfect street mugging. The whistleblower walking back home alone from a dinner date with friends, the mugger taking all his money, credit cards and even his wedding ring and wristwatch. The police speculated that the whistleblower had resisted and got a knife in the ribs for his pains.

The homicide detective stood over the crumpled body in the alley and shook his head over the mugger's luck in hitting the heart with one thrust.

It wasn't luck. Outlaw had practiced that move thousands of times in training and hundreds of times on live bodies on mission.

Had the whistleblower been taken out by a sniper's bullet, the police would have looked closely at his affairs and would have found material incriminating Munro, who would have had some explaining to do, which would have made pointless the hundred thousand dollars Munro had transferred to Outlaw's bank in Aruba.

As it was, the police couldn't track the knife on which there were no prints and after a fruitless two weeks, the whistleblower's file was already a cold case.

That hit had made him. He became the go-to guy for anyone in the financial sector who had a problem that couldn't be solved by throwing money at it, including divorcing wives where there was no prenup.

Outlaw had had more than twenty jobs in the past five years, all executed perfectly. A study of the terrain and the subject, a quick in and out, using methods that varied widely, and no one was the wiser. He had even put together a team of former soldiers, good men who, after giving their all to Uncle Sam, were now up for earning real money.

Outlaw had learned from the finance guys, too. Corner a market and charge big. He was up to five hundred grand a pop now, plus expenses.

Outlaw had given Munro a cell phone number on a card, knowing Munro would spread it around. Munro lived in a world of men used to winning, no matter what. And if they didn't have the necessary set of skills to do specific jobs, they simply hired men who did.

The call came as he was looking out over the hundred acres he'd bought in Georgia, less than an hour from the hub that was Hartsfield International. The land was extensive enough to have firing ranges, a shoot house and endurance courses for his men, while offering complete privacy. The perimeter was surrounded by sensors sensitive enough to detect a jackrabbit, with webcams every five feet.

In essence, Outlaw had his own country.

He'd built an enormous house that offered every comfort he could possibly want. Standing at the huge reinforced plate-glass window sipping a Jack Daniel's, he answered his cell. It was his business cell phone, never used for anything but clients with jobs.

Well good, he thought. *Time to make me some more money.*

"Are you the man known as Outlaw?" The voice was soft, not deep, standard American.

"Yeah." He didn't ask who was calling. It didn't make any difference. The guy would lie anyway.

If necessary for the job, Outlaw could find out. Otherwise, he didn't give a shit as long as the money landed in the bank. "What do you need?"

"Ah, a man who comes directly to the point. I like that."

"Well, since I've got myself a rep as a straight shooter, let me tell you straight out I'm not moving until my fee is in my bank."

"I was told about your . . . style, Mr. Outlaw. If you check your bank account, you will find your fee. Plus. I will send you the information on the person of interest in ten minutes, once you've ascertained this."

Outlaw didn't need ten minutes. Inside a minute, he'd logged onto his bank account and yes, there it was, 500K with an extra 100K thrown in for goodwill.

Outlaw knew his employers lived, breathed and died for money. Extra money meant this was extra important.

After ten minutes, a beep from his cell phone. He had a text message.

Nicole Pearce. Translation agency, Wordsmith. Morrison Building, San Diego, California.

Nicole Pearce received data in e-mail sent from Marseilles on June 28. Retrieve hard disk, possible flash drive, search for backups, eliminate computer, eliminate Nicole Pearce. Strict timeline. Job must be completed by July 2.

Okay.

Get a hard disk from a woman, snuff woman.

He'd done harder things in his life. He checked the website of this business, Wordsmith. After half an hour, he had a handle on what it did and he'd gotten a good look at Nicole Pearce.

Christ. She was a fucking looker. One of his men, Dalton, was perpetually horny. If Dalton had been on this op, he'd toss Dalton this Pearce babe to play with for a while. Make him grateful.

He checked Vital Statistics and saw that she lived with one Nicholas Pearce, her father, not her husband.

Outlaw purged his search history from his computer, stood up and stretched. He finished his bourbon looking out the window at his little fiefdom.

He loved this life. He loved the heft and feel of it, the money and the power. He loved having hard skills and making soft men pay through the nose for them.

Outlaw stood at the window, watching the planes from Hartfield climb into the sky, one after another, like clockwork. In his own way, he was as precise a technician as any pilot or surgeon.

He'd go down to his state-of-the-art gym and give himself a good workout, get limber, then would have a light lunch with water. No more booze. He was now officially on Op Time, dedicated solely to the mission, and would be until the job was done.

He had a private plane at his disposal. He'd book it for 3 P.M., give him time to research the person, the hit.

His eyes lingered on the lovely face on his computer screen.

Christ, a real beauty. Who was about to be sacrificed to the money men.

Sorry, honey, he thought. *I don't know how you did it, but you just stepped on the wrong toes.*

Chapter 7

San Diego
June 29

Sam put the phone down for the bazillionth time, teeth grinding. Nicole wasn't answering. She hadn't picked up the phone the first time he called, she wasn't picking up the phone the thirtieth or fortieth time.

He knew that the definition of insanity was doing the same thing over and over, expecting a different outcome each time.

Was he insane?

God only knew. He sure wasn't entirely sane. He'd been pinging off the walls of his own brain ever since he'd woken up in a post-coital glow unlike any he'd ever had before, only to find that Nicole had sneaked out while he was sleeping.

Without a word, without even a goddamned *note*.

He must have been in a coma, because no way

the noise of even the quietest person on earth dressing wouldn't have woken him up. In the field, he'd heard in his sleep a dislodged rock tumble down a hillside half a klick away, and when the tangoes got to the campsite, they were met by only the embers of a fire and an ambush.

Not to mention the fact that his security system sent off a message to his cell phone each time the front door opened. He'd slept right through that, too.

Everything about the morning was off, askew, after the most fabulous night of sex he'd ever had. At first, he'd stumbled blearily from room to room, foolishly expecting to find her . . . somewhere. Out on the balcony. In the bathroom. Maybe in the kitchen sipping a cup of coffee.

It had taken him two circuits of his house before it hit him upside the head that her clothes were gone. Together with Nicole.

He'd rubbed his chest when he realized that. It hurt, as if he'd taken a sharp blow.

That was when he'd placed his first phone call, to her house, kicking himself in the ass because he'd been too involved in his dick to think of asking for her cell phone number. Well, a quick search of a semi-legal database took care of that.

The cell phone voicemail message was a canned one, from the company, inviting him to leave a message. Which he did, repeatedly.

At the home phone number he'd gotten his first taste of, *"You've reached the Pearce household. We can't*

*come to the phone right now, but please leave a message
and we'll get back to you as soon as we can."*

Rule number one in business—don't believe a
canned announcement. It's right up there with
The check is in the mail. But man, he'd believed it
and left a long, rambling message, the basic tenor
of which had been *Come back to me.* While stumbling to the shower, he'd kept a cordless by his
side so he wouldn't miss her call.

Because of course, she'd make the call as soon
as she could. She wasn't calling right now because
she was . . . in the bathroom or something. Or
maybe tending to her father.

So he'd called again five minutes later, timing it
to the second. Because, well, hanging up and calling again right away would be a tad . . . obsessive.
Wouldn't it?

It wasn't until the tenth time he'd called, while
he was driving in to the office, that it occurred to
him that it wasn't that she wasn't answering because she was busy.

She wasn't answering because she didn't want
to talk to him.

Jesus.

She was avoiding him.

She'd also switched her cell phone off.

The last ten calls to her house had been from the
office. Each one answered by *"You've reached the
Pearce household . . ."*

Sam stared at the phone, drumming his fingers.

He had an estimate to get out, for a client who
was very rich, as dumb as a rock, and would

doubtless provide a good revenue stream over many years to come.

He had some security equipment catalogues to go through.

He had e-mail to answer.

He had next year's budget to go over.

He had to call his accountant.

He drummed his fingers again and blew out a frustrated breath.

Fuck.

Sam picked up his cell phone and called Mike.

"Yo." Mike's deep, calm bass settled him a little. Mike was always cool, but he was especially cool with the ladies. He'd never get in a sweat or a panic because a woman disappeared after a night of hot sex. Nights of hot sex were Mike's specialty.

Not that Sam was in a sweat or a panic. No, no.

"Hey." Sam's voice was scratchy. He cleared his throat. "Listen, I've got a favor to ask you."

"Shoot." It was one of Mike's favorite expressions—ironic, coming from a sniper.

"I need you to show up at a woman's house. I want you to pull up in a patrol car, lights on, dressed in your SWAT suit, the whole friggin' deal. Be armed. Look scary." For Mike, that wouldn't be hard. The special-issue body armor turned his barrel chest into a massive wall. You didn't want to fuck with Mike. You particularly didn't want to fuck with him on duty, fully suited up and armed.

Exactly what Sam wanted. He wanted Mike to scare the shit out of those two scumbags. Every hair on his body had stood up when he'd seen them come out onto the porch to stare at Nicole, hooting and whistling. The way they looked at her had had his gut churning. Their behavior had been classic predator behavior. Circling warily, coming ever closer. One of the fuckheads had touched her car while she was in it, Nicole had said. The next step was touching *her*. And the step after that was a snatch and grab, the next time she came home after dark, and rape.

Over his dead body.

Sam had no illusions about the way the world worked. The strong preyed on the weak and in this world, the weak more or less included all women and all children. He'd seen enough women and children beaten into submission growing up to know that someone perceived as weak, without a protector, was going to attract violence, sooner rather than later. It was inevitable. He'd spent his entire life putting himself in front of the weak, standing for them. The three of them, Sam, Harry and Mike, had spent their lives trying to stop something that could never be stopped, only slowed.

Nicole was like a lamb staked out as bait.

Whatever the house had been like in her grandmother's time, now it was smack in the middle of a neighborhood that degenerated daily. With the recession so bad, he'd bet that every other man there was unemployed. Out of work, resentful men, many high on booze or drugs, with nothing to do all day but fantasize—well, those weren't the best neighbors for a woman to have.

Especially a woman like Nicole.

Off-the-charts gorgeous, living alone with a housekeeper and a sick father. Oh yeah, to men like those two fuckheads on the porch, and probably others in the run-down neighborhood, she was ripe prey.

Well, Sam would put a stop to that. First, Mike would drive by for a couple of days and make it clear that Nicole had friends on the force and that they were looking out for her. And then, whatever happened between him and Nicole, Sam was looking forward to a little chat with those two. And they could pay their own goddamned hospital bills.

First Mike. "I need you to go to 346 Mulberry Avenue. It's the house of a woman called—"

"Nicole Pearce," Mike said, only not into his cell, which he was slipping back into his jacket pocket. He was standing in the doorway to the outer office and Harry was right behind him. Harry, much taller, towered over Mike. "Yeah, I know."

They both came in, settled down in the two armchairs across from the sofa where Sam was sprawling. Both hunkered down as if it would take bolt cutters and a crane to get them out of there.

Oh Jesus, the double whammy. All three of them had been on the receiving end of that one, at one time or another.

One of them got in a mess and the other two ganged up on him. Looked like it was his turn. He sank lower in the sofa, knowing what was coming and knowing it was not going to be fun.

Sam looked at them, at his brothers, men he relied on, men he loved, men he'd kill for, men he'd unquestioningly die for, and wished them both gone. Poof. Disappeared in a puff of smoke.

But the whammy part could wait because first he needed to take care of business.

His gaze fixed on Mike.

"Yeah. Nicole Pearce." He'd rather die than let them know that just saying her name hurt. "Right across the street is a boarding house, at Number Three twenty-one. There are two dickheads, one black and one white. Dreadlocks, pant crotches down to their knees, the usual. They've fixated on Ni—Ms. Pearce, harassing her. I want you to drive by and make a show of force. Walk up to the house. Make it clear she's protected, that the police are looking out for her. That anyone who messes with her will be real sorry. And I want you to do that for the next couple of days. I want to make sure the fuckheads get the message. Loud and clear."

Mike nodded. "Sure thing."

Harry simply looked at him pensively, long fingers under his chin. Harry looked awful, like he hadn't slept in months. He'd been on the receiving end of the double whammy a lot since he'd come home, particularly while he tried drowning his sorrows in beer.

Sam and Mike tried to get him into physical rehab but when Harry refused, they simply hired a guy Mike knew. Bjorn looked like a wrestler and started whipping Harry back into shape, whether

Harry wanted it or not. Harry was moving just a little more easily, and not like an eighty-year-old now. Harry bitched endlessly about Bjorn, the therapist, and called him the Nazi, though Bjorn had emigrated from Norway. Harry tried every trick in the book, including not answering the door when Bjorn showed up with his bag of massage oils and what Harry swore were his instruments of torture. Sam simply gave Bjorn a copy of the key to Harry's apartment and everyone ignored Harry's bitching until it eventually stopped.

Sam forced him to come into work and it did Harry good. He was even starting to put some weight back on, though the sleep thing wasn't going well, to judge by the huge blue-black bruises under his eyes.

Harry was the poster child for messed up. If he was double-tagging with Mike, it meant they thought Sam was more messed up than Harry.

Well, hell.

Harry fixed him with his fierce yellow-brown gaze. "Would this be the same Nicole Pearce you've been calling every five minutes all morning?"

Sam gritted his teeth.

"And the one whose office doorbell you've been ringing every quarter of an hour?"

Sam sank even lower into the sofa.

She hadn't come into work this morning. That was the thing that was driving him crazy. He could barely stay in the same room with the thoughts that were exploding in his head like grenades.

There was no good spin to put on Nicole Pearce

not showing up for work, none. Every single option he could think of was bad. The worst, the very worst was—he'd hurt her. She was lying in bed in her home or was—God!—in a doctor's office or hospital. He talked himself down from that one because he knew he couldn't possibly have hurt her enough for medical care, but like a rabid dog, it was a thought he couldn't keep away. It kept circling back at him, snarling and snapping.

There were times last night when he hadn't been gentle. And his memory wasn't always clear.

Sam had an excellent memory, a native ability that had been honed by training. He could remember a map he'd seen once well enough to navigate by it, he could remember a face no matter how long ago he'd seen it; once he'd driven a route, he never forgot it.

But bits of last night were shrouded in such heat and electricity it was as if he'd shorted parts of his brain. He remembered his cock plowing her endlessly, but he couldn't remember what his hands had been doing. Holding her down? He had strong hands, all of him was strong. Had he somehow used that strength against her?

He'd never muscled a woman before, but he'd never before in his life been as excited. Had he somehow hurt her? The thought made his insides roil.

Second in his little list of nightmares was that he hadn't hurt her but had somehow . . . disgusted her. Because otherwise, why was she avoiding him? Those little blackout moments might not have been violent, but maybe she thought he was some kind of sex maniac or sex addict. The kind you read about on the internet. The kind who go to 12-step programs.

Hello, my name is Sam and I can't keep it down.

Because, well, if she thought he was a sex maniac, he could understand why. His cock hadn't gone down once all night. Not even a bit. It was like he was plugged into her and as long as she was around, he was aroused.

Neither thought was a happy one, though having her believe he was sex crazy was marginally better than having her think he was violent.

"Because if it is," Harry continued in his calm voice, "if this is the same woman, then you're pretty much the dickhead I always suspected you were. Because clearly, the lady isn't answering. Her phone *or* the door. And she might not be answering because you're calling every five minutes." He shrugged and spread his hands in a "don't knock the logic" gesture.

Mike's sharp gaze went from Harry, then back to Sam. "So . . . the mission is to protect the hottie from across the hall. Who's not talking to you. Looks like fucking her once wasn't enough . . ."

The rest of the sentence was choked in Mike's throat, right behind Sam's forearm, pressing him against the wall with it. It had happened without any thought, without any planning, in an instant out of time. The words came out of Mike's mouth and Sam launched himself. He hadn't even felt his feet as he jumped Mike, throwing him so hard against the wall his head bounced. It wasn't planned or premeditated. He just found himself trying to punch Mike through the wall by his arm across Mike's throat. Dimly, he was aware of Mike turning red, his hard punches that had no effect, Harry's shouting, Harry pulling at his arm . . .

The noises grew louder, finally penetrating the wild static in his head. Bits of him were coming back. He started feeling Mike's punches, Harry's hold.

They wouldn't have made any difference except for the fact that a little sense was seeping back into his head together with the voices, and he realized that he was doing his damnedest to throttle his own brother.

He dropped his arm, stepped back.

"Hey man," Mike wheezed, voice raw. He bent forward, hands on his knees, drawing in breaths in loud whoops.

"Sam . . ." Harry growled. Harry shook him once, then released him. All three of them had spent their childhoods gauging men on a rampage. Harry instinctively knew the storm had passed and that a little bit of sense had come back into Sam's head.

Jesus.

Sam's hands were shaking. What the fuck was he doing? This was *Mike*, his brother. And he'd wanted to kill him.

Except no one talked about Nicole that way, as if she were just some casual fuck. Particularly not

Mike, who had women tripping into and out of his bed nightly. Mike was a "love 'em and leave 'em" kind of guy. So was Sam, except for now.

When he'd been loved and left.

Sam and Mike stared at each other, both breathing heavily. Mike owed Sam an apology. And Sam owed him one. Sort of.

Who was going to go first? Their gazes were unwavering, stances hostile. Two old bull moose on a tear. Damned if Sam would be the first to break.

The aroma of good whiskey filled the room.

"The hell with this," Harry said, thrusting shot glasses of whiskey into their hands. "Back off, both of you, and drink up. Maybe alcohol will knock some sense into your hot heads."

Mike had relaxed his stance, got his breath back. "But it's ten o'clock in the morning," he observed. Mike was a carouser, but he had his standards. No alcohol till after midday, he always said.

"It's afternoon in New York," Harry said, and Mike nodded, curling his hand around the heavy crystal glass.

Sam blew a breath out. Another. Looked with disgust at Harry holding the bottle, pouring so fast the whiskey gurgled. "Go easy, man. That stuff costs two hundred bucks a bottle."

"Yeah?" Harry perked up. "Then I'll take the bottle home with me. It's wasted on you two."

They stood, knocking back the whiskey with satisfied sighs, the tension lowering as the level of liquid dropped in the bottle.

Silence. Mike and Harry looked at Sam. There was no censure in their gaze, no recrimination, which was awful, of course, because Sam had acted like an ass. And he'd attacked his brother. They should be ganging up on him, chewing his ass off. But they weren't. They just stood there, silently, two strong men saying nothing at all, letting Sam stew a little.

Sam loosened his shoulders, drew in a quick breath. It had to be done. "Sorry," he muttered to Mike. "I was way out of line."

Mike dipped his head, eyes fixed on Sam's face. "She means something to you."

Well, duh. Of course Nicole meant something to him, though he'd bite his tongue before he said it out loud. Sam didn't want to say anything because saying it out loud somehow . . . nailed it down. Made it real and raw and scary. Articulating what were batshit crazy feelings he barely understood himself.

"Well, let's just say I don't want her beaten up by the fuckheads across the street."

That shut Mike up. Harry too. They'd both seen lots of brutality toward women in their lives. They knew what a beaten-up woman looked like. No one wanted to see a black-and-blue Nicole, with swollen eyes and broken bones.

"Yeah." Harry's jaw muscles worked. Sam knew he was thinking of his mother and sister, lost to violence. He turned to Mike. "Do what you need to do to keep her safe."

Mike nodded curtly. "I'll stop by a couple of

times. Make sure they see me. Make sure they know who they'd be messing with."

Goddamn US law enforcement, that's who.

Mike put the glass down. "So. Any messages you want me to give her? Anything I should say from you?"

Answer your phone, goddammit. Don't shut me out. Talk to me. I want to see you again tonight, and the night after that and the night after that. I haven't even begun to get you out of my system.

Sam's jaw clamped shut on the words. His throat was tight and dry. He couldn't have spoken if he wanted to.

He shook his head and Mike left. With an odd glance at Sam's face, Harry left, too. Without saying anything, or overanalyzing the situation, which was a miracle.

He was alone. Alone in his big, expensive office that he'd worked so hard for. Alone with at least three urgent reports and requests for ten quotes for new business. Alone with his fucking thoughts.

He was behind in everything. He should be diving into work and instead here he was, playing with his dick.

He winced.

Do not think of your dick.

Too late.

It rose, urgently, as if he hadn't fucked his brains out last night.

Oh Jesus, just the memory of her was enough to set him off. That face, under his, moving slightly up and down on the bed in time with his thrusts.

Those huge cobalt eyes gazing into his. He'd never seen eyes that color before, a blue so intense it glowed.

Nicole Pearce was, hands down, the most beautiful woman he'd ever fucked. The most beautiful woman he'd ever even seen. But there had been something else in the bed with them. Some kind of . . . connection, however crazy that sounded. There'd been intensity, yes, of a kind he'd never experienced before. But there had been other things, too. Things he had no word for, really, because they were new. But if you put a gun to his head and forced him to find a word, one might be *affection*.

Though that was crazy, because they had spent the night fucking like bunnies.

However much they'd fucked, though, it wasn't enough. It wasn't even in the same ballpark as being enough.

He missed her, fiercely. Missed her smell, fresh and clean at first. Afterward, she'd smelled of sex, of course. But somehow, her juices and his mixed together smelled good, real good. He missed her smile, her intelligence. She got him, got everything he said. There hadn't been even one of those awkward moments Sam often experienced on first dates where the woman had no clue what he was talking about. He'd always put them down to those man-woman differences all the books went on and on about.

His Y chromosome made him say things the woman's two X's didn't equip her to get. And oh man, vice versa. Sam couldn't count the times he'd listened, baffled, as the date du jour went on and on about things he barely understood and couldn't care less about.

Nothing like that with Nicole. Even blasted by lust over dinner, Sam found what Nicole had to say interesting. She'd *understood* Lebanon, a country he loved. Her caring so intensely for her father made perfect sense to him.

In bed, it was as if she had been tailor-made for him, moving lithely to his rhythms. Not one awkward moment, just sex so intense he thought he'd pass out at times and yet fun at the same time and . . . his mind skittered away from any further definition of the feelings he had.

This was way too much introspection for him. Bottom line—he missed her, he wanted her, he wasn't in any way ready to let her go.

If he'd done something, he would apologize.

If she was reticent, he'd convince her.

Giving her up wasn't an option, not even close.

He picked up the phone and called her home number again.

"You've reached the Pearce household . . ."

Nicole sat in the tiny pantry off the kitchen that had been converted into a home office. She stared at the words on-screen, listening to the phone ring. Again. The housekeeper had strict instructions to let the answering machine pick up. From the suspicious look thrown Nicole's way, Manuela clearly thought it was someone Nicole owed money to. Not that there weren't plenty of those.

The answering machine clicked, went through its little spiel about them not being home then clicked again. *Nicole*, a deep voice said. *Pick up—*

She switched the whole thing off then pulled the plug from the wall. Sam had graduated from the tentative messages at the beginning of the morning, with lots of *pleases*, to a peremptory tone.

Tomorrow. Tomorrow she'd go into the office, ring his bell and talk to him, adult to adult. Not today. Oh God, no, she couldn't face him today. Not on no sleep and after the most intense sexual experience of her life, which had left her so shaken and off-balance.

Just listening to his deep voice leaving messages had made her stomach muscles clench, her thighs quiver. And worse.

Nicole had shared a dorm room once with a funny, smart girl from Seattle who had a crazy, wild sex life. She cut a swathe through the university, basically going to bed with everyone with the right plumbing. When a man particularly attracted her, she'd whisper to Nicole, "Whoa, that guy makes me *cream*."

Nicole hadn't really understood until now. Now she knew exactly what Sharon had been talking about.

Listening to Sam's voice loosened a wave of moisture in her sex that was embarrassing. As if her body were preparing itself for him to walk through her door and fling her on the couch. Just from listening to the man leave a damned message on her answering machine!

She stared at her screen, incomprehensible words swimming in front of her. A report of the board of directors' meeting of a Luxembourg bank. Something she could do with her eyes closed, though not, apparently, while blasted by leftover lust from the night before.

She blew out an impatient breath. The report was due tomorrow and she was only halfway through it. They were paying her very good money, more than the market rate. If she wanted the bank as a customer, she had to deliver that translation by tomorrow.

She forced herself to sit up straight, concentrate. She reread the paragraph for the millionth time and finally started typing, forcing herself to focus on the translation and not on Sam Reston.

"Darling?" The quavering voice cut through Nicole's attention. She sighed and rose from her workstation.

"Coming, Pops," she called. This was one of the reasons she couldn't work from home. He called her a thousand times a day. Though there was a housekeeper on call and though a registered nurse stopped by twice a day, if Nicole was around, Nicholas Pearce wanted his daughter.

Nicole knew why. Manuela was an excellent cook, kept the house gleaming and wore a perpetual smile, but she didn't know how to handle her father. Once, she'd insisted on helping him get up and he'd fallen to the floor.

The nurse who stopped by twice a day was super-efficient but had never cracked a smile in her life. Certainly never in Nicole's presence.

Nicole had learned how to physically care for her father. She never let him fall, she knew exactly which muscles were sore and how to massage them, she could dress him smoothly and quickly. She also took care to smile, to be upbeat, no matter how hard it was.

The downside of that was that when she was home, Nicholas wanted her, and only her, by his side. Nicole understood completely. If she could have afforded to, she would have dedicated herself exclusively to her father in the last waning months of his life.

Unfortunately, she couldn't afford to do that. The oncologist had mentioned a brand-new, incredibly expensive treatment that wouldn't cure but could possibly halt the progression of the disease. Nicole had enrolled her father in the experimental protocol and was waiting for him to be called up.

The new drug cost almost $1,500 a month and the protocol called for a three-month cycle.

Wordsmith was doing well, even in the downturn. She was gaining new customers by the week. She was growing, earning more each month. But the expenses went up each month, too, in a horrible spiral.

Her father was in his wheelchair in the living room, a big book open on his lap. His head lifted when he saw her and he smiled. "Ah, darling, there you are. The light seems to have dimmed, could you open the curtains a little more?"

Her step and her smile faltered. There was plenty of light in the room.

The doctors had told her that Nicholas Pearce's brain was "peppered" with tumors, bilaterally. Too many to count. And one was pressing down on an optic nerve. At times his eyesight dimmed, sometimes dramatically. It terrorized him.

Nicole opened the drapes wide and switched on a floor lamp, angling the light over his lap, hand on his shoulder so he'd feel her touch.

"That better, Dad?"

"Oh, yes, darling. Thank you." He reached up and placed his hand on hers. "You're so good to me."

The one thing left to him was his voice—deep, strong, steady. Tears pricked her eyes. She squeezed his shoulder lightly and opened her mouth to ask how he was getting on in reading through the definitive history of medieval Japan, when the doorbell rang.

Frowning, Nicole went out into the hallway to the front door. Through the side windows she could see a police car parked in front of her house.

Oh God. What now?

The man who stood on her porch had been staring at the house across the street. He turned and took off aviator sunglasses to reveal piercing blue eyes. Fiercely intelligent eyes. He was dressed in a dark blue police uniform, with—oh my gosh—body armor. And about a ton of hardware on his belt, some of which looked suspiciously like weaponry. And a big side holster strapped to his thigh carrying a big black gun that definitely was weaponry.

She opened the door.

He wasn't much taller than she was, but she'd never seen shoulders as broad as his. Everything about him was broad and strong and unyielding.

"Are you Nicole Pearce?"

"Yes," she replied. "Yes, I am. Is there something wrong, Officer?"

"No, ma'am, not at all. My name is Mike Keillor, with the San Diego PD. I was asked by a mutual friend of ours, Sam Reston, to stop by. Make my presence felt." He stopped, looking at her so intently it was as if he were walking around inside her head.

The mention of Sam's name jolted her, threw her off her stride so much she barely heard the rest of his sentence. She hit rewind and heard what he'd said all over again, puzzling over it.

Sam had said—

"Oh!" Of course! Sam had sent over his policeman friend, the man who was like a brother to him, to intimidate the creeps across the street. Though the entire effect was wasted if they weren't home. "Yes, thank you so much." He wasn't answering, just standing there, looking at her. Nicole resisted the urge to wring her hands. She'd been trained from childhood to deal with unexpected, even awkward encounters, but all her savoir-faire deserted her.

Just the mention of Sam Reston flustered her so much that manners went straight out the window.

She backed up, holding the door open. "Please come in, Officer. Or would that be Sergeant?" A lifetime in the diplomatic corps had taught her the importance of getting titles right.

"That would be Sergeant, yes ma'am. But please just call me Mike."

"Okay, Mike. Would you like to come into the living room?"

He ducked his head. "Thank you, ma'am. But first, I'm going to walk back to the patrol car and get my long gun. I'm going to do it slowly, so whoever's watching across the street will realize I mean business."

"Sam—" God, it was hard just to say his name. "Sam said that these two men who are . . . who are bothering me will be deterred by you. I hope so. I also hope they're watching right now, or else it's an exercise in futility."

"They're watching, all right." Mike's voice was grim. "Second floor, third window from the right."

Nicole's eyes flew to the window in question. She blinked. There were closed grungy-looking Venetian blinds over the window. And—yes—a tiny peephole created by someone holding the slats slightly open. You had to look carefully to see it.

He turned and walked slowly back to the patrol car. Across that extra-wide bodybuilder's blue back were stenciled big white letters. SWAT.

He reached into the car and brought out a rifle. A big, bad-looking weapon that looked like cool, deadly business. Once he'd closed the car door, he just stood with his back to her, staring across at the house of her nemeses. Holding that big gun with complete familiarity, like a mother holds a child.

Finally, he turned around and walked back up to the house, following her in. Once the door was closed, he stored the gun, upright, in a corner, said, "It's not loaded, ma'am. But they won't know that," and stood at rest, impossibly wide shoulders back, hands folded neatly over his crotch.

She'd seen a thousand Marine guards in embassies all over the world assume that stance. Sam had mentioned that Mike had been a Marine, but even if he hadn't, it was unmistakeable.

"Were you in the Marines, Sergeant Keillor? Mike?"

He looked startled. "Yes, ma'am. Six years."

She smiled faintly. She'd loved the embassy Marines, always so polite and no-nonsense and utterly, completely competent. Unlike most of the political officers.

"Can you stay for a cup of coffee, Ser—Mike?"

He fixed her with a ferocious light blue gaze.

"Yes, ma'am, thank you, ma'am. I need to stay long enough to establish that we're friends, that you've got a police officer looking after you."

She called the housekeeper. Manuela appeared in the doorway, smiling, wiping her hands on her apron.

"Manuela, could we have coffee served in the living room, please?"

"Yes, ma'am."

She turned to Mike. "Come into the living room, then, and we'll have our coffee."

Her father had dozed off in his wheelchair. The officer looked a question at her. Nicole smiled. "Don't worry about my father. We won't bother him. Household noises don't wake him up." Pain would eventually wake him up, as it did regularly. For now, if he was sleeping, the pain had subsided. He needed his rest.

She watched his sleeping face. The skin now hung off his beautiful bones like a too-large garment. His once magnificent head of black hair was bald, with only a few tufts clinging here and there, the effect of the last course of radiation therapy to the head.

During the day, her father put on a brave face, but what he felt was there, not hidden, in the sleeping man. He was exhausted and in pain and it showed.

Dying, she thought with a pang.

Nicole turned to her guest and indicated a chair. Mike Keillor sat stiffly, back upright, hands on knees. Nicole sat on the sofa, facing him.

It had to be faced. "So. Um. Sam sent you?"

"Yes, ma'am. He said you were having trouble with two fu—guys who were escalating."

"I beg your pardon?"

"Escalating. Becoming violent. It's a process, and it's always the same. I'll bet they started bothering you by staring, then shouting insults or lewd invitations. Am I right?"

She sighed. "Yes, since the day they moved across the street. Every time I left the house, it seemed they were there."

"Because they were watching out for you. But after a while it wasn't just words, was it? There were probably gestures. And the gestures got cruder and cruder. Then they walked down the porch steps. Then they came to the edge of the property."

Nicole stared. "Yes. Exactly that. How did you know?" She thought back to her conversation with Sam. "Sam told you."

"No, ma'am, he didn't have to. It's behavior as predictable as the seasons. Sam said they touched your car. Is that correct?"

Nicole shivered at the memory. "Yes. I mean, one of them did. Just knocked on the window of the car, but it—it scared me." She gave a half laugh. "I've lived in third-world countries, I'm not usually such a wuss."

His jaw tightened. "You're not a wuss, ma'am. Not at all. The next step is touching *you*, and once they do, they won't stop. Sam recognized that. It's why he sent me. Believe me, we've seen this behavior over and over. They're bullies when they sense someone is weaker than them. But deep down, they're cowards. They won't want to mess with the police. I'll keep coming around. Might actually have a little heart to heart, in full gear. Scare the shit out of them." He bowed his head. "Pardon the language."

Scaring the shit out of them sounded just fine. Fantastic, in fact.

He sat there, broad and square and tough as hell, actually frightening to look at. Dangerous. Not to her, but to anyone he might deem an enemy. Those heavy muscles moved with athletic grace. He was SWAT. He more than knew how to handle weapons. Creepy and Creepier might very well try to attack a woman, but not one with this level of protection. He'd put himself and all the resources of the police department at her disposal.

He'd just made her safe.

A deep-seated tension dissolved. She hadn't even admitted to herself how much Creepy and Creepier frightened her. How she'd had to steel herself to walk out her front door every morning.

Nicole smiled. "Well, thank you very, very much, Mike. I must say I feel relieved. So far, they haven't done anything I would report, and half the time I thought I was exaggerating their importance in my mind, but you're right. I guess I felt that one day they might do something . . . violent."

"They would have done something violent, and

soon. Count on it. But I'll make sure they get the message. Mess with you and they're in deep sh— trouble." His blue eyes fixed on hers. "And don't thank me, ma'am. Thank Sam. He's the one who sent me. He's the one making you safe."

Nicole's heart thumped as a wave of heat washed over her. Oh my God. Did he *know*? Did she have something on her face that showed she'd spent the night making frantic love with Sam Reston? And that she'd been avoiding him all morning?

"Ah—" she began, her voice a croak.

"Señora. El café està listo."

Nicole turned gratefully. Manuela stood in the doorway with a tray holding a pot of her world-class coffee and three cups, bless her. If her father woke up, he would enjoy a cup.

Manuela put the tray down on the coffee table and Nicole leaned forward, looking a question at Mike.

"Black, no sugar, ma'am."

She smiled. "Manuela's coffee is strong enough to wake the dead, Mike. Are you sure you don't want sugar? And please call me Nicole."

"No. The stronger the better. I like the taste of bitter coffee. Reminds me of the field."

His shoulders relaxed just a little as he accepted the small cup. It looked tiny in his huge hands.

Well, she wasn't a Marine. She added two heaping teaspoonfuls of sugar and stirred, watching as he downed the coffee in one gulp.

His eyes widened. She couldn't say it would

put hair on his chest, he already had that. There were thick tufts of dark hair showing in the *V* of his open collar, but no doubt that hair just got thicker.

"Yes, indeed," she said, smiling. "Manuela's Cuban, and her *corto* is famous in a couple of countries."

Maybe it was the smell of Manuela's coffee, maybe the sun that had shifted in the sky, shooting a hot beam of light into his lap. For whatever reason, her father snorted slightly and woke up. His head lifted, turned.

"Darling?"

Nicole's heart sank. His voice had turned weak, shaky, a sign that the pain was coming. Not immediately, but soon.

She rose, coffee cup in hand. "Here, Dad." She put the cup in his hand, her own hand cupped under his in case he spilled it, her other hand lightly on his shoulder, in reassurance. His grasping strength was erratic. At times, he couldn't hold on to things. "Manuela's finest. Drink up. If you ask nicely, I imagine she's got some *pasteles* in the kitchen."

Nicole plastered a smile on her face, pretending not to notice the bird-like bones of his shoulder under her hand. Or his trembling hand as he brought the cup to his mouth. Or the sound of his breathing, loud in the quiet room. The effort of holding a cup to his mouth was enormous.

Her father had been such a handsome man. People turned their heads when he walked by, even when they didn't know who he was. He had had such a regal bearing, one of nature's aristocrats.

Now he was crunched in a wheelchair, often in pain, barely able to feed himself.

Dying.

This was breaking her heart.

Mike had stood, doing that straight-shouldered hands-over-crotch thing again. Her father took one look and nailed him immediately.

"Marine, young man?"

Nicole rushed to make introductions. "Daddy, this is Mike Keillor, former Marine—good call, you still have a fantastic eye. He's with the San Diego Police Department now. He's the friend of a friend of mine. Mike, this is my father, Ambassador Nicholas Pearce." She shot Mike a hard glance. *Don't you dare say the real reason you're here.* She would kill him with her bare hands, body armor or no body armor, if he said he was here to ward off troublemakers. The very last thing her father needed was to worry about her and her safety

Mike gave an imperceptible nod. "Pleased to meet you, sir. I just stopped by to say hello to Nicole."

Her father brought the cup to his mouth again with shaking hands, Nicole's hand under his so he could sip. He loved Manuela's coffee. She'd asked the doctors what he could eat and drink. His oncologist, a wise and humane man, told her to let him have his pleasures for as long as possible.

Nicole had understood quite well what the gentle oncologist was saying. *It won't make any difference. He'll die soon, anyway. Let him enjoy what he can while he can.*

Nicole fixed her father whatever he wanted, whenever he wanted, happy if he could enjoy something.

So she let him have Manuela's coffee, and the Calvados he'd learned to love in France and his Cuban cigars, as often as he wanted, and was happy that they made him happy.

The trembling was worse. No surprise there. Everything about him was worse. Day by day. Nicole cupped her father's jaw, briefly, then blinking back tears, bent to kiss the top of his head. Something she did a thousand times a day. It was a miracle that there wasn't a shiny spot on the top of his head from all her kisses.

She straightened and turned to Mike Keillor. He was staring at her with a peculiar intensity that she couldn't decipher.

"Would you walk me to the car, Nicole?" he asked. He hadn't shifted out of his modified parade-rest stance.

She blinked. "Sure."

Outside, at the patrol car, he turned to her. "I'll need for you to embrace me. Maybe kiss me on the cheeks. I want them to get the message that we're real good friends."

Oh. That made sense.

Nicole leaned forward and put her arms on his

shoulders. Around his shoulders would have been impossible, they were so wide. It seemed to her that there was no difference between the hard unyielding feel of the body armor and the hard unyielding feel of the muscles of his shoulders.

She'd held a man like this in her arms all night long.

Nicole kissed Mike's cheeks and stood for a moment, arms outstretched on his shoulders.

"I'll stop by again tomorrow morning. You let me know whether they bother you again. If they so much as look at you, let me know." Mike's voice was grim, face drawn tight, deep grooves in his cheeks. "And tomorrow, I'm bringing a can of Mace and a police whistle for you. Burn their eyes out and bust their eardrums if they try anything."

He was making a real effort for her. She had a feeling Creepy and Creepier would think twice before bothering her again.

Nicole smiled. "I really appreciate this, Mike. Thanks so much."

His jaws worked. "Like I said, don't thank me, thank Sam. He's the one who sent me. He's worried about you."

Nicole froze, feeling another wave of heat wash over her. What could she possibly say? She opened her mouth and closed it, completely incapable of speech. Sam was watching over her and she was avoiding him because she didn't have the faintest clue how to deal with him.

With enormous effort, she didn't wring her hands.

Mike stood still, silent, watching her.

"Yes, um," she said finally. Oh God. "Will you—will you thank Sam for me?"

"No, ma'am, I think you should thank him yourself." He dipped his head, touched a finger to his forehead in salute, got into the patrol car and drove off.

Chapter 8

Outlaw landed at the General Aviation side of Lindbergh Field Airport at 4 P.M., local time, carrying a small arsenal.

Oh, the joys of working for the Masters of the Universe, even if they'd been taken down a notch or ten and their plumage was not as bright and as full as before.

If you were a CEO and earning $170 mil a year instead of $240 mil, it gave you bitching rights down at the club, but it didn't really make a whole lot of difference.

Included in the contract was reimbursement for private jets to take him anywhere he wanted to go. And the good thing about private jets was that no one was going to ask any questions at all.

He was definitely dressed for the part. He'd studied his clients like it was a mission and just as he could camouflage himself for a sniping mission in the desert or a quick infil into the African jungle, he could pass muster among the rich. He'd learned the camouflage well.

The human eye is overwhelmed by input from the brain. It won't "see" a sniper in camouflage with mottled, disruptive patterns. It perceives the sniper and his surroundings as a continuum and can't see the contour around him. A good sniper becomes invisible, whether in mountain terrain or in forests or in the desert.

The same here. He was dressed in the equivalent of his ghillie suit. A ghillie suit of the rich. He was dressed from the skin out in silk, Egyptian cotton, cashmere and new virgin wool. Look the part, be the part. What was underneath the $8,000 suit, a steel-tough, scarred body, couldn't be seen.

The mission called for speed, otherwise Outlaw would have spent the day at a spa, to achieve that ruddy, pampered look. But there'd been no time.

It had given him enormous pleasure to put his Remington sniper rifle—he would use it only if he had to, to complete the mission—and his Kimber 1911, three magazines, tactical gear, body armor, powerful laser light, lockpick gun, K-bar, karambit knives and vial of acid all in matching Louis Vuitton carry-on hand luggage and briefcase.

No one would think to question it.

It was simply a different world, the world of the *über*-rich. They were as invisible in their way as the homeless. Outlaw had been both, under cover.

People avert their eyes from the homeless, particularly if you were smart and pissed on yourself. Eau de bum. But they avert their eyes from the super wealthy, too. As if the rich gave off a special glare too bright for the eyes of ordinary people.

Outlaw had the bearing of the super-rich down, too. God knows he'd studied his clients enough and he knew the rules. You could never be too arrogant or act too entitled.

He drew up in a limo, which he exited without giving the driver a second glance. The pilot was at the top of the stairs and Outlaw passed by him with only a terse nod.

It was behavior so expected, he was invisible.

The flight was smooth, the weather excellent all the way into Southern California. He'd spent the entire trip studying the Google Street View of the Morrison Building, hacking into the blueprints on file in the San Diego County office and the building management company's files. The office of Wordsmith was tiny, 500 square feet, and the rent was $2,200 a month. Nicole Pearce had a two-year lease and had never been late in payment.

Outlaw then hacked into a Keyhole satellite and checked out the roof of the building. He spent an hour on close-ups of every inch of the roof and had a viable game plan for getting into and out of Nicole Pearce's ninth-floor office, and a backup emergency plan, by the time they landed.

He rented a Lexus and drove himself to near the Morrison Building. An hour after landing, he was parking the Lexus on a side street.

The street view had been astonishingly clear, but the Google cameras hadn't been able to penetrate the smoked-glass windows of the lobby.

Outlaw watched the entrance for a quarter of an hour from a trendy café across the street. He monitored the ebb and flow of people, timed it and strode into the expensive glass-and-brushed-steel expanse of the large lobby together with an intake of men. He wore large wraparound sunglasses and walked with his head down. There were security cameras all around the walls, but their angle was such that if you walked straight down the middle of the 11,000-square-foot floor, chances were they'd only catch his feet. He put himself in the middle of a crowd of excited business executives who'd just come back from some seminar.

Like many Special Ops soldiers, Outlaw wasn't a big man. He was of medium height and wiry rather than broad. He placed himself between two big, beefy executive types, keeping pace with them across the large lobby, wishing men still wore hats. A wide-brimmed fedora would have been perfect to cover his face.

No one paid him any attention at all. He was one more businessman who'd just come from the plane with his carry-on luggage, walking briskly to a meeting in the building.

The security cameras at the bank of elevators were all tilted at the same angle, calibrated to cover an area about seven feet from the doors. Which just proved to Outlaw all over again how incredibly stupid civilians were. Especially rich civilians. No drug lord or criminal worth their weight in cocaine would have set up security cameras like that. The angles would have been staggered to ensure maximum coverage, to make sure not a fly got past security. But those were hard men, who paid for lapses in security with their lives.

These rich civilians lived in a soft world, where just the *idea* of security cameras and guards was cool, and enough. In a glance, Outlaw had seen the guard in the big U-shaped desk made of maplewood and brass. Good haircut, good-looking guy, trim, with an elegant uniform.

Security as fashion accessory.

This was going to be a cakewalk.

Nobody paid him the slightest bit of attention as he rode to the seventh floor. He walked the floor, head down, just another executive deep in thought about an upcoming IPO. It was a matter of vibes. When he wanted to, among men who understood the signals, Outlaw was good at emitting "don't fuck with me or I'll cut your balls off" vibes. But here it would be like broadcasting radio waves to a TV station. No, in this kind of environment, the equivalent was *I'm too busy and important to worry about worms like you, so don't bust my balls.* With that attitude, he was invisible.

It was going on 7 P.M. The building was emptying of all the clerical workers, the secretaries and gophers. Offices would have a skeleton crew, and only those busy on a big deal or wanting to show off for the boss would still be working. And most of them would quit by nine.

Outlaw met no one as he walked the length of the building to the fire stairs at the other end of the hall. Few of the offices had cameras outside their doors, and most of them were turned off.

Outlaw shook his head as he walked. Jesus Christ. Turning a security camera *off*? What the hell was *wrong* with these people?

In the huge, empty stairwell, he took the stairs two at a time to the ninth floor, pulling out his laser light, holding it in the cup of his hand.

Office 921 was halfway down. And, he saw at a glance—no security camera outside the door. So Ms. Pearce hadn't coughed up the extra amount for extra security. Wonderful.

There was a security company right across the hall, though. Its camera was definitely on, and it covered half the hallway. Outlaw walked close to the wall on the other side, and just to be sure, flashed the laser light into the camera as he walked by. Anyone viewing the tapes afterward would just see a blanked-out section, like a glitch in the tape.

Okay, he'd reconnoitered; time to go to his hide.

It was twenty-eight floors to the roof, and Outlaw took them at a run. He'd be sitting immobile for a couple of hours, so the small bite of exercise felt good.

At the top, on the landing, he changed into his tactical Nomex suit, readied his equipment and hunkered down next to the door leading out onto the roof.

He checked his watch. Seven twenty. Less than two hours to wait. He wanted to go in at nine. Nine was a perfect time. Almost everyone gone, not so late he'd catch the attention of the night security guards.

Waiting was never a problem. He was a sniper and patience was a big part of it. He was good at waiting. He could slow his breathing, bring his heart rate down, put himself into a state of vigilant rest, yet remain ready to kill at a moment's notice.

Outlaw rested his head against the wall and shut down.

The whole afternoon was a washout. Nicole got exactly zero work done. This was terrible. She had the bank deadline, ten texts to distribute to her network of collaborators and new texts to look at and quote prices for. She couldn't afford to take a day off, staring into space, thinking of Sam Reston.

However hard she tried to concentrate, though, his strong features swam into her monitor, crowding out the description of a new French manufacturing technology of airplane components, which was the text after the Luxembourg bank board meeting.

Every cell in her body squeezed tight as his image blossomed in her mind—dark face intent inches above her, focused on her so tightly she felt the lines of attraction between them could become visible.

Her body tingled with remembered sexual desire, but with a little time and distance, something else impinged on her consciousness. Something important about last night. There'd been something elusive, something she hadn't felt in a long time.

She'd been . . . happy.

It had been so long since she'd felt that way, it had taken her a whole day to recognize it. Her entire being had been bathed in joy and, well, sexual delight. The sex had had a lot to do with it, but something about Sam himself, beyond his formidable power as a lover, was involved.

She was drowning in problems, up to her neck in them, sinking fast. Her father was dying, day by day. Piece by piece. When working, Nicole tried to wipe that thought from her mind but it was there, constantly, this huge dark hole that sucked everything down into the black pool at the bottom. It was her first thought on waking up and her last thought at night.

Helping him die was eating her alive. And eating up all her financial resources. She didn't know which would finish first—her father or her money.

She didn't care at all for herself, but she was terrified at the thought of her father spending the last months of his life without the comforts she killed herself to provide for him.

She'd already been to the bank to see about taking out a mortgage on the house and they'd laughed at her. Whatever resources she could use to ease her father's life had to come from Wordsmith, the company she was struggling to keep afloat.

The terror that her father would be less than comfortable at the end of his life was like a sharp nail hammering into her head, hour by hour, minute by minute. Each time she saw a medical bill a vise tightened around her heart, squeezing hard.

Except for last night.

All of that had been utterly wiped from her mind during the hours she'd spent in Sam's arms, all that worry and darkness replaced by heat so intense it scorched her. Part of her was ashamed that she'd been able to simply toss her problems overboard for a couple of hours while drowning in sensuality, and part of her had reveled in it. She hadn't thought of any of it—sick father, money problems, trying to get Wordsmith off the ground—all the constant overload of worry that ate at her every waking moment.

Gone, like smoke. While she had a godzillion orgasms.

Nicole watched the cursor blinking on the screen. She'd translated a sentence and a half in the past hour. It was eight in the evening and the translation should have been finished.

This was crazy.

With a sigh, she closed the computer down, extracted the portable hard disk and went to the dining room that had been converted into a hospital room for her father.

The night nurse looked up from the magazine

she was reading and stood. Nicole waved her back
in her chair.

"How's he doing?" Nicole asked softly, walking
to his bedside, avoiding the IV tree pumping God
only knew how many chemicals into him.

"Blood pressure normal, heart rate normal. He's
mildly sedated. He'll sleep through the night." The
nurse's voice was low, brisk, objective. Nicole appreciated that. She was efficient and unemotional,
which Nicole needed. Manuela sometimes broke
out in tears at unexpected moments and it didn't
help. The nurse's quiet calm was soothing.

"Good." Nicole gently laid her hand over her
father's. The IV line was in the other hand, where
they'd finally found a vein. The backs of both
hands were darkly mottled where the thin veins
broke. It was increasingly difficult to find a strong
vein for the IV fluids and medicines that were
keeping him alive.

Nicole knew that the next step was a minor operation to open up a subclavian IV catheter line,
which would create its own problems of blood-
stream infection.

Her father's hand was cold and still. He was
always cold, no matter what she did to keep him
warm. His body simply no longer had the energy
to warm itself.

She looked down at him, her last living relative
on this earth, the person she loved more than anyone in the world.

He was leaving her, a little each day, and there
was nothing she could do about it. Not all her

tears, not all her care could halt the disease's progress. In the beginning, she'd read up ferociously on brain cancer, joined internet forums, talked endlessly online with patients, with the doctors. Read everything about brain cancer until the words blurred and until finally, she could read no more.

They were past all that. There was nothing science could do for her father, and the only thing she could do for him was to love him with all her heart and make sure he was as comfortable as she could possibly make him.

Often, if she held him long enough, she was able to transfer some of her young warmth to him. It pleased them both. She'd been holding his hand for ten minutes, but his hand wasn't warming up. So that had been taken from them, too.

"I'm going out," she told the nurse. "I'll be gone a couple of hours, maybe more."

"That's fine." The nurse settled back in the chair with her magazine. Nicole knew that she would spring instantly into action at the first sign of distress from her father. She was a good nurse and had passed many a sleepless night with Dad.

He was in good hands.

Nicole grabbed her briefcase, quietly closed the front door behind her and headed for her car. She stopped for a moment, breathing in the late evening air. The extreme heat of the day had dissipated but it was still pleasantly warm. It felt good to be outside after spending the day working. Trying to work.

It was a quarter to nine—rush hour was long over. Traffic would be light, she could make it into her office in less than twenty minutes.

Just the thought of her office, so pretty, so ordered, so silent, with no demands on her other than work, calmed her. She had a Pavlovian response in her office, focusing on work immediately with no outside distractions.

Four or five hours' solid work there would more than make up for the lost day. She suddenly yearned for the cool calm of her office the way a desert straggler yearned for water.

She was in the car, pulling away from the curb, before she realized that something was missing. That slight edgy feeling in her gut that Creepy and Creepier would come out and harass her.

But nobody had. The two seemed to live to watch her come and go from her house but tonight there was silence.

Thanks to Mike.

Thanks to Sam.

Whoa.

No, no. She'd done way too much thinking about Sam. Tomorrow she'd have to face him, make some kind of decision about him, but today she was going in circles and had to stop.

Don't think about Sam. Her new mantra.

The next few hours had to be about the job. She resolutely focused on what needed to be done as she drove into town, making good time on the almost-empty roads. She had mentally drafted her to-do list, sifted through priorities and decided which translation went to whom, by the time she pulled into her slot in the underground garage.

Being good at her job, making Wordsmith a success, had a direct bearing on her father's well-being. She had to remember that. Stay focused.

As always, she enjoyed the ride up in the elevator. It was usually full in the mornings and evenings as the building filled up and emptied out. Tonight it was empty, a big, wood-and-brass cube with bronze internal doors so polished they were as reflective as mirrors.

She looked at herself and winced as the elevator smoothly rose. Thank God it wasn't office hours. She made such a point about meticulous grooming on the job, it was a good thing no one saw her. Hair pulled back in a messy ponytail, no makeup, jeans, a white shirt and flats. She looked at her face reflected in the doors. She looked tired and worried. Which was as it should be, because she *was* tired and worried.

The elevator whooshed to a stop and pinged as the doors opened. She walked down the corridor, itching to get to work. The evening cleanup crew hadn't arrived yet. The flower arrangements were drooping; there was a streak on the floor where someone had dragged something heavy.

Tomorrow morning it would be pristine. Nicole loved that, that there was something in her life that someone else took care of.

She stopped in front of her door, in the middle of the corridor. Though she ached to reach the sanctuary of her office, she instinctively turned left, as if compelled by a powerful magnet.

She stood before a door exactly like her own except that the little shiny brass plaque read *Reston Security* instead of *Wordsmith*.

Nicole reached out a hand to touch the cool, smooth wood.

Sam's office. Tomorrow morning he would be behind this door.

She'd ring the doorbell and he'd open the door and . . . what? The next few minutes were a complete and utter blank in her mind. What would she say? Sorry?

Sorry, Sam, I just freaked. Couldn't deal with you at all.

Would he forgive her?

She was so tired. Not just from last night and today. She was tired from wrestling with her problems day in, day out. So tired some barriers in her mind were coming down, crumbling to the floor, leaving her naked and raw and defenseless.

She stood, head bowed, hand on the door for a few minutes, coming to terms with the fact that she was looking forward to seeing Sam Reston again tomorrow. To absorbing some of the heat and strength that he seemed so happy to share with her.

Tomorrow. Tomorrow something might change in her life. But for tonight, she had work to do.

Feeling somehow better, Nicole turned back to her own door, fit her key in the lock and pushed it, feeling for the light switch as the door swung closed behind her.

Suddenly, hands grabbed her, slammed her against the wall so brutally it knocked the breath out of her. A cold steel circle ground so hard against her temple, the skin broke. A drop of blood slid down her cheek, dripped off her chin.

She couldn't breathe, couldn't see.

A puff of breath against her ear and a low, vicious voice. "Scream, and I'll blow your head off."

Chapter 9

Sam knew it was stupid staying late in the office when he wasn't getting any work done and he had a perfectly good home to go to. But the thought of walking into his house without Nicole, without having spoken to her, made his stomach clench. Would the house still smell of her? The sheets would. God, he'd ground her into his sheets. They would smell of her and taste of her. Shit, if he went home without her, he'd just wander around his living room with a sad boner and nowhere to go with it.

He had to go home sometime, though. Harry and Mike were keeping tabs on him. If he was still here at midnight, they'd come to take him away, probably to some bar somewhere to get him drunk, then they'd get him home.

It was a thought. Getting shit-faced, oh yeah. Maybe pick up someone in the bar, fuck her, start getting Nicole out of his head.

Nope, that wouldn't work. The thought had no appeal at all. Zero.

Jesus, this was scary shit. His cock hadn't even stirred at the thought of fucking another woman. If anything, it shriveled, balls curling up into his groin. If his dick could talk it'd tell him only Nicole would do, which was bad juju, since the lady wasn't talking to him.

He'd finally stopped calling her office and her home around midday, when she'd taken her phone off the hook. Cell phone still off, so he was stymied.

Mike had reported back on his mission to put the fear of God into those two scumbags but he'd been annoyingly closemouthed about Nicole. When Sam had asked him how Nicole looked, he'd answered, "Beautiful."

Yeah, thanks Mike. If there was one thing Sam knew in the world, it was that Nicole Pearce was beautiful.

Mike also said that Nicole loved her father very much.

After that, Mike just zipped it, leaving Sam hanging.

Sam sat behind his big desk, a big, fat, shiny success symbol that went nicely with the big, fat, shiny success symbol that was his office, and contemplated this huge curveball life had thrown at him.

Ever since his eighteenth birthday, when no one had any legal power over him anymore, he'd gotten everything he wanted out of life. It hadn't been easy, fuck no, especially becoming a SEAL, but by Christ, if he set his mind to it, if hard work and intelligence and perseverance could get it, it was his.

He'd never failed a mission he set for himself.

Except right now, when failure was staring him in the face. He'd rarely wanted anything in his life the way he wanted Nicole, but she'd slid right out of his grasp, and he didn't have the faintest idea what it would take to get her back.

He was dying, here. Just sinking down into some black hole, with no clue to where a hand-hold would be.

Sam sank further into his extremely comfortable, $6,000 designer chair he'd been embarrassed to buy but the decorator had insisted on.

Fuck. He was *whining*. Good thing Mike and Harry couldn't see him now, because they'd knock all this self-pity right out of him.

But the thing was, in every mission he'd ever had, he knew exactly what it would take to get what he wanted. Hard work and willpower usually, things he was capable of in spades.

But Nicole wasn't graduating BUD/S or surviving a firefight or founding a company. She was a woman, with a woman's totally unfathomable heart, and Sam simply couldn't see his way clear here. It was like being lost in a fog.

He second-guessed every move. Call, not call? Well, that was blown out of the water when he spent all morning punching out her home number.

That hadn't worked well.

What would she want? What would help?

Send flowers? What kind? He'd read somewhere while waiting in a barbershop that roses were over. No one wanted roses, they showed that a man had no imagination. So, fuck, what else was there? He racked his brain for other flowers and all he came up with was daisies. Weren't daisies associated with death?

Christ, he didn't recognize himself. This wasn't him. He was . . . dithering. Sam Reston, dithering. He didn't do dither. He did action.

Only not tonight, he thought with a sigh. Showing up on her doorstep would just alienate her, not to mention the fact that her dad was really sick and Sam might disturb him if he was sleeping. Man, he'd never seen anyone look the way her dad did, ready to step over the threshold of death at any moment. Sam had seen death before, but usually it came in the form of a bullet, shattering a healthy young body.

No, if Nicole's dad was sleeping, or had taken a turn for the worse, she wouldn't appreciate his ringing her doorbell. If there was one thing that had been made real real clear to him, pounded into his thick skull, it was that Nicole loved her father and had made him her top priority, and that wasn't going to change.

It was a real pity that it only made him admire her even more.

Jesus. Maybe it would be a good idea to go back to Plan A, getting shit-faced with his brothers.

Yeah, that would—

Sam froze. He had a bank of monitors on the short side of his L-shaped desk, one showing the corridor outside his door. It had gone blank about an hour and a half ago, and he'd made a mental note to have it fixed, toot sweet, as Nicole would say.

The monitor showed Nicole, right outside his door. Looking troubled and tired and unbearably beautiful. Long, slender hand outstretched, touching his door.

That's right, honey, he thought, rising. *Oh yeah. Knock on my door and walk straight into my arms and we can pick up where we left off.*

She stood, clearly tempted, but then she turned around and he lost her. She'd gone into her own office.

Shit.

Well, she was here. He wasn't going to have to wait till tomorrow to see her. Whatever was going on inside that complicated, beautiful head of hers, he'd find out in the next five minutes.

Sam shut down the office and walked across the hallway.

He was about to ring the bell next to the door when he stopped, frozen.

Oh *Christ.*

He could hear a man's deep rumble, though he couldn't make out the words. Shit! Of all the scenarios he'd run through his head, the fact that she was seeing someone else simply hadn't occurred to him. But if she was going out with someone else, then why the fuck had she accepted his invitation to dinner? Gone to bed with him?

He turned his head, good ear towards the door. Oh yeah. That was a man's voice. Unmistakeable. He stood there, as if someone had encased him in cement, trying to process this thought. Nicole was with another man.

Then he heard a high-pitched cry of pain and Sam forgot every ounce of training, every second of experience he'd had as a soldier. It had been drilled into his hard head by men with equally hard heads, over and over again, that you do not go blind into a battle situation. Ever. Any instructor would have had his ass if he'd done in training what he now did.

If he'd been able to use his brain to think instead of being instantly filled with terror at the nightmarish image of Nicole being hurt he'd have gone back into his office, where he had a shitload of weapons in his gun locker, picked up his Glock 19, checked to see the load, get a pair of restraints in case he didn't kill the fucker, used his thermal imager so he'd know where Nicole was, and make a dynamic entry.

He'd have taken a few seconds to run through the scenario in his mind and it would have gone smooth as shit through a goose, something he'd done a thousand times before, though never on his own, without a team by his side.

There'd been only one male voice, and Sam would pit himself against any man alive in combat.

Training said to wait and to go in prepared and with the right gear.

But the hell with training. No one knew better than Sam how much damage an angry man could do to a woman in just a minute. Broken arms, broken jaws, a punch so hard it reduced the liver to pulp . . . he'd seen it all in his childhood.

He'd touched every inch of Nicole last night and though she was toned and sleek, she didn't have the muscles of someone who knew self-defense. She was helpless.

Nicole cried out in pain again and Sam operated out of pure, wrenching terror, picking the lock in a second and launching himself into the room and, oh Christ, it was his worst nightmare.

A man in tactical gear, holding a gun against Nicole's head, one arm around her throat. They both turned, and Sam would never, ever forget the look on Nicole's face. She'd been struggling in despair and when she saw him her face simply lit up, with joy and hope. Blood dripped from where the muzzle broke the skin of her temple.

"Sam!" she choked and moved instinctively toward him, only to be caught up short by the man holding her.

"Oh no, you don't," the man growled, tightening his arm. "Stop right there," he said to Sam and Sam stopped. Fuck fuck *fuck*! They were against the wall, with Nicole's desk between them. There was no way Sam could rush him. The man was holding a Kimber 1911, safety off, finger in the trigger guard. He looked like he knew how to use the gun. And he looked like he would use it in a heartbeat.

"Who the fuck are you?" The man tightened his left arm even more around Nicole's throat, caught inside his elbow. Sam could hear her struggling for breath. It was a hold he knew and he tried not to let panic overwhelm him because it was a hold a trained man could use to snap her neck in a second. A lift of the forearm, a push to the left from the gun hand and the delicate bones in the neck would snap. It was a hold Sam had used. On men who dropped lifelessly to the ground.

Terror iced his veins. This was no casual thief he could maybe trick. This was an operator. Sam circled to the left, but the man kept something between them—the desk, a client chair.

The man shook Nicole. "I said, who are you? Tell me or her brain will be decorating this pretty desk."

Jesus. Sam knew exactly what a bullet through the head looked like. He had to exercise all his self-control not to visualize Nicole, red mist where her head used to be, collapsing to the floor.

Time. She needed time. He held his hands up. *Look, no weapons.* Christ, it was true. Not even a fucking knife. "Sam Reston," he said.

"Reston, huh." He shook Nicole a little. "Stay still, bitch." The man's dark gaze sharpened. "The guy with the office across the way?"

Sam nodded, eyes never leaving his. Nicole was fixed on him, eyes pleading, but Sam didn't dare even look at her. Every cell in his body was focused on the man, watching his every movement. All Sam needed was the barest chance, even a second's drop in attention.

But this guy was good. He moved carefully, completely unmindful of the fact that he held a desperately wriggling woman in his arms. He was circling toward the door, dragging Nicole.

Her chest was bellowing in a useless attempt to pull in air. Her lips were turning blue.

"You're choking her." Sam kept his voice low and even, watching the man's eyes. "Ease up a little."

The man didn't even answer. He jerked his head toward the back wall. "Get over there behind the desk. Sit down and put your hands on the desk."

Sam hesitated. Nicole's eyes were starting to roll up in her head. Maybe he should just launch himself at the fucker, see what happened. Nicole was going to be dead in a few minutes, anyway, if he continued choking her. Maybe the fuckhead would switch the gun to the big guy rushing him and away from the woman. If he didn't get off a head shot, maybe Sam could take the bullet and live long enough to snap the fucker's neck . . .

"Now!"

Except maybe the intruder would go for a head shot. The guy could drop him in a second and then Nicole would be at his mercy. As long as Sam was alive, she had a chance. He moved to the chair and sat.

"Hands on the desk. Palms down, fingers spread."

Jesus. Sam didn't even have a knife. He was good with a knife, almost better than with a gun. He could have his K-bar through this guy's eye and into his cortex in a half second, dropping him dead so fast that the instruction to his trigger finger to fire a bullet into Nicole's head would never make it past the first synapse.

But he was weaponless. His hands and feet were weapons but he had to get to the man first and right now, that was impossible.

The intruder was moving toward the door, dragging Nicole with him. Her wheezes sounded painfully loud in the silence of the room. Her feet scrabbled for purchase, heels drumming against the guy's ankles. He didn't even flinch. Sam dropped his eyes to the man's feet. He was wearing combat boots. Nicole was trying to kick him, hurt him, and he wasn't even feeling it.

Nice try, honey. She was nearly passed out from lack of oxygen and she was still fighting.

The two had reached the door. The guy was going to try to escape with Nicole, but he wasn't going to get far, dragging a woman kicking and screaming. Sam would catch up with him soon enough, it would be . . .

Sam was mentally reviewing his options, none of them good, when the man loosened his arm from around Nicole's throat, picked her up bodily and hurled her across the room, straight at the big plate-glass windows of her office on the ninth floor.

* * *

"Honey, honey, stay awake. Don't go away again, that's a good girl. Look at me now. That's right, open those beautiful blue eyes."

Strong fingers, tapping at her cheek. Annoying. It was really annoying, when all she wanted to do was sleep. Some small memory in the back of her head told her she'd been drifting in and out of consciousness.

She was on her back, head in someone's lap. Someone she knew . . .

Another tap and her eyes opened. Strong features, face drawn, deep brackets around his mouth.

"Sam?" Her voice came out a raw whisper. It hurt to talk. Hurt to swallow, she discovered.

"Yeah." Sam's own voice was harsh, hoarse. "Yeah, it's Sam."

"What—" Nicole brought a hand to her throat. God, it *hurt*. "What happened?"

Sam's face above her was grim, nostrils pinched with stress. He looked pale, stressed. Ten years older.

"Someone was waiting for you in your office, honey. He was hurting you. When I came in he was holding a gun to your head. He tossed you across the room." His jaw muscles worked. "You nearly went out the window. Of the ninth floor." His eyes closed. "Just about gave me a fucking heart attack."

Flashes of memory blossomed in her mind, like scenes under strobe lights. A gun muzzle, tightly held against her temple. A strong, unyielding arm around her throat, cruelly tight, cutting off air. Sam, still and dangerous-looking, ignoring her, carefully watching the man holding her like a cat watches a mouse.

Being picked up, flying through the air, limbs flailing, caught at the last minute by Sam . . .

"Where—" Nicole raised a hand to her head. The blood at her temple had dried. "Where did the man go? Did you catch him?"

"No." Sam ground his teeth, hard. She could actually hear the enamel grating. "I was too busy catching you. Your windows aren't bulletproof. They're just simple glass. Nine stories is a hell of a long way to fall. Luckily, we didn't find out what a nine-story fall looks like."

Nicole stirred in his arms, groaning. She seemed to be one big sore muscle. She might not have fallen out of the window, but she'd definitely banged against some furniture.

"Shhh." Sam held her more tightly. "Don't move. The EMTs are on their way and so are the police. They should be here any minute."

Nicole's hand sought, and found, Sam's. "That's nice," she said drowsily, eyelids drooping. She ached all over and was so tired. "I think I'll just rest my eyes for a moment."

The next time Nicole felt that annoying tapping against her cheek, her office was filled with light and people and noise. She sat up, Sam's hand to her back helping her up. It took her a second to realize her head wasn't swimming.

"Ma'am?" A young face thrust itself in front of hers. Thin, short hair, clever eyes. He shot a glance at Sam. "Sir, you're going to have to give me some space here or I can't do my job."

With visible reluctance, Sam let her go.

The medic shined a light in her eyes, took her pulse.

"Shouldn't she be strapped to a stretcher?" Sam asked. He hadn't gone far, crouched on his haunches next to her.

The medic shot him an ironical glance. "She was sitting upright when I got to her. If she has a spinal injury, it's too late."

Sam closed his eyes and winced. "Jesus, I didn't think of that."

Nicole reached out and closed her hand around his. "That's okay, Sam. I don't have any serious injuries, I promise."

Sam's eyes met the medic's. "She was tossed across a room. Didn't go out the window by a miracle, but she hit the bookcase. God knows what kind of internal injuries she has."

The miracle was Sam. He'd caught her just before she'd have gone crashing through the window to her death nine stories below. She shuddered at the thought.

Nicole took a quick internal check, as the medic took her pulse and shined a light in her eyes. Did she have internal injuries?

Most of the momentum of her flight toward the windows had been blocked by Sam's body. Her shoulder and back had slammed into the bookcase and she'd had the wind knocked out of her, like the time she'd fallen out of the swings when she was ten. She still remembered that horrible feeling as she lay on her back, staring at the bright blue Greek sky, unable to move and unable to draw a breath.

It had been terrifying, but a minute later, she was on her feet again, and ten minutes later, she was back with her friends on the swings, the incident totally forgotten, until now.

She'd had the wind knocked out of her, badly. Her shoulder hurt and, knowing how delicate her skin was, she'd be badly bruised. In the next couple of days, there would be a rainbow of colors on her shoulder, the palette dominated by black and green.

But that was it. She took in a deep breath and felt no pain at all. She felt shaken, a man had broken into her office and threatened her with a gun to the head. Feeling deeply rattled was only natural. And she was tired, because she was now going on thirty-six hours without sleep. But there was nothing broken inside her.

Another man entered the room, crouched next to her, a familiar face. Mike the cop.

Sam frowned at him. "What the hell are you doing here?"

"Word travels, bro. Cop shop jungle drums. Harry's here, too."

Sam swiveled his head. Behind Mike was a tall man with lines of suffering on his face, on crutches.

He was an unhealthy pale color, big-boned but painfully thin, the emaciation of illness or injury. Nicole recognized it immediately.

The medic stood. "Okay. Vital signs are good, but we're taking you in for observation, ma'am. It would probably be a good idea to stay overnight, just so we can be sure you're not concussed."

"No," Nicole said calmly.

The medic had been beckoning to someone at the door, but he turned around at her tone. "No?" It was as if he'd never heard the word before.

"No. No question. I'm not going to the hospital." Nicole had spent two months accompanying her father to the hospital for radiotherapy, every single day. Just walking through hospital doors and inhaling the smell of formalin and alcohol made her nauseous.

She didn't need the hospital. She was shaken and scared but not hurt, not seriously. Staying in a hospital was not going to make her feel better. "I know myself. I had the wind knocked out of me, that's all. I'm a little bruised, but there's nothing broken inside. I'm just fine."

Sam's jaw muscles jumped. He was literally biting down on words. "You could be concussed." Each word sounded pulled out of him by red-hot pincers.

"If I'm concussed, being in the hospital won't help." But she wasn't. She hadn't bumped her head. Her muscles hurt, not her head.

"You're coming home with me, then." Sam's deep

voice was belligerent, as if spoiling for a fight. "And at the first sign of something I don't like, you're going to the hospital. That is non-negotiable."

Usually, Nicole was like a cat. You did not order her about. Under normal circumstances, her pride, if nothing else, would have made her refuse Sam's orders. But actually, going home with Sam sounded wonderful. If she went back to her own home, she'd have to face the night nurse and, maybe, her father. The last thing he needed was to see her bruised and shaken.

Going home with Sam, maybe sleeping a few hours in his arms, sounded like heaven right now.

"Okay," she said softly. "Deal."

Sam had assumed a fighting stance, legs apart and braced, clearly ready to put up a fight. He blinked, the wind taken out of his sails. He relaxed a little and nodded, eyes never leaving hers. "Deal."

"Ma'am? I'm Lieutenant Kelly. Do you feel up to answering a few questions?" Nicole looked at the man standing next to Mike. Lieutenant Kelly looked tired, as if just coming off a very long shift. He was tall, heavyset but very fit-looking, dressed in a rumpled gray suit that matched the gray at his temples.

She had to twist her neck painfully to look up at him as he walked around her, pulling up one of her client chairs. A Louis IV, which she'd had covered in *Antico Setificio Fiorentino* dark green brocade. It was exceedingly pretty and fragile. He sat on it gingerly as if hoping it wouldn't crack under his weight. She sat on its twin, turning it so they were face to face, almost knee to knee.

Sam pulled up another chair, placed it as close to hers as it could go, and sat down.

Lieutenant Kelly leaned forward, elbows on knees, holding a worn notebook. At his soft instigation, Nicole gave her name, address and office, home and cell phone numbers.

"Do you want to tell me what went down, Ms. Pearce?"

"Yes. Of course." She took a deep breath, marshaling her thoughts. "I, um, didn't go into work today. I wasn't, um, feeling very well, so I worked from home. Or tried to." Next to her, she could practically feel Sam vibrating. The lieutenant was watching her carefully, bruised-looking gray eyes fixed on her intently. Nicole hoped with all her heart the man didn't have telepathic powers, because she would die on the spot if he figured out exactly why she didn't come in to work today. Because she'd been rattled by the most intense night of sex of her life. Whew.

He simply nodded at her, made an annotation in his notebook, then looked back at her. *Go on.* He didn't betray any impatience, but the words hovered in the air.

God, she was tired. A sudden wave of debilitating exhaustion swept over her. She looked down in her lap, horrified to see her hands shaking. She clutched them, hoping the detective hadn't noticed.

He'd noticed.

So had Sam.

Sam reached over and curled one big hand over her clasped ones, stilling the trembling. But she was trembling all over now and felt cold, chilled to the bone.

"Oh God." She clenched her jaw to stop her teeth from chattering. "Sorry. I don't know what's happening to me."

"Adrenaline dump," Sam said, tightening his grasp. His hand felt so warm.

The lieutenant nodded. "It's perfectly understandable, Ms. Pearce. You've had a terrible experience and your body's reacting. We can take this downtown. Or do this tomorrow, if you want."

"No, no, I want to do this now. I want this man caught. I want him caught and punished to the full extent of the law. Not only for breaking and entering but also for assault." The lieutenant looked over at Sam, a brief electric glance of male understanding.

"What?" she said, indignant. "You don't think you're going to catch him, do you?" The thought chased the chill away. The intruder had violated her space, threatened her. She wanted him *caught* and put behind bars for scaring the living daylights out of her. Oh, and for trying to toss her out of a ninth-story window.

"Well, we'll do our very best, ma'am," the lieutenant said calmly. He looked down at his notebook. "So . . . you weren't able to work from home today. And you decided to come in after hours, is that correct?"

"Yes, that's correct." Nicole got a grip on herself.

To catch this awful man, she had to get past her emotional reactions and give the police as much information as possible.

Grow a backbone, Nicole. She sat straighter in her chair and willed the trembling to stop. Sam's hand around hers was like a small furnace. She concentrated on that warmth until she could marshal her thoughts.

"Do you know what time you came in?" The lieutenant bent his head over his notebook. He had a crewcut so severe she could see the scalp beneath the hair.

"No, I don't—" she began, then stopped. "Wait. It was exactly 9:05 when I walked out of the elevator. I remember seeing the big wall clock at the end of the corridor. It's digital so it gives the exact time. That means it probably would have been 9:06 by the time I entered my office." She snatched a sideways glance at Sam. "This time I made sure I had my keys with me."

He nodded, unsmiling.

"And you opened your door with your key?" Nicole couldn't imagine what the lieutenant was writing, but he was scribbling away.

"Yes. I, um, I entered with the key and—oh!" She cried out. The other men in the room, the fingerprint tech, the medic and Sam's friends Harry and Mike raised their heads. "How stupid of me! I didn't notice. I always engage the deadbolt when I leave my office. Always. And yet when I opened my door with my key, I didn't have to turn my key more than once. So—"

"So someone was in your office and you waltzed right into an ambush. Goddammit, woman. That wasn't smart. You could have gotten yourself killed." Sam's deep voice was harsh, his face stiff with disapproval. His jaw muscles bunched as he clearly bit back further words. Probably a lot of adjectives, like *idiot* and *airhead*, were rolling around in his mouth like marbles.

No, it hadn't been smart. Nicole wanted to snap back at him, but the truth was, he was right. If she'd been paying any attention at all, she'd have backed away immediately. But this wasn't the kind of thing she paid attention to. She paid attention to her father and to her work and not much else these days. This was just way, way outside her attention zone.

Besides, she'd been tired, confused about her feelings for Sam, worried about her father . . . and she'd walked right into a burglar trying to steal God knows what from her office.

"Sam, dial it down. This isn't helping." The lieutenant shot him one of those looks men used to quell each other. "Now, ma'am." He turned back to her. "So the deadbolt wasn't engaged, but you didn't notice that."

"No, not at all." Oh God, the shame. Single women weren't supposed to be so clueless when it comes to their personal security. "What can I say? I was thinking about the work I had to do and I simply wasn't paying attention. So I just turned the key and . . . and reached for the light switch, but then a man slammed me against the wall, put a gun to my head and said that he'd shoot me if I screamed."

She shivered. Sam leaned over, planted a soft kiss in her hair and whispered. "It's okay. You're okay now."

Mike and Harry exchanged glances.

"It—it was horrible. I was so scared and I had the breath knocked out of me. I couldn't breathe, I couldn't think. I didn't know what to do, I was paralyzed with fear."

It was something she'd never forget—the feeling of utter helplessness. Of knowing that he was stronger than she was and his strength gave him permission to do anything he wanted to her. She'd lived twenty-eight years on this earth without feeling like helpless prey and she never, *ever* wanted to experience it again.

She turned to Sam. "I want you to teach me self-defense. All the moves possible to break someone's neck. Or at least an arm." She thought for a moment. "And maybe how to shoot or something. I never want to feel that helpless again."

Sam closed his eyes and nodded. His eyes opened and stared fiercely into hers. "Count on it. An intense course in self-defense, several martial arts, we'll find the one best suited to you, and also use of firearms . . ."

"And knives." How satisfying it would have been to stick a knife between his ribs. Or cut off the man's balls. "I want to know how to use a knife. A big one. Big black one. The kind that reaches the heart in a second." She'd wear it in a thigh sheath, like Lara Croft.

"Knives, too, then. No question." For the first time, a ghost of a smile crossed his lips. He bowed his head gravely.

Nicole nodded her head. She probably wouldn't train, but right now the thought that she could, that she could turn herself into a mighty she-warrior, comforted her.

The lieutenant was immersed in his notebook, clearly as riveting as any best seller. "Then what happened?"

"He—he switched on the light."

The lieutenant looked up at that. "Did you recognize him?"

"No." Her voice rang with conviction. "I've never seen him before in my life."

"Can you give me a description?"

Nicole closed her eyes. It had all happened so fast. "Um, I didn't see him for very long. He had short light brown hair, light brown eyes. Dressed in this funny black jumpsuit." She thought, then shrugged. That was about it. "I'd probably recognize him in a lineup." Maybe. She'd been so terrified, her mind had simply blanked with blind panic.

The lieutenant switched his gaze to Sam.

"Five ten, one eighty, brown and brown, Nomex tactical suit, combat boots, K-bar in thigh sheath, Kimber 1911, three mags on the belt, latex gloves, so your guys probably won't find prints. He left in a real hurry, maybe my security cameras caught his face. You could run it through the FBI's facial recognition software, maybe come up with a hit." Sam frowned. "Come to think of it, my security cameras just outside the door fogged up around seven thirty and then a few minutes before nine. I didn't think anything at the time, but he could have been using a—"

"Laser light," Harry and Mike said at the same time.

The lieutenant grunted. "An operator."

"Oh yeah," Sam answered. "An operator. Got in and out real smooth."

The lieutenant rested his elbows on his knees and fixed Nicole with a weary gaze. "So, we've got a pro breaking into your office, Ms. Pearce. What was he looking for?"

Nicole shook her head. The sixty-four-thousand-dollar question. "I have no idea, but he was definitely looking for *something*. He kept saying, 'Where is it?'" She cleared her throat delicately. "Actually, he kept saying, 'Where the fuck is it?' I have no idea what he was talking about. I tried to say so, but he just ground the gun more tightly against my head."

All the men looked at her temple. "It's okay," she said to the room. "Just some torn skin, nothing serious."

Sam closed his eyes in pain.

"So, the intruder was looking for something. For what? He didn't come to steal those pretty knickknacks you've got, he was looking for something specific. What?" the lieutenant prodded.

Nicole shrugged her shoulders, baffled. "I can't imagine. I don't think he was after the watercolors or the silver." It was true that she'd decorated the office very nicely, with two or three good pieces of family furniture, a little collection of solid sterling pen holders and an Art Déco leather desk set, all attractive pieces without, however, any real resale value. The watercolors were lovely, but they were by her mother, who'd been talented but had never exhibited. They had zero value on the open market. Nothing in the room had any real value if fenced, except maybe her desk. But who would enter an office and steal a *desk*?

"Has anything been taken?" the lieutenant asked.

Nicole looked around her office and shook her head.

"Do you feel like checking that?"

Would her legs support her? Yes, they would, she found as she rose. Sam rose right along with her and shadowed her as she walked the perimeter of the room, opening drawers, carefully scrutinizing every surface. Sam stayed so close she could feel his body heat.

Finally, she made it back to the lieutenant.

"Okay. Everything's where it should be. It looks like he didn't have time . . ." Nicole's voice died away as she looked at her computer, head tilted. She kept her desktop on a separate table, where she worked, and kept only her laptop on the desk, where she dealt with clients. She used a Knoll office chair on wheels when at her desktop computer, and it was pulled away from the table. "That's not right."

All the men looked at her.

She walked over and touched the chair back, a foot from the table. "I am absolutely positive I pushed the chair in under the desk before leaving. I always do. I like leaving the office in order. Do you think the man was after something in my computer?" Nicole looked up at Sam, then at the lieutenant.

Sam was already settling into the chair, reaching down to press the button that would turn the processor on. He pressed it and waited, frowning. He turned his head up to Nicole. Everyone had gathered around her computer. "I think he trashed your computer, Nicole."

"No." She pulled her portable hard disk drive from her purse. "I use portable hard disk drives and always take them home with me, together with my laptop and backup files on a flash drive. I make my livelihood from my computer and I never leave anything behind in the office. My computer has some valuable software and can deal with a fairly broad range of alphabets, so I'd hate to lose that. Plus, most of our contracts contain a confidentiality clause, so I make sure there's a minimal degree of security."

At the word *confidential*, the lieutenant, Sam, Mike, Harry, the fingerprint tech and the medic pointed their faces at her monitor like hound dogs flushing birds.

"Fire it up," Sam growled.

Nicole slid the portable hard disk drive into the designated slot and pressed the button to turn on the processor. There was utter silence in the room as the computer pinged and whirred its way to the home page of Wordsmith.

"Password," she said, and the men averted their eyes while she entered the password to access her files. She had her files organized into clients, languages and translators. The men stared at the screen as if it could render up the secrets of the universe.

"What are we looking at here, ma'am?" the lieutenant finally asked.

Nicole gently nudged Sam with her hip and slid into the chair when he stood. "Okay. What Wordsmith does is translate texts, from ten languages into ten languages. We work from English, French, Spanish, German, Dutch, Italian, Russian, Chinese, Polish and Hungarian into the same languages." She thought of Aidan Berry, who'd been one of her best friends at the Geneva School of Translation, had fallen in love with a painter in Reykjavik and used to work at an Icelandic bank, which, like all the other Icelandic banks, had gone belly-up. "We also would offer economic translations from Icelandic into English, if Iceland still had an economy."

She sat back, pleased. Wordsmith, her baby. It was pretty special. "Well, there you have it. It's a fairly straightforward business."

Six utterly blank male expressions. "What?"

The lieutenant pinched the bridge of his nose.

"Could you sort of run that by me again, ma'am?" He nodded his head at the screen. "Show us what we're seeing? I can't make any sense out of what's on that screen, and we need to make sense of it. Maybe a man was willing to commit murder for what's in your computer."

He was right. If the intruder *had* been at her computer, he'd gone to a lot of trouble to get something. And if he was after something . . . she drew in a shocked breath, swiveling her chair around to face the men. "Oh my God. If he wanted something from my computer, he didn't get it because the hard disk was in my purse. That means—"

"He's coming back," Sam said harshly. Nicole looked at the grave faces surrounding her. They'd come to this conclusion well before she had. She twisted her hands in her lap, suddenly icy cold.

This was not over.

Sam laid large, warm hands on her shoulders. "He's not getting to you again, though, honey. I can guarantee you that." She looked up at him. He wasn't smiling at her reassuringly, trying to make her feel better. He looked grim. And deadly. Which actually did make her feel better. "You're coming home with me and you're staying with me until this fu—asshole is caught. We straight on that?"

Sudden panic had slowed her thought processes, but one thing was clear. "I can't leave my father, certainly not if he is in any danger. I simply can't do it."

Sam shifted until he could see her eyes. "Someone might be coming after you. You don't want to take that danger to your father, do you? If this guy is willing to hurt you, believe me, he won't balk at hurting your father."

Oh God, no, he wouldn't. Nicole remembered clearly the cold command in her attacker's voice, the menace that emanated off him like vapor off ice, the utter steadiness of his movements. He wasn't a petty thief, frightened and in over his head. *An operator*, Sam had said. By that he meant a man used to violence. Nicole was not going to lead him to her father, but . . .

"He'll need protection." Just the *thought* of someone hurting her father made her stomach clench, cold sweat break out between her shoulder blades. "I can't possibly leave him alone to face danger."

"Mike?" Sam pivoted slightly to look his friend in the face.

Mike turned to the lieutenant. "Lieutenant?"

The lieutenant sighed. "Yeah, yeah, I hear you. Okay, I'll post a couple of men around Ms. Pearce's house. No one will get to her father."

"Triple shifts," Sam said.

The lieutenant winced. "Yeah. Christ, I don't know where I'll get six men from, but okay, I'll try, at least. I can't guarantee more than a couple of days, though. Couple days nothing happens, that's it, you're on your own." He shrugged. "Sorry."

"I'll provide security after that," Sam said. "I know some good men."

Bodyguards, around the clock, indefinitely. Oh God, how could she afford this? Nicole balanced possible danger against certain bankruptcy and turned to Sam. Before she could open her mouth, though, Sam squeezed her shoulder. "I'll take care of it," he said softly.

The lieutenant had been speaking quietly into his cell. He flipped it closed and looked at Mike and Sam. "Six men, rotation of eight hours, for two days. Best I can do. They'll be in place inside half an hour."

"I'll pick it up after that," Sam said.

Nicole started to object, out of principle, when the lieutenant interrupted. "Now that we've got that out of the way, let's see what the guy could have been looking for. So, show me how your system works, ma'am."

Nicole switched gears. Wordsmith, her baby. The best way to describe it was to show it.

Nicole went to her files and clicked on the folders. "This is the way my business operates. A client sends a text to be translated. The client would have contacted me beforehand and we would have agreed on a quote. The price varies in relation to the degree of technical difficulty, the rarity of the combination—Dutch into Chinese is going to cost you a *lot* of money, for instance—and the urgency. So when I receive the text, the client has already been given a quote and I know exactly how much the file he sent me is worth. If it's from Spanish or French into English, chances are I'll do it, though lately the workload has increased, so

I send what I can't handle to a friend of mine at the Monterey Institute of Languages. Everything else is sent to one of the translators in my network. I negotiate the price, receive the text, forward it to the appropriate translator, who will have the requisite languages and field of expertise, I take care of the billing and client relations. For that I take a fifteen percent commission. It's not a huge business; it's only a year old, but it's growing."

The lieutenant grunted. "Show me some of the files. Starting from, say, three days ago. We don't know where the guy came from, maybe he had to travel to get here."

"He was American, though," Sam said quietly. "No doubt about that. Probably ex-military."

"American." The lieutenant nodded. "So—let's go back three days. How many files?"

Nicole had a chronology function and went back to June 26. She spoke with her eyes glued to the monitor. "Okay, over the past three days I've received twenty-two files. Two hundred fifty pages of a travel guide to St. Petersburg from Russian into English." She clicked the file open and the men stared at the Cyrillic text. "My Russian isn't very strong, but the title of this is *St. Petersburg, Jewel of the North*. It was sent to a professor of Russian at the University of Chicago who rounds out his salary by doing translations."

She clicked on another folder. "This is a hundred twenty pages of text that is an analysis of the German bond market, to be translated into English. I sent that off to the appropriate colleague. And here's a text from Chinese into English, which costs a premium because good Chinese-into-English translators are rare. A survey of the banking sector in China. This is the project for the enlargement of the Port of Marseilles. I'll take that one myself, the Marseille Port Authority is an old client of mine, I worked for them just out of school, before applying to the UN." She did some calculating in her head. "In all, a total of almost four thousand pages."

"What came in today?" Mike asked.

Nicole pointed. "Since this morning, eighty pages of a novel, Spanish into English, the publisher is hoping for a sale to foreign markets at the Frankfurt Book Fair in October. The publicity for a trade fair in Buenos Aires, a short treatise on Napa wines to be translated into French, an Italian paper on microsurgery and a treatise in Polish on the miracles of Pope John Paul the Second. Tomorrow I should receive a technical manual on DVD recorders, Japanese to English—that's going to cost them—which I will send to a student at MIT." Nicole sat back. "That's it."

"Has anything else arrived since the last time you looked?"

She leaned forward, typing quickly. "I don't know . . . nope. The only thing that has arrived is a copy of a contract and an e-mail from a girlfriend in Geneva. Who has probably broken up with her boyfriend again."

Silence. She could almost hear the men thinking.

"Do you have any military contracts for translation? Come to think of it, the military has dealings all over the world. They might outsource some translation stuff."

"No. I'd have to apply for a security clearance for myself and my collaborators. I've thought about it, a lot, but have never gotten around to it. I will, though. There's a lot of work with the military, it's a big field."

"State Department?"

"The State Department has its own internal translators, a really good service. They don't outsource anything."

"What about industrial espionage?"

"I beg your pardon?"

"Do you get translations—texts—that someone could make money knowing? Some industrial secrets?"

Nicole was shaking her head. "We're too young a company for that. We do good work, but any corporation that had industrial secrets someone would be willing to steal at the point of a gun— well, they wouldn't send them to us. I guarantee a certain degree of confidentiality, there's a non-disclosure clause in the contract, and my firewalls are pretty good. But any corporation that entrusted me with truly valuable secrets, well, they'd be so foolish that presumably just about anyone could access them. Someday I'm going to set up the company to guarantee a maximum degree of confidentiality, including encryption, but that kind of software costs a lot of money and I'd have to up my price considerably. Now is not the time to do that."

Silence, male cogs whirring.

Finally the lieutenant stirred. "All this banking stuff. Is any of it—" his cell rang and he held up a finger. He listened, grunted, closed the cell. He looked at Nicole. "My men are in place, your father's protected."

Nicole slumped, letting out a long breath. "Thank you."

Sam's warm hand on her shoulder reminded her that she was protected, too.

"Hey." The tech who'd been dusting for prints lifted something that looked like a thick plastic string. "Look what I found. Guy must have lost it off his utility belt."

The men turned to look. Sam's hand tightened on her shoulder.

"Jesus," Harry breathed. It was the first word he'd spoken since coming into the room.

"What?" Nicole looked around at the grim male faces. "What is it?"

"A goddamned restraint," Sam said, the words falling out of his mouth like stones.

"A what?"

"A restraint." He turned, eyes burning into hers. "He was planning on handcuffing you."

"Why would he—" Nicole began, then stopped. There were all sorts of reasons an intruder would be willing to handcuff her, none of them good.

Sam nodded. "Yeah. So let's fucking figure out what the fucker wanted so fucking badly, so we can fucking go get him."

Nicole sat back, a little shocked at the idea that Sam had foiled a plan that not only included guns but also included handcuffs. And, if they included handcuffs, it probably also included pain.

A part of her also noticed that Sam's language deteriorated badly when he was stressed.

"You seem to do a lot of banking stuff," the lieutenant said again, breaking the silence.

Nicole nodded. "Yes, we do have a great deal of economic expertise."

"Could there be anything someone would be willing to kill for in those bank reports? Sometimes a lot of money can be involved in these things. Maybe someone was looking at losing millions."

Nicole was shaking her head before he finished. "I can definitely rule that out. Most of the economic texts we translate are to fulfil legal requirements, for board meetings and such. In Europe, the record usually must be in the language of the meeting and English, so foreign shareholders can read it. No one would send us information that would involve a lot of money. We're simply too small and too young for that kind of data. Our work is strictly routine."

Silence.

"Okay. I think we might be done here." The lieutenant was staring at her, face closed like a fist. He blew out a breath. "Can you send me a copy of everything you've received over the past three days? No, make that a week."

Nicole hid her wince. It was borderline unethical, her clients definitely would not want her to be sending out their documents. But this was the police, and they certainly wouldn't be broadcasting them. "Yes, of course, though most are in foreign languages."

The lieutenant looked pained. "Yeah, that will be part of the fun." He stood. "I think we've done everything we can here. Jansen—" he indicated the young fingerprint tech, "will be taking your prints for comparison purposes. Will we find anyone else's?"

Would he? Nicole thought about it. "I don't know. I actually don't think so. The last client in here was Maxwell Rubens, the software guy, to discuss an ongoing contract for translations of his programs into Chinese. But he was here ten days ago, and the cleaning service has been in here at least three times since then. So if you find prints that aren't mine, they might be Mr. Rubens's. And anyway, as Sam said, the intruder wore gloves."

"We'll check anyway." The lieutenant gave her his card. "If you remember anything, anything at all, call me. Day or night."

Nicole understood very well that she was getting special treatment because of Mike. No way would a botched burglary, where nothing was actually stolen, be getting all this attention. Not to mention a police lieutenant giving her his private cell phone number and authorization to call him day or night if she needed something.

She put the card in her purse and held out her

hand. "I cannot begin to thank you enough, Lieutenant."

His grasp was firm and dry. "No problem." He nodded. "Sam, Harry. Mike, you're with me."

A source of energy left the room with him, the medic, the young tech guy, and Mike. Nicole felt suddenly drained, exhausted beyond measure. She swayed slightly, then felt Sam's strong arms go around her. She leaned into him, into his strength, leaning her forehead against his chest for just a second, inhaling the scent that had been imprinted on the primitive part of her brain all last night.

Harry cleared his throat and she straightened, suddenly ashamed of her weakness, but Sam held her tightly before she could pull away.

He spoke over her head to Harry. "I'm taking her home. You look after things here."

Harry nodded.

"And check our security cameras, I'll bet you anything we caught him as he was running away."

"Yeah. I'll freeze a couple of frames and e-mail them to the SDPD. They've got facial recognition software, just like the FBI. If the guy's in the system, we'll get him. I'm on it." Harry closed the door softly behind him. They were alone.

Sam tightened his embrace and bent down to her ear. "Let's go home, honey." His voice was so low, she felt the vibration in his chest more than heard the words. His breath washed over her ear and she broke out in goosebumps.

She pulled away and looked up at him. At that

strong, unhandsome face. Of course she was going home with him. There was no question of that. He'd come for her in her hour of need, without hesitation. He'd saved her life. In some important, primordial way, a way that was blood and bone deep, she now belonged to him.

Chapter 10

Escaping hadn't been hard. For someone who'd graduated SERE with only a busted shoulder to show for it, getting out of the fancy building with the pretty, pretend security had been a cakewalk.

Up the fire escape, and up onto the roof. It was night and the satellites that passed weren't equipped with infrared cameras. That was for war zones.

Outlaw was seriously annoyed at having his work interrupted, though. And by someone who knew what he was doing. Fuck, another few minutes and the lady would have talked. She'd been terrified. He could still feel the deep tremors running through her. He'd even been tempted for a second there. The bitch was a real looker and Outlaw liked his women just a little scared. Made them real accommodating.

But he knew better than to mix sex with the job. It was the kind of mistake that could have gotten him killed in the service and the kind of mistake that would cost him money in his new job. So sex while working was off the table, always.

The job wasn't done. He'd just sat down to her computer when he'd heard the key in the lock and had barely made it to the door and turned out the lights before she walked in.

And a couple of minutes later, the big asshole from across the way picked the lock and came in and the whole mission had gone FUBAR in a second.

It was a very good thing that the guy cared about Nicole Pearce. Outlaw had seen it in an instant and realized that she was his get-out-of-jail-free card.

He'd tossed her at the window, knowing that if the guy didn't catch her, she'd fall nine stories to her death and he'd never get the info. But he also knew the guy would rather catch her than him.

Up on the rooftop, Outlaw went to the southern edge of the building. Only two feet separated this wall from the next building. He tossed the trolley suitcase and his briefcase over onto the next roof and jumped.

This building had a service elevator from the roof to the garage, and a quarter of an hour later, Outlaw was dressed in his banker's suit and driving away in his rental.

Next stop—Nicole Pearce's house. She would either go home and he could get the job done there or if she didn't, he'd grab the dad and force her hand.

Outlaw had never understood the hostage thing. There wasn't anyone in the world he'd give something up for. You could blow up any head you wanted and he didn't care. But for the rest of the world, it was a surefire winner. There were people who'd give up anything if you held a gun to a loved one's head. Or knee or elbow, promising to shoot the hostage to death, piece by piece.

Ah, yes. That always got results.

Outlaw parked two blocks from Nicole Pearce's house, then made his way in the dark to the back of the Pearce house.

It wasn't a wealthy part of town. The houses were small, about sixty years old, most of them badly kept.

He knew how to move in the dark, it was in his bones. He ghosted from tree to shrub to wall, ending up crouching behind the Pearce house, looking out over the backyard. It was the best-kept house on the street, sporting a fresh paint job. The garden was well tended, with neatly trimmed shrubbery and flowering plants and a recently mown lawn. Someone worked hard.

There were lights on in every room downstairs. It was ten thirty. Pretty soon the household would be going to bed, if there was an old man in the house. Outlaw would make his move a few hours after lights out, when the father would be deep in sleep. He leaned his ear against the wall. There were voices in the room, a male rumble and the lighter tones of a woman, but he couldn't make out the words.

Well, he'd come prepared. That's what they paid him for.

He entered the combination to open his suitcase. Inside the lining was a soundless electric mini-drill and a snake mike with inbuilt microcamera. He carefully drilled a hole through the exterior wall of the house, the drill so silent he could barely hear it inches away. He broke through at floor level and threaded the mike and camera into the hole.

Shit!

The room was set up like a hospital room. There was a high cot surrounded by medical instruments, an IV tree, a bedside table with pills, a man in a wheelchair. A woman in a nurse's uniform bending over him.

Outlaw pulled his eye away and sat with his back to the wall.

Well, *fuck*. Nicole Pearce's father was sick. How the hell could he have known? It's not as if it was on her website. That complicated things, because the geezer might die on him and he'd instantly lose his leverage. And that bag hanging from the IV tree would probably have a sedative in it. Outlaw could end up having an unconscious hostage.

Not to mention the fact that the nurse was contractually obliged to stay awake and by his bedside all night.

Shit. This was supposed to be fucking *easy*.

At least the nurse would be easy. And he had a preloaded syringe of adrenaline he could always shoot into the geezer. It would work.

He'd wait until all the lights went out, then
break in. The place had no security, none. No
cameras, no burglar alarm and he'd seen the locks
on the front and back doors. Pathetic. These people deserved what was going to happen to them.

Outlaw settled with his back to the rear left-
hand corner where he could keep an eye on the
front and back of the house, stretched his legs out,
preparing to go into sniper's lethargy for a couple
of hours, when every cell in his body went on red
alert.

A squad car pulled up outside the Pearce house.
Two cops in the front seats. The passenger window rolled down and Outlaw could hear the
squawk of the radio. The guy riding shotgun pulled
a mike from the dashboard attached to a curly
wire, put it up to his mouth and talked, staring
out the window at the façade of the house. The
cop listened to a static-filled voice, then got out of
the car, hand on the grip of the Beretta 92 in its
holster, clearly preparatory to doing a look-see.
He was wearing body armor and he looked alert.

He started walking toward the side of the
house.

Jesus fucking Christ.

Outlaw melted into the shadows, moving beyond the cop's vision, thinking furiously.

Now there were two cops to take out, besides
the nurse. Count in Nicole Pearce and her father,
that made five fucking bodies. His usual fee didn't
cover that. Particularly not snuffing cops. Cops
never gave up on cop killings. There was no such

thing as a cold case when a cop was offed. It remained hot till the end of time.

Outlaw's hits were carefully planned and even more carefully executed. No improv, no surprises. He'd avoided capture so far because he left nothing to chance. No prints, no DNA, nada. He was meticulous, almost surgical in his precision.

Tonight he was being forced to work on the fly, leaving behind a trail of dead bodies, two of them cops.

Furious, he pulled out his Blackberry and sent an encrypted message.

> Job now requires taking out two cops, a nurse and sick old man. Will need backup. Awaiting instructions.

He was well hidden behind a neighbor's tool shed and was prepared to wait all night for instructions, but it wasn't necessary. Fifteen minutes later, he had an answer.

> Check your bank. Then do it. Expenses OK.

When he checked his bank account, there was a payment for $1,000,000 there. Shit, for a cool million and a half, he'd off an extra two cops, a nurse and a sick geezer. Particularly since he had the element of surprise.

Killing two cops was serious stuff, though. He'd have to take the money and disappear for a while. A year, maybe more. There was a small property he'd bought in Costa Rica. He could add to it, make himself real comfortable. Dollars went a long way there. He could stay off the grid for a long time.

His gun was untraceable: he'd loaded the magazines wearing latex. He turned everything over in his mind, planning it step by step until he knew it was feasible.

It was a go.

He waited. The cops rang the doorbell and talked to the nurse, then went back to the patrol car and called in a report.

He quietly made his way back to the rental Lexus and pulled out. A couple of minutes later, he was pulling up beside the Crown Vic parked outside the Pearce home.

He buzzed down the window, a smile on his face. He knew what the cops were seeing. A perfectly normal guy in a suit driving an expensive car, clearly lost. He pasted a sheepish expression on his face.

"Good evening . . . officers." He let his eyes go wide, as if just noticing they were in uniform.

"Sir," the uniform in the driver's seat said.

Outlaw widened his smile. "I need some help here. I think I'm really off base. My GPS is on the fritz. I'm looking for the Gaslamp Quarter, and I've been driving around in circles for the past hour."

"Well, you're going in the wrong direction. You'll have to—" The cop never finished the sentence. A red hole blossomed on his forehead and a halo of pink mist surrounded his head. The pink mist erupted around the other cop's head, too. There had only been the softest of sounds, completely inaudible to anyone even five feet away.

There was no one within five feet. There was no one within a hundred feet.

Outlaw had heard the cops checking in. This would be a routine surveillance. They'd only check in a couple of times in the shift, but it would be well to move fast now. As sure as hell as soon as the two cops didn't report in, this place would be swarming with cops.

He wanted the whole job over fast. They'd be searching airports, bus and train stations.

Time for backup.

Outlaw had a list of collaborators, ex-military all. Men more than willing to use their gifts and training in the private sector.

He didn't need to check a Rolodex or his cell address book. Every number he needed in his life he had committed to memory. He pulled out his Thuraya satellite cell phone. The records were kept in Saudi Arabia. The US government could not eavesdrop and could never requisition the records. Not even the NSA could listen in.

The phone at the other end was picked up immediately. It was past midnight, but the voice was alert. Warren Wilson, ex-Army, specialist driver, good mechanic, good shot. But above all, he had a boat and he lived in San Diego.

"I'll need a hand for twenty-four, maybe thirty-six hours. Fifty grand." Outlaw kept the amount low to leave room for negotiation.

"You got it. What do you need?"

"A safe place for a couple of hours for an interrogation. Then a boat to take me to near Cabo San Lucas in Baja and a car from there."

Silence for a moment, then Outlaw heard tapping sounds, someone on a keyboard. "Okay. I'm sending you the GPS coordinates of an abandoned waterfront warehouse right now. My boat will be anchored right outside. I'll get a buddy of mine to meet us at Cabo with a car. It'll cost you, though. $150,000 because I need to give something to my buddy down in Baja."

"Deal." Outlaw flipped the cell closed. That went well. He'd been willing to go up to two hundred grand.

He parked the car right in front of the Pearce house. Even if someone noticed it, it didn't matter. The rental had been with fake ID and Outlaw had switched plates with another Lexus at the airport. By the time they straightened it out, he'd be south of the border.

He walked calmly around the house, gun held down by his thigh. Time to pick that pathetic back-door lock, get rid of the nurse and get the old man to the warehouse.

He had to move fast. It was late and he wasn't even halfway through tonight's killing.

* * *

"You okay?" Sam asked for the millionth time. He shot another worried glance over at Nicole, noticing all over again how fucking pale she looked. Every time he saw the dried blood on her temple he winced, because it could have been worse than some broken skin and clotted blood. It could have been a hole.

He knew exactly what that beautiful head would have looked like if the fuckhead had pulled the trigger. Gun residue stippling the creamy pale skin surrounding a neat round hole that wouldn't be so neat and so round on the other side of her head.

Sam had seen so many dead faces, dead people in his time, hundreds of them. So it wasn't hard to picture a Nicole with a hole in her head, collapsed to the floor of her very small, very pretty office where she created miracles with languages and was working hard to develop a fascinating young company. Sam knew exactly what her dead face would look like, he could see it on the insides of his eyelids when he closed his eyes.

Her eyes, so lively—the irises that amazing cobalt blue—lifeless, like beautifully colored marbles. Her skin, ivory with the rosiness of good health right underneath, would be the color of ice, and just as cold. All that grace, all that beauty, gone in an instant.

That was if she'd had a bullet blown through her head. Being thrown out of a ninth-floor window conjured up an entirely new set of ghoulish images.

Sam had watched, helpless, as the carabineer of a good friend snapped open during mountain training in the Cascades, dropping the man 150 feet to crash onto the rocks. Sam and the rest of the team had gone back down the mountain to pick up the remains of their fellow soldier. Every bone in the body had been broken and it had been like a sack of marbles except for the torso, which had cracked open and spilled out about a yard of intestine.

Nicole, after plunging nine stories to the sidewalk. Christ, that one was enough to give him nightmares, too.

Nicole turned and drummed up a smile for him. Something in his face must have betrayed what was going through his mind, because she laid a hand on his arm. "I'm okay, Sam. Really. Just a little shaken up."

Not as shaken up as he was. His fucking hands trembled.

Whoa.

There was no such thing as a nervous or overly sensitive SEAL. They just didn't grow them nervous, and if they were, they were weeded straight out in selection.

Sam was known for being cold-blooded. During training in the shooting house with live ammo, a pencil-dick geek had come and wired them up and taken blood samples after each session. Doubtless sent by Christians In Action. CIA refused to reveal the findings of the study but Cakewalk Potowski, who never met a computer he didn't like and couldn't crack, found the results buried deep in the heart of Langley.

Turned out the SEAL team's heart rate and the cortisol and catecholamine levels—the stress hormones—remained stable even under live fire. Sam's heartbeat hadn't altered even when a flash-bang went off in the room.

The geek, with an alphabet soup of letters after his name, had concluded the report with the morose observation that "efficient counterterrorism agents appear to have an essentially inhuman nervous system, not subject to the normal flight or fight reflex that has been part of the human legacy for ten thousand years."

Fuckhead called them *aliens*?

Well old pencil-dick would have been astonished to see him now. His heart was pounding in his chest, still. Every time he started to calm down, he'd get an image of a dead Nicole right there in front of his eyes—head blown apart or body cracked open, take your pick of nightmares—in living color, and he'd start sweating all over again.

Sam was normally a fast, good driver, but right now, he was driving as if carrying sweating TNT.

He could barely concentrate on the road. Nicole in the car with him just ate up all his hard disk. Having her by his side and driving seemed like mutually exclusive things.

He didn't want to hurt her in any way. Sam had intercepted her on her way toward the window, but her right side had crashed into a bookcase. Sam turned corners like a seventy-year-old grandmother because he couldn't stand the thought of her jostling against the car door.

"You're not okay." Sam ground his teeth. "You nearly died. Twice." Just saying it made his heart rate pick up even more.

"Yes, I know. Believe me, I know." She gave a deep sigh, her slender hand tightening on his arm. "But I didn't. That was entirely thanks to you. You have no idea how grateful I am that you can pick locks like a pro."

"Well, goddammit, that's another thing," Sam said heatedly, aggrieved. Happy that anger chased a little of the fear away. "Why the fuck didn't you put in a security system? The guy just fucking waltzed into your office, just about anyone off the street could just fucking—"

His cell phone rang and he put it on speakerphone. "Yeah?" he barked.

Mike's deep voice came through, slow and reassuring. "Our guys gave a perimeter check outside Nicole's house, talked to the nurse, checked on Nicole's father; everything's okay. They'll be relieved tomorrow morning and another two-man team will take over."

Nicole slumped in relief, eyes closed. "Thanks so much, Mike."

"Yeah. No problem." His voice grew louder. "So the old man's taken care of, Sam. You hold up your end. Make sure nothing happens to Nicole."

"Oh yeah. Count on it." If Sam had to tie her to a chair and stand guard, he would. "Did you get a face off our camera?"

"Yeah. Harry got two really good shots, one full face, one in three-quarter profile. He sent it as a JPEG here to headquarters. It's already in the system. If this guy so much as jaywalked in the past ten years, we'll know about it. I'll stay here until we get an answer, and I'll let you know right away."

That made Sam feel better. Once they got the fucker's name, they could find an address and he could go kill him. Discreetly. He'd take care of it himself. Just disappear for a day or two, do the job and then nothing else would ever threaten Nicole again. He wouldn't let it.

"Good," he grunted. "Stay on top of it."

"You bet. Harry's with the building night guards right now, trying to figure out how he got in and out. We'll nail him. Don't worry about that." He closed the connection.

Nicole turned to look at him. "I'm really grateful for all you're doing for me, Sam. And all that Harry and Mike and Mike's police officer friend are doing."

A bruise was starting to blacken at her temple and he could see dark flesh under her light white shirt along her right shoulder.

He shuddered.

"You've stepped into something nasty, Nicole." He picked up her hand and raised it to his mouth. "We've got to keep it far away from you and from your dad while we track it down. But you've got to help us, honey. You've got to come up with what he's looking for. We need to know that to keep you safe."

Nicole rubbed her forehead with her free hand, looking troubled. "You think I don't understand that? I do, believe me, I do. I keep running over everything that might be in my computer and I come up with basically nothing that could possibly be of interest to anyone. Wordsmith simply doesn't get vital or confidential texts to translate. Though we will, you can count on that. And we'll charge top dollar for them. Oh yeah." She smiled at the thought.

Sam was struck anew by just how different she was from other beautiful women. She simply exuded intelligence and purpose. He'd never met a woman quite as physically gorgeous as she was, but he'd met and bedded his share of attractive women and none of them was like Nicole. Beautiful women had a powerful weapon at their disposal and they grew up using it, often.

Sam didn't blame them. The instant he put on his spurt of growth, he'd used his size and strength to get what he wanted whenever he could. Life was tough; no one knew that better than he did. You used whatever goddamned tools life gave you and hoped like hell you came out ahead.

But Nicole was somehow different, though she didn't need to be. She had, like, a fucking nuclear bomb at her disposal. The most powerful weapon in the world—female beauty that was off the scale. He couldn't even begin to imagine any heterosexual male ever saying no to anything she wanted. In essence, she was a princess.

And yet there was none of that in her interactions. She didn't assume any kind of female superiority or expect special treatment. She worked hard for everything she got and didn't whine or look for protection when life got tough.

Amazing.

A woman in a million and she'd become his. So he better goddamned keep her safe.

"Go back a little further," Sam urged. "Maybe he's looking for something that came in a week ago, or two weeks ago. Is there anything that could raise a red flag?"

"No, Sam." Nicole shook her head. "I keep telling you. I'm simply too new at the game. Confidential or even economically important data is either translated in-house or would be given to a partner of long standing with access to high-level encryption, not to me. Wordsmith is a year old. No one's going to send me anything sensitive. It's true that we get a lot of economic texts but as I said, most of them are to comply with European Union rules that require a version in English, and we get the work because, frankly, I charge less than a European translation agency, and the dollar's really low right now. So we get a lot of legally mandated translations of board meetings, some company prospectuses, the odd literary translation. Some technical stuff." Nicole lifted her shoulders helplessly. "That's about it."

He wanted to pound the steering wheel, pound someone's head, pound *something*. If they couldn't get a handle on what the fuckhead was looking

for, they could never stand down from the Defcon
I level of alert they were at now.

Defcon I was a level that was preparatory to
war. Sam didn't mind going to war. He'd sure as
hell go to war to defend Nicole, but he needed to
know who he was fighting, otherwise he was just
spinning his wheels. Not to mention the fact that
you couldn't keep up a maximum level of alert forever, not unless you were a soldier. Nicole would
eventually chafe at staying forever by his side—
his left side to keep his shooting hand free.

Sam was used to worst-case scenarios because
in his personal experience, the worst thing that
could happen often did. He was alive to danger at
all times, but he was also aware that it came off as
paranoia to civilians.

Right now, Sam wanted to keep Nicole in his
apartment, lock her up nice and tight till he had a
better handle on this thing. He defied anyone
who wasn't Special Forces, and using C–4, to get
through his security and even then, he had a built-
in emergency signal sent to his cell in case of a
breach.

But he couldn't keep Nicole locked up in his
house forever, much as he'd like to. She wouldn't
stand for it. And the police wouldn't stand guard
outside her house forever, either. Sam could pick
up the slack after the police stood down, but he
couldn't station his men 24/7 for an indeterminate
amount of time; he didn't have the manpower.

If they didn't figure out what the fuckhead who'd
attacked her wanted, Nicole would walk around

with a bull's-eye painted on that beautiful smooth forehead, because she simply wasn't the kind of woman to cower, to stay put when he said *stay*.

"Maybe I was wrong," Nicole mused. "Maybe I did leave the chair pushed away from the desk and this guy was looking for something else entirely. Like money, or . . ." Her voice trailed off as she turned to him. "Well, that's the thing," she said, blowing out a little breath of frustration. "I don't know what there could possibly be worth stealing in my office. I never keep money there and there's just nothing that has much resale value. But maybe he wasn't looking for something specific, maybe he was just a thief making the rounds of the offices that were easy to break into. God knows mine seems to have an invisible sign that says, 'This one's a snap to break into—come and get it.'"

She slanted him a wry glance.

"No." Sam was already shaking his head before she finished talking. "It would be nice to think that, but he wasn't a common thief, honey. Burglars don't carry weapons. It's like a kind of rule. The sentence for armed robbery is more than twice that of burglary. This guy was armed to the teeth." It had to be asked. "Do you think—do you think he could have been waiting there to rape you?"

The thought had of course already occurred to him and it was horrifying. Not as bad as the thought of her being killed, but it was right up there in the same ballpark of horrible things in a world in which horrible things happened on a regular basis.

Nicole stared out the window for a long moment, face somber, thinking. "No," she said finally. "I don't think so. I think if somebody wanted to—to rape me . . ." She swallowed heavily. "I think if that was what he wanted then he'd have been already, um, aroused. I think he'd have made it clear in the first second that's what he wanted. He held me tightly against him, but I didn't feel, um, an erection. So, I'd say no, rape wasn't what he wanted."

Sam's grip loosened slightly on the wheel. It was a miracle it hadn't snapped off in his hands.

So rape was out. That was good.

Now he only had murder to worry about.

Chapter 11

They turned off the road to drive down into Sam's underground garage. The last time they'd done that—was it only last night? It felt like a million years ago—he'd turned off the main road and swooped in, fast, with panache, into his building's grounds and down to the underground garage. He drove like he did everything physical. With grace and speed and utter confidence.

Not now. He'd driven them from their office building to his house as if he were ferrying a load of eggs. Driving slowly, braking carefully, taking the turns wide. All in an effort to spare her any discomfort. And she was grateful, because her shoulder was throbbing and there seemed to be an ache in every muscle of her body.

Once he came to a slow, rolling halt, braking gently, Sam muttered, "Stay put," and came around to her door, helping her out of the car as if she were an eighty-year-old grandmother.

She had the feeling that if he could slow down

the elevator's ascent, he would have. His big body was completely still at her side, arm around her waist. She could feel his tenseness. It was only when his bank-vault-level security of his apartment was engaged, the door quadruple-locked behind them, that he relaxed a little.

"Come here," he murmured. He turned her into to him, big hand covering the back of her head, the other around her waist. Nicole leaned into him for a long moment, grateful for his strength. It was like leaning into a warm, muscled wall that would stand forever and she simply soaked that strength up.

They stood in the nighttime quiet, the only sound that of the low wavelets lapping the shore through the open balcony windows. She was so glad he wasn't the kind of person to keep air-conditioning on all day and all night. The night-time breeze was warm and welcome, bringing the fresh smell of the sea with it, so much more re-freshing than chilled canned air.

"So, what do you want first? To eat, or to take a shower?" She could hear his deep voice rumbling in his chest.

It was a tough decision because the instant he said *eat*, she realized she was ravenous, having skipped lunch and dinner. But the thought of a shower . . .

Sam had one of those huge modern showers with a showerhead that looked as if it would re-lease a sinful amount of water that was like a warm massage, a huge, square bronze showerhead that would ease the kinks from her sore muscles, light-years away from the trickle that came from her grandmother's sixties-era shower that was an exact replica of the one in *Psycho*, where Janet Leigh was hacked to death.

She pulled away and looked up at him. From this vantage point, he was all clenched jaws and high cheekbones, heavy five-o'clock shadow and dark, piercing eyes.

"Shower," she decided. "Followed immediately by food. I'm really hungry."

"Roger that," he said calmly, and swung her up in his arms.

"Sam!" Nicole scrambled to hold on to his shoulders. "I can walk!"

"Yeah," he rumbled. "I know you can. I, ah, I just—" his jaw muscles bunched and he looked away for a second, breathed deeply, turned back. "I really need to be touching you right now, and this works for me."

He stopped on the threshold of his huge bathroom, bending his head toward hers until their foreheads touched. "I was scared shitless back there," he confessed.

"Yeah." She huffed out her breath in a little half laugh, tightening her arms around his neck. "Ditto. Did I mention how grateful I am you picked my lock?"

That earned her a small smile. "You did mention it, a couple of times, in fact. Gratitude's an interesting concept. Just how grateful are we talking about here?"

She smiled back. "Major, major gratitude. Name-your-price grateful."

He moved sideways through the door with her in his arms so he wouldn't jostle her against the doorjamb. Once inside, he put her down by gently removing the arm under her knees, holding her steady as she slid down his body. "If I can name my price, make me a happy man and promise me you won't ever get into trouble like that again."

"I promise," she said fervently, etching a huge X over her left breast.

She was steady on her feet, but she hung on to his arms just the same. He seemed to be happy touching her and man, it was reciprocal. Touching him made her feel a whole lot better. Being close to that big body simply radiating heat was enough to dissipate the chill of fear and danger.

With Sam right in front of her, hands on her waist, looking at her as if he wanted to eat her alive, cold and danger and fear were all far, far away.

Head bent to her, a serious frown between his eyebrows, as if he were solving the most difficult calculus equation in the world, he started carefully unbuttoning her blouse. The buttons were small and though his hands were huge, they were deft. In a moment, her blouse hung open.

Nicole stood quietly, making no move whatsoever. Whatever he wanted from her, she wanted to give it to him.

He lifted his hands to her shoulders. The light linen shirt billowed to the floor. A second later, her bra followed.

She saw him wince, touch her shoulder and back lightly. "That's going to be a spectacular bruise tomorrow. Does it hurt?"

It did, but not so much that she wanted him to stop touching her. "A little sore," she admitted. "It's okay."

He shook his head briefly, as if to say *no, it's not okay*, then reached for the zipper of her pants. He pulled them down gently, together with her panties. He knelt, lifting one foot by the ankle, then the other, taking off her sandals. "Brace yourself on my shoulder."

In a moment, sandals, pants and panties were on the bathroom floor. Sam rose slowly. His big hands had encircled her ankle. As he rose slowly, his open hands ran along her ankle, shin, knee, thigh. The skin of his hands was rough. By the time his big hands cupped her hip, the hairs of her forearms were standing up.

Suddenly, Sam froze, making a low, shocked sound. He even stopped breathing for a moment, eyes fixed on her hips.

"What?"

"My God," he whispered. "*I* did this."

Nicole craned her neck to see. There were four faint bruises on her hips, both sides. She wouldn't have understood where they came from if his big hands weren't touching her. The bruises matched precisely with his fingertips.

A sudden flush raced through her body, head to toe. She remembered exactly how she'd gotten those bruises. Sam had held her hips tightly as he rammed into her the last time they made love, when he'd lost control, just a little. She'd been so excited she hadn't even felt the grip of his hands.

She was excited now, completely naked in the bathroom. The memory of their night together, his big body so close to hers, made heat blossom in her, made her bones loosen, started drawing her into a spiral of desire.

Nicole lifted her face for a kiss, then stopped, frowning when he didn't meet her halfway. What was this? He didn't want to kiss her? Since when?

Sam was staring at her hips, at the small bruises which were nothing in comparison to what was going to be a real doozy on her back tomorrow morning.

He looked absolutely horrified.

"Sam?"

"I did this," he said again hoarsely, eyes glued to where his hands framed the small dark spots. "These bruises came from me. From my hands."

She covered his hands with hers. "It's okay. I bruise easily, don't worry about it. "

He was breathing heavily, face tight with some strong emotion. He raised his eyes to hers and she winced at the pain in them.

"Is that why you ran?" he asked hoarsely. "Because I hurt you? Because you were afraid I would hurt you some more?"

Nicole opened her mouth to answer, appalled that he could even think such a thing. She'd run because she was a coward and couldn't face her feelings for him.

"No, God no, Sam. I—"

But he drowned her out, his voice strong and adamant. "Because I don't do that. Could never do that. I don't hurt women." His jaw muscles bunched, he opened his mouth, then clamped it tight, throat working. It was as if he wanted to say more, but nothing else besides that stark statement would come out.

Nicole started to say *Of course you don't hurt women*, but stopped when she looked closer at him. He looked like a truck had run over him. As if something had scraped him raw.

In Nicole's world, of course men didn't hurt women. That went without saying. The man she knew best, her father, had been the most gentle, loving and affectionate of fathers and husbands. She couldn't even begin to imagine her father raising a hand in anger to her or to her mother. Or to any woman or child for that matter. It was simply unthinkable.

But that wasn't where Sam had grown up. Sam had grown up in the feral underbelly of the world—a place of brutality and cruelty, where men regularly beat up women and children, simply because they could. And because no one stood up for them. At some point in Sam's childhood, something strong in him must have risen up, rebelled against the cruelty and the violence around him, led him to make his stand and forged him into the man he was.

I don't hurt women.

The words had clearly come from the deepest bedrock of his being.

Looking up at him, at that strong face, now trying to mask how deep his feelings were, something big, something important shifted inside her.

Sam Reston. At first she thought he was a low-life, a thug, the kind of man a woman instinctively avoided. Then he turned out to be the sexiest man alive. Last night had been, hands down, the most incredible sexual experience of her life, a potent combination of heat and laughter and pure hormonal overload.

She'd been wildly attracted to that Sam Reston, the man who had taught her more about sex in one night than in all her twenty-eight years taken together. Attractive and attracted, sex on a stick. That Sam Reston had turned her on so powerfully he'd turned her inside out.

But this Sam Reston—the man who protested hoarsely that he didn't hurt women, as if the very blood in his veins would stop if he did . . . Well, that man was more than an incredibly hot date.

The feelings he aroused in her were like a complete realignment of her being, right down to the molecular level.

The French had a name for it—*les atomes crochus*. Where the very atoms that made up your being hooked up with another person's, so that you were one, permanently, irrevocably.

The night of amazing sex had somehow sparked off the process, and Sam's horror at the idea he could have hurt her set it ablaze. The violence in her office had been a defining moment, watching Sam come to her rescue, unflinching even with a gun in his face.

He'd defended her with his life.

His hands were stroking her hips, right over the bruises. Gently, so gently, as if he could somehow wipe the bruises away. He watched his hands, face tight and grim, etched in regret at what he'd done.

There was nothing wrong with what he'd done last night. She'd been with him every step of the way.

He'd given her so much. Wooed her, seduced her, protected her, defended her. It struck her that she had the power to give something back to him, something he desperately needed.

His pride. His knowledge of himself as a man who didn't hurt women.

"That wasn't why I ran, Sam," she said softly, holding his beard-roughened chin in her hand, forcing his head up so she could meet his eyes. His gaze kept going in horror to the small bruises on her hips.

She took a deep breath, looked at him solemnly, shoulders back, standing ramrod straight.

He stared at her, unblinking, jaws clenched.

He was hurting. It was so clear, now that she had eyes to see. This big, strong, tough, magnificent man was hurting.

She couldn't stand another second of it.

His mouth worked and he finally managed to get a few hoarse words out. "So why did you run?"

"Because I was afraid—" He was already wincing. "I was afraid of what I felt for you. Last night—it was just so intense, it was like there was another woman in the bed with you. When I woke up I ran, because I could hardly recognize myself."

She leaned forward, kissed his chest right over his heart. She could feel its slow, regular beat.

She tipped her head back to study his face and told him the stark truth. "I was so rattled by you, by what was happening. It just scared the hell out of me."

Nicole rose on tiptoe, cupped his shoulders, lifted herself up against him and bit his lower lip until he let her in. It wasn't a slow kiss. She took it straight from zero to a hundred in a second.

She was naked and could feel everything that happened to him as she kissed him. At first he froze, surprise coming off him in waves at the unexpected kiss. She was plastered against him.

The sudden sharp breath, the heavy erection trying to rise under his jeans against her lower belly, such a powerful movement it made her vagina contract in desire. His hands on her hips moved to her buttocks as he pulled her tightly against him, positioning her to rub against his penis—and he froze. Carefully, as if he were handling something full of nitroglycerin, he eased back and away, the only connection between them his hands still loosely at her hips.

Nicole's eyes fluttered open, the heat that had flared up so fiercely and brightly slowly dissipating.

"Sam?" she whispered. He was pulling away? But he was aroused, massively. She had felt it against her own skin.

"No."

"No?" she echoed hollowly.

"Not right now. Not yet, anyway." He looked down at her, at the drops of blood on her white shirt on the floor. "You need to be ready."

Ready? She was ready all right. Blood pooled heavily between her thighs, her breasts felt full and heavy. She didn't need any foreplay.

"I'm ready, Sam." If Nicole hadn't felt the words leave her lips, she would never have believed that that throaty, velvety voice laced with sex could possibly be hers.

"Mmm."

Shifting sideways, Sam did something complicated to the complex shower control and a rush of hot water came flowing out, steam billowing out in the room, shrugging off his shirt. "First things first."

He bent to kiss her cheek.

He was moving slowly. Last night, half the time he had moved at warp speed. So this was going to be his show and he was going to take it slow. Okay. Some of that sexual tension relaxed a little. They were going to make love, but clearly not right away.

He picked her clothes up from the floor, put them on a chair together with his own shirt and rose, big thigh muscles flexing, jeans clinging to him like a lover. Oh wow. Who knew she could be so susceptible to beefcake? Who knew that his enormous chest could take her breath away, that watching his thigh and stomach muscles contract as he rose slowly from a crouch could make her own thigh muscles twitch?

He shot out a hand to test the temperature, grunted, then eased her into the stall as if she were the queen of Coronado Shores.

Ah, the hot water pummeled her sore muscles. It felt wonderful. She turned under the showerhead, face uptilted, eyes closed, savoring the sensation.

She opened her eyes and saw that he was getting drenched. He still had on his jeans.

Nicole gave a half laugh and pointed at his jeans. "Shouldn't you take those off?"

Sam's dark eyes gleamed as he opened a bottle of shampoo and poured a little into his hand. "Nope. Denim chastity belt. Best in the world. Worked in high school, works now. Boner's got no place to go. Now turn around and tilt your head back."

She obeyed, sighing with pleasure as his strong fingers began working up a lather. A strong scent with a deep note of sandalwood washed over her. Sam's shampoo. She remembered smelling it in his hair as she ran her fingers through it, then clenching her fists in his hair as she started coming. Scent memories are locked into the most primordial part of the brain, she knew, and this one nearly knocked her off her feet as she remembered the hot feelings connected with this smell. She moaned.

"What? Did I hurt you?" His large hands stilled. Oh man, this was embarrassing. She was being turned on by his *shampoo*.

She leaned against him heavily, head tilted back onto his shoulder. "No," she said, as the water rushed over her. "You didn't hurt me."

"Good," he grunted. His strong hands went back to kneading, fingertips digging in, somehow knowing exactly where the knots of tension were. She could feel every inch of him against her naked back. The dark swirls of chest hair tickled her upper back and she could feel his tight abs contract as he moved to pour more shampoo into his hand.

His penis was huge behind the wet denim, hard and hot enough to radiate heat through the stiff material. She wiggled her bottom and felt him surge against her, fingers stilling in her hair.

That denim was less of a chastity belt than he thought. She wiggled again, rolling against what felt like a moving hot steel rod in his pants.

He made a noise deep in his chest and she smiled. She held all the power here and it made her feel . . . whoa. Ten feet tall.

The man who'd held her prisoner against his body had used his strength against her. It had been a terrifying, horrific experience and, deep down, a humiliating one. Nicole had never been manhandled before, never physically forced to do anything.

The intruder had overpowered her with contemptuous ease, and it burned. Everything about the experience had been—*I'm stronger than you and you will do what I want.* Brutal and primitive.

Sam's body language was exactly the opposite, though he was even stronger than the intruder. Sam was the strongest man she'd ever seen. She'd held him in her arms all night and she knew how deeply powerful he was. If he wanted to, he could force her to do anything, bend her completely to his will.

But with every move, he gave all the power to her. Even now that she was being deliberately provocative, rubbing herself against his arousal, she could sense, could *feel* his self-control, so deeply a part of him.

"Close your eyes." She could feel the vibrations in his chest of his deep voice through the skin of her back. She obeyed, and he pulled her gently right under the showerhead until all the shampoo was rinsed away.

The water stopped. "Stay there."

Nicole stood watching as he got two big, blindingly white towels from a cabinet and held them, waiting for her to get out.

"No conditioner?" she asked as she emerged dripping. He looked blank. "And moisturizer? I don't think I've ever taken a shower without moisturizing."

"Ah . . ." Panicked, Sam looked around, as if conditioner and moisturizer could suddenly, magically appear.

Most of Nicole's previous lovers had been good-looking, vain metrosexuals who used the same products she did from the same houses, only the male version. Her last lover, Sergey, had had every Clinique men's product on the market and Nicole had never had any problems with sleepovers. All she'd needed to bring with her was her tooth-brush.

Sam had towels, soap, a toothbrush and tooth-paste in view and she somehow suspected that was it. Looked like she was going to have to stock Sam's bathroom with some essentials.

She looked him straight in the eyes. "Be pre-pared to have your bathroom full of creams and lotions. Do you think you can handle that, big guy?"

His mouth lifted on one side as he wrapped her hair in a big towel. "Honey, I survived Hell Week. You have no idea what I can handle. Hold out your arms." She obeyed as he gently patted her torso and arms dry.

"Tough guy, huh?"

"Hmm?" He'd been staring at her breasts and suddenly lifted his gaze to hers. She nearly stepped back at the blazing heat in his eyes. Though he was almost smiling, the skin over his cheekbones was pulled tight, his eyes narrowed. "Yeah, I guess I think I'm pretty tough."

Nicole reached out her hand and curved it over his penis and squeezed. "Not that tough, big boy."

Sam's big body froze, breath hissing in as if she'd done something painful to him. The big column of male flesh she could feel beneath her hand was moving, becoming even longer, thicker. A little moan escaped his lips and his penis leaped once again under her hand.

He looked like he was one second from coming. Nicole nearly laughed out loud.

This was so *delicious.*

Everything in her life was so . . . wrong. Her father was gravely ill, dying a painful death. Her company was trying to take off, but kept sputtering when she had to take attention away from it for her father. Some unknown assailant had trashed her office, searching for God knew what and would presumably keep searching until he found it or she was hurt, whichever came first.

It didn't get worse than that.

And yet right now, all those terrible problems were like flies buzzing in the distance. Her battered mind and body just gave up on all her anxieties and worries and urged her to live this moment. This magical moment out of time when a big, tough warrior was handing over his body to her for her own use. Giving himself over to her.

Sam kneeled again to dry the rest of her off and she rested her hand on his shoulder for balance. Oh God, the feel of him was so wonderful. She knew from experience that there was no give in him at all, anywhere. She curled her fingers into the bare skin of his shoulder and it was like trying to make an impression on a piece of warm steel machinery. The heat coming off that big body was amazing. It chased out any residual chill of the attack in her office.

She watched as Sam slowly stood, one big hand drifting up over her body as he did so. He was masculinity personified, and yet his movements were also so graceful. He rose with the grace of a world-class athlete, a man whose body would never let him down.

He looked her up and down, hot eyes moving over her slowly, the gaze so intense, it felt like hands caressing her body. Every cell in her body felt full, replete, warm, the aches and pains completely forgotten. Amazing. Sexual desire for this man was better than a day at the spa.

Nicole stretched up to put her arms around Sam's neck in hopes of getting one of those amazing kisses of his, the one that was way sexier than even intercourse with other men, but then gave a little yelp as he picked her up.

"What are you—" she began, then stopped. It was clear what he was doing. He was carrying her to bed. Fine. Perfect. In bed with Sam was exactly where she wanted to be.

Nicole could almost feel what was coming next. Sam laying her down, then coming down on top of her, his heavy weight grounding her, his legs opening hers.

She frowned. Those wet jeans would have to go, though. Wet denim, in bed. Gah.

He lay her gently on the bed and stood for a moment, looking down at her. She smiled and held up her arms, expecting to feel him settling on her, fitting himself to her. Her skin tingled in anticipation.

And yet he was simply standing there looking at her, the dummy. What was he waiting for?

He walked to the end of the bed, tugged her legs until they were almost off the edge and kneeled.

He wanted *foreplay*? Nicole had never been so aroused in her life. Well, except for last night. She didn't need foreplay right now. As a matter of fact, she probably wouldn't need it ever again. Sam's very presence was potent foreplay, calculated to drive any red-blooded woman's hormones to fever pitch.

Nicole started to tell him that when she felt his mouth on her, right on her most sensitive tissues and the only thing that could possibly come out of her mouth was a sigh.

He was kissing her there, exactly as he kissed her mouth. As if he would die if he didn't get more of her, right now. She was so incredibly sensitive, she could feel his mouth and tongue all through her body. He nipped her very lightly with his teeth and she jumped at a pleasure so intense it bordered on pain.

Her arms were up around her head, back arched with delight, her entire being concentrated on the wet aroused tissues between her thighs. He was French-kissing her, thumbs holding her open for his mouth. The sight of his dark head between her pale thighs was intensely erotic.

He gently bent her left thigh with his hand to

give him better access and when he gave another long, languid swipe with his tongue, her thigh started trembling.

She looked down at herself, at the heavy heartbeat she could see in her left breast. She was already close to orgasm after only a few minutes. The big room was utterly silent except for the delicious sounds his mouth was making against her. Even the sea had stilled. She couldn't hear the waves—or maybe her heartbeat was drowning the sound of the ocean out.

He stopped just as a long tremble ran through her, the beginning of that luscious free fall into blinding pleasure. Sam lifted his mouth from her, though his eyes remained fixed on her sex. His dark skin was flushed, mouth wet from her body, face tight with arousal.

"You're so beautiful," he said hoarsely, his finger tracing the lips of her sex. The callused skin of his finger was intensely exciting. "Here, too. All pink and puffy, and here—" He ruffled through the hair of her pubis and laid his hand on her lower belly. "Here you've got this Snow White thing going. Ivory and ebony. Amazing." He lifted her leg higher and took her foot in his big hand. "Even your goddamned *feet* are gorgeous." He brought her foot to his mouth and nibbled on the instep, sharp little bites that raised goose pimples all over her body.

Oh heavens, they were *right*! Feet were erogenous zones! She'd never believed it up until now, until Sam Reston nibbled and bit his way over her foot and toes. She'd have thought his mouth would have tickled, but it wasn't ticklishness she felt, it was pure sex and it shot straight to her groin.

One particularly sharp nip and her vagina clenched, along with her stomach muscles.

He saw it. Of course he did, he was incredibly observant. His eyes shot to hers then right back to her groin.

Sam didn't grin with triumph at arousing her so intensely that she shook, as any other man would have done. Instead, his mouth tightened and his eyes narrowed and fixed on where he was touching her. Gently, oh-so gently, the tip of his finger sliding around and around her opening, so that she started squirming. Needing his touch to be stronger, to be *there*—

An electric current ran down her spine when he inserted a big finger inside her and her vagina erupted in convulsions so strong it was as if her entire body were having an orgasm. Her open thighs trembled and her whole body shook, clenching tightly against his finger.

Nicole's eyes had closed but she saw lights against the lids. Short, sharp pants that were almost moans came out of her throat, the contractions going on and on as he kept his finger inside her, thumb slowly circling her clitoris that had become so sensitive it was almost—but not quite—painful.

He kept her going for what seemed like forever and when the contractions started dying down, he bent and put his mouth to her again, lips and tongue tasting and feeling her climax.

It was so intense she struggled against it, but his big hands pressed on her hips, just over the hip bone, holding her down, his hold gentle but implacable.

She couldn't move, she couldn't pull away, she could only feel the keen edge of pleasure lancing through her like shards of steel, held hostage in a place out of time, her body not her own as it convulsed, again and again.

Finally, her body subsided. Sam pulled away and looked at her gravely. Every inch of her skin was covered in sweat, so sensitive she could feel the weight of the air. She was panting, throat dry from pulling in air that never seemed to be enough.

Oh God, it had been way too much, way too intense. He laid his hand on her belly again, big hand covering her almost from hipbone to hipbone, the weight and warmth grounding her after that incredible experience.

She was wiped out—utterly exhausted, incapable of movement or thought. She held his gaze as she blinked once, twice, then couldn't lift her lids again.

She turned her head and went out like a light.

Well, so much for relaxing her, Sam thought wryly. He'd relaxed her so much she'd gone straight to sleep. Now what the hell was he supposed to do with his boner?

He winced as he stood up. His cock was stiff, his muscles were stiff, he could hardly breathe from tension. He walked around to the side of the bed and just looked at her, the delicate lines of her, like a dream of a woman instead of a real woman.

She'd fallen asleep with her legs open and he could see deep pink flesh peeking out from the dark cloud of soft hair between her thighs. She was soft and wet, he knew that because he'd felt it, with his tongue and his hand. She was ready for him and Christ, he was ready for her. He could feel his cock weeping beneath the denim, aching for him to stretch out on top of her and slide right in. Exactly as she was, long delicate arms arched over her head in a pose of sensual abandon that would rouse a man from the dead.

And he was far from dead. He felt alive in every cell of his body, and every cell wanted her, right now.

She'd welcome him. He knew that the way he knew the sun would rise in the east tomorrow morning. When he mounted her, she'd smile, eyes closed, and her entire body would welcome him. Long legs twined around his, arms crossed over his back, mouth open to him.

He shook with desire. His entire body felt parched and cold, deprived of something only she could give him. He'd just wanted to relax Nicole a little, give her a little pleasure, reassure her that he could control himself.

Before he jumped her bones.

He'd obviously been way too good at his job. She was completely out, not even a flicker of her eyes under her eyelids.

For a second, he was tempted to shuck his jeans, stretch out on the bed, roll her a little toward him, lift her leg over his hip and slip right into her. Ah, yes. She was wet enough, from his mouth and from coming. It would work. She'd wake up with his cock in her, moving nice and slow and easy, no better way to wake up.

He put his hands to the brass button of his jeans, then stopped.

She'd fallen into a very deep sleep, the sleep of the exhausted. There were faint purple stains under her eyes. Her cheekbones were sharper than usual and it seemed to him that her slender torso had become even more slender. Could she have lost weight in twenty-four hours?

And then another thought occurred to him, like a sledgehammer upside the head. If he could have kicked himself in the ass, he would have.

She'd been hungry. She'd asked for food and a shower. It was altogether possible she hadn't eaten today. She'd told him how rattled she'd been last night. Some women stopped eating when they were rattled.

Not soldiers. Soldiers never lost their appetite, because who knew where the next meal was coming from? And who knew whether this meal might be the one to keep you alive in the field those extra hours waiting for help to come?

Nicole had been *hungry*.

Sam felt a chill rush over his skin at the thought of Nicole going hungry. In his *home*. It made him sick with shame. No one knew better than him what it was like to go hungry. He'd spent half his childhood scrounging for enough food to keep up with his growth spurts. Keeping *Nicole* hungry, just because he wanted to fuck her, was shocking to him.

He'd fallen for her from the first moment he'd set eyes on her, blown away by her beauty. Well, that had been lust. But now that he knew her, had seen firsthand what a fine woman she was, had felt her warmth, it seemed impossible to him that he could ever desire another woman.

This was it. Nicole was it.

And how did he treat her? Well, last night he'd nearly fucked her to death and tonight he ignored the fact that she was hungry.

He was going to get one shot at this, so he'd better start shaping up. No more jumping her like a rabid wolverine. Or at least not until all her other needs were taken care of.

He'd have to keep his lust in check. Some. When necessary. When he could.

Sam had never had a woman of his own. He'd fucked a lot, but even when they lasted weeks, they'd been essentially one-night stands for several nights. He'd grown up around hugely dysfunctional people and he'd seen couples nearly kill each other with rage. What could he know about being part of a couple?

But he'd lifted himself out of all that, made himself into a fine soldier and now a good businessman. He'd taught himself how to do that and he could teach himself how to be the partner of a woman like Nicole. He could do it. He could learn.

And step number one was to take care of her needs. She was tired, so he had to let her sleep. She'd been hungry, so he'd fix her a hot meal. And hope it wouldn't poison her.

He was halfway to the kitchen when his cell phone buzzed from his jacket pocket.

"Yeah?"

What the hell did he have in his kitchen cabinets? Anything warm he could cook for her? What would you feed a traumatized woman? Soup. That was it. Soup was what they fed the sick. Only how the hell did you make soup?

"Sam, it's Harry."

"Uh-huh."

So maybe soup was out. Presumably it took ingredients and time and some skill. Would a grilled-cheese sandwich do?

"Sam, we've got a Fed in the office."

"A *Fed*?" Soup and sandwiches fled from his mind. There could only be one reason a Fed would be in his office. "They got a read off the vidcam."

"Roger that. And the news isn't good."

"It never is. Shoot." Holding his cell between his ear and shoulder, Sam shrugged his shirt back on, his shoulder holster and jacket. The jeans were still wet but what the hell. Things were moving fast and so would he.

"The guy's ex-Special Forces. Ranger, for ten years. Dishonorable discharge five years ago, accused of stealing and selling base weapons, fell off the grid. But the Feds have linked him to one murder for hire and have been on the lookout ever since. He was red flagged, that's why the FBI got here so fast."

This was bad news. Special Forces soldiers had an extra gear. About a million dollars of training went into each soldier and they were worth it. To a man, they were smart, relentless and capable of devastating violence delivered with surgical precision. An SF soldier gone bad was tragic news. An SF soldier gone bad and after Nicole was terrifying.

"Coming in," Sam said and flipped his cell closed. He went to his gun locker and chose a Glock 19, slotted in a full magazine and picked up another two magazines he put in his jacket pocket. He slid the Glock into the shoulder holster. There was more firepower in the office, but it just felt good to be loaded for bear right now.

He took the time to stare for a full minute at Nicole, stretched out on his bed, in a deep sleep. What would waking her up achieve? Nothing. There was nothing she could do right now and learning that a highly trained bad guy was after her would only make her more anxious. The best thing she could do for herself right now was to rest. Her father was safe and by God, if there was one place in all of San Diego where Sam trusted the security, it was his house.

It had top-of-the-line features, triple backups and a small separate generator to keep the alarm system going even if the electricity was cut. He would swear in court that he and Harry and Mike were the only ones who could get in.

He scribbled a note—*Honey, I had to go into the office, call me on my cell when you wake up. Be back as soon as I can*—and left it on the dresser.

Sam was in a rush to get back to the office, but still he stood for a moment on the threshold of his bedroom, just looking at her, naked, stretched out on his bed. He could see every single detail of her slender, curvy body. Could see the delicate collarbones, the sharp points of her hip bones, the long lines of her legs.

A stunningly beautiful woman. A head turner. The kind of woman who'd have made a fortune modeling.

But more than just a beautiful woman. She was smart and strong and kind and funny and fiercely loyal in a way he appreciated down to his bones. A woman in a million, and she was his.

He was going to keep her safe.

The fuckhead after her might have been a Ranger, but Sam was a SEAL, which trumped that to hell and gone. As long as he was alive, no one would ever hurt her.

And he was a hard man to kill.

Chapter 12

The man who came, Wilson, was fast and good. He'd given his bank account number, and by the time he drove up in a nondescript-looking off-white Transit van with the logo of an electrical-supplies shop on the sides, Outlaw had had the money transferred. Outlaw believed in paying well. You got what you paid for. And anyway, it was the client who was paying. He'd just add that amount to the bill.

It was the wonderful thing about working for the money men. They could fucking well afford anything. All they wanted was for their problem to go away and they were willing to throw money at it to insure that it did.

Outlaw did his briefing inside the van as Wilson drove them to the warehouse. The old man was trussed up in the back. Getting him out of the house had been a snap, he'd weighed as much as a girl and he'd been sedated. The nurse's body was in the back, too, and would be weighted with heavy chains, abdomen slashed open. It was improbable given the weight of chains attached to her, but the gases that formed in the stomach could possibly carry her to the top. Slashing her open took care of that. Outlaw never took chances.

"We'll get the geezer set up and then get his daughter here. I'll have her meet up with you. As soon as I get what I need from her, we'll just drop them over the side of the wharf. Where is it exactly that we're going?"

"South side of town," Wilson said. "The docks around Fleetridge. This warehouse was impounded because the owners were using it as a drug clearinghouse and now it's slated for demolition. Next month, in fact. There won't be anyone there. There won't be anyone in a three-mile radius this time of night."

"Perfect," Outlaw said. His instinct had proven correct. Nothing beat local knowledge. And Wilson was proving real efficient. Outlaw liked men who did what they were told without unnecessary talk.

He'd made it a habit to hook up with former soldiers and so far it had worked out fine. He'd refined his search parameters even further, sticking to men who'd tried out for Special Forces and hadn't made the grade. They were perfect. Depending on where in the long, grueling process they dropped out, they'd had the best training on the planet without that fuck-you, my-way-or-the-highway attitude all Special Forces soldiers developed. To a man, SF soldiers only followed orders when they made sense to them, which made them useless to Outlaw.

Outlaw didn't need for his men to understand, just to obey.

There was also the fact that a man who had been an SF soldier had his pick of civilian security jobs, low-hanging fruit for all of them. There didn't need to be anything else on the resumè. If you'd been a SEAL, a Ranger, Force Recon, that's all anyone needed to know.

There were plenty of guys who'd nearly made it, but when they mustered out of the military, no one would give them the time of day. If they were lucky they became rent-a-cops, low-level security, cheap bodyguards for minor punks. Not a one who didn't need money.

They'd trained and trained hard, and yet, since they couldn't make that final cut, their lives were over. But they were manna from heaven for Outlaw, who didn't need that razor edge the elite soldiers had. All he needed was good, solid muscle with some brains behind it.

Outlaw had mostly uncomplicated jobs to do for clients who had to remain anonymous. The SF dropouts were efficient, took orders and were glad for the work, since they were shut out of the top-tier security work Special Forces soldiers gave each other once they were out of the military.

They wouldn't give the dropouts the time of day. Outlaw had once seen a former SEAL cross the street to avoid a man who'd rung the bell four days into Hell Week.

He treated his men with respect, paid them above market rate, and got excellent service.

He'd learned well from the money men.

She was swimming in the Pacific, way out beyond her comfort zone. The strong tide was slowly carrying her out to sea, however hard she fought against it.

It was getting dark, the last slice of the sun drowned in the vast ocean's blackness and there were no lights on shore. A wind started up, blowing from land, creating wavelets rippling out that would reach all the way to China. Never a strong swimmer, she was tiring fast, swimming as hard as she could to shore, yet never coming closer.

The wind intensified, grew cold, sapping her strength. A wave crashed over her head unexpectedly and she drank water, icy salt water. She surfaced sputtering and frightened and shivering.

She drew in a deep breath and set out once more for shore. For what she hoped was shore, a big black mass rising out of the dark sea, cold and unforgiving. She tried to speed up her strokes, but it took all her strength merely to resist the increasingly strong tide.

Another wave crashed over her head, driving her under, and she crested the surface just as her breath gave out, gasping and treading water, looking around her in a panic.

It was all black, all dark now. Which way was shore, and safety? It was impossible to tell. She struck out again, hoping it was the right direction, her strokes uneven. She fought down the waves of panic, the deadliest enemy at sea, as she fought the strength of the waves that wanted to carry her out, away, toward the vastness of the open sea.

Exhausted, she gulped in air, only to find it was salt water instead. Her limbs were flailing now, she was so cold it was hard to coordinate her movements. She treaded water, turning in a full circle, fighting panic.

Darkness, everywhere. No lights, no sounds from shore to orient her. No ships on the horizon, nothing.

Staying still like this, she rode the waves as they grew taller, trying to time it so she wouldn't dissipate her strength. Rising, rising, a faint ripple of light as the wave crested in foam, then the drop to the trough, over and over again. Up, cresting, plunging down . . . another wave crested fast over her. She hadn't expected it, she had no air in her lungs.

Oh God! It was pitch-black beneath the waves! The swirling water had tumbled her into a somersault and now she didn't know which was was up and which was down. She tilted her head back, but there was nothing to see, not even reflected starlight on the surface.

She started kicking, arrowing as fast as she could . . . up? Please God, let her be kicking upward. In a last spurt of strength, she scissored her legs harder and faster, lungs burning, aching to pull in the breath that would fill her lungs with salt water. She had a second left, maybe two . . .

She was going to die here, all alone, in the cold, dark ocean, everything so silent except for her beating heart. It thumped against her rib cage, hard, as she kept her hands outstretched, hoping to break the surface, but all her hands encountered was cold water.

She was dying, panic ringing in her mind like a bell, ringing, ringing . . .

Nicole sat up in bed with a gasp, sweating and shivering, completely disoriented in the dark. With a shaking hand, she groped until she found a lamp and turned it on, blinking blankly at the room.

The ringing continued, on and on. Her cell phone!

Nicole dove for her purse, lying on the floor, scrambling for the phone. Maybe it was Sam. He wasn't here. The house had an unmistakeable empty feeling. And, she now saw, there was a note on the dresser from him.

She glanced down at the little window. Not Sam, her father. Was something wrong? Had he taken a turn for the worse?

"Dad?" she said breathlessly. "Are you okay?"

"Not your father, bitch." A low, deep, man's voice. Slightly raspy, somehow familiar . . .

"Who is—" And suddenly she knew. That low, raspy voice had spoken vicious things in her ear only hours ago. The intruder.

"Look at your screen."

Nicole turned the phone so she could see the

screen and gasped. It showed her father, pale as ice, tied to a chair. He was trembling badly. Not fear, those were muscle spasms unchecked by the medication he'd clearly not had a chance to take. While Nicole watched in horror, a large man's hand offscreen took a knife and traced a long line down her father's face, from temple to chin.

At first she thought he'd brought the wrong edge of the blade to her father's face, as an admonishment. *Look what we could do to him if we wanted to.*

But then a small red line appeared, growing larger and larger, gaping open, blood starting to drip off her father's jaw onto his pale gray pajamas. Looking more closely, Nicole could see that the knife had cut deep into the flesh, possibly to the bone.

"Stop it!" she screamed into the cell phone. "Don't you dare hurt my father!"

The hand reappeared, this time holding a gun. A big black gun that looked enormous next to her father's frail figure. Deadly black metal against her father's pale, wrinkled skin. The gun angled downward until the muzzle pressed into her father's knee. It was driven so hard into her father's flesh she could see the material of the pajama pants ruching around the muzzle.

Then the screen went dark.

"Oh, we'll do more than just hurt him," the deep, vicious voice came back on. "You saw that gun."

Nicole listened, heart pounding.

"I said—*you saw that gun!*" the voice roared.

Nicole tried to get her voice to work but her mouth and throat were too dry. No sound would come out. She coughed, managed to croak, "Yes. Yes, I saw the gun."

"Good. Remember that gun. Now listen carefully. This is what I want you to do." The voice was back to cool and calm. Giving instructions as if indicating which way to Balboa Park. "Call a taxi, tell him to take you to Fleetridge, to the Westwood shopping mall parking lot there. Keep this line open so I can hear and see what you're doing, otherwise your father will pay the consequences. If you don't come alone, your father's dead meat. He's dead meat, anyway, anyone can see that, but I'll make him suffer before he goes. If you don't do exactly as I say, I'll disappear with him and you'll never see him again, but you'll know that every second of what's left of his life I'll be hurting him. Is that clear?"

The temperature in the room had suddenly dropped. Nicole was shivering with terror and cold. "C-clear," she whispered.

"If you call anyone, if you signal anyone, if you don't come alone, your father will pay first, then you. At the parking lot there will be someone to meet you. Is that clear? Deviate one inch from this and your father gets a bullet in the knee, first thing. I don't have to tell you how excruciatingly painful that would be."

"No, no!" Panic exploded in her head. "Don't do that! Oh God, please! Don't worry, I'll follow your instructions to the letter."

"Of course you will." That horrible voice, now sounding genial and chirpy. "Oh, and pray that you find a taxi right away, because I'm giving you twenty minutes to get to the meeting point, after which I start shooting bits of your father off."

"N-no." Her teeth were chattering so hard she could barely get the words out. "D-don't. Pl-please."

"Then bring me what I want."

Oh God. What was it? "I don't know what you want!"

But she was talking to dead air. He hadn't hung up, though. He was keeping the connection open.

So terrified her hands wouldn't work properly, Nicole tried to pick up Sam's cordless handset, fumbled it badly and watched as it bounced on the floor. It took her trembling hands three tries before she could hold it, and she ripped a page out of the telephone book pawing through it to the Ts. It took her two tries before she could punch in the taxi service's number. While waiting for the call to go through, she fumbled her shirt on and pulled her jeans up, sliding her feet into loafers, picking up her purse.

The instant she heard the taxi dispatcher tell her that a car would be arriving in four minutes at the front gate, she rushed out to the bank of elevators, punching the button over and over again in her anxiety.

Her skin prickled with panic as she got into the elevator and punched for the ground floor. The damned thing was so *slow*! When, after a million years, it finally reached the ground floor, she shot out and ran across the lobby and into the landscaped front garden, checking anxiously along the dark road for a car with a taxi sign on top, trembling with anxiety.

It was 2 A.M. and the residential area was quiet, the vast darkness of the ocean across the road silent and oppressive.

She was holding her cell phone in her hand, gazing at it longingly. *Sam.* Sam was at the other end. All she had to do was close this connection and call him. He'd come running. Oh God, *Sam.* For just a moment she yearned with all her heart to be able to listen to that deep, reassuring voice. Sam would know what to do, would know how to help her father.

But that cold implacable voice had been very specific. *Don't make any calls. Keep the line open or your father will pay.*

She couldn't risk it. She'd give anything in her power to communicate with Sam, but not if her father was going to pay the price. A small voice somewhere inside her said that her father was going to pay a horrific price, anyway. And so would she. But she had to play this according to the rules set down by that sadistic bastard.

The man had been willing to casually slice her father's face open just to make a point. If he felt that she wasn't obeying his orders . . .

It didn't bear thinking about.

She hopped up and down, chilled to the bone in the dark night, checking the time feverishly, obsessively. Twenty minutes. He'd said she had twenty minutes to get to the mall parking lot and five had already gone by. Another couple of minutes and they couldn't possibly make it in time.

Ah! Bright headlights and a taxi sign on the roof, traveling fast on the empty road. Inside a minute she could see the taxi sign clearly and heaved a sigh of relief as the yellow cab pulled to the curb. She rushed out, wrenching the cab door open.

"I'll pay you double if you can get me to the Westwood shopping mall parking lot in Fleetridge inside of fifteen minutes." Her voice was high, hysterical.

The driver looked like a student, clean-cut and very young, a bit astonished at the wild woman flinging herself into the backseat.

"You got it," he grunted, taking off so fast the tires squealed against the asphalt.

She stared out the window at the black ocean disappearing from sight as the driver turned inland, making good time on the empty streets.

Sam, she thought again. She wanted to hear his voice with a ferocity that astonished her. A tear rolled down her cheek and she brushed it away impatiently. Tears wouldn't help. Nothing could help.

She shuddered as she thought of her father in that man's hands. Her dad was barely kept alive with all the love and care in the world, and all the tricks the medical profession could pull out of its bag. Being held against his will by a violent man capable of hurting him . . . it could kill him. She might be speeding toward a place where she would only find her father's corpse and a violent thug willing to harm a helpless old man. A thug who wanted something from her, though she had no idea what.

She imagined he wanted her computer files, even though there was nothing in her hard disk that could possibly be of any use to anyone besides her and her clients. When the man discovered this, discovered that she didn't have what he wanted, whatever it was, he'd kill her. She was speeding toward her father's possible death and her own certain one.

The young cab driver reached the parking lot and entered with a dramatic turn, slewing slightly on the gravel of the soft shoulder. The lot was empty except for a dirty off-white van, a man standing outside the driver's door. The lot was illuminated with streetlamps except for the one directly above the van, so she couldn't make out the man's face.

"There you go," the driver said cheerfully, stopping the meter. It read $15. "Fifteen minutes on the dot."

Nicole didn't trust her voice. She simply threw a twenty and a ten at him and climbed out of the car on rubber legs.

Nicole crossed the parking lot slowly, her legs barely holding her up. By the time she reached the man standing by the van, he had his hand out.

It wasn't the intruder. There were at least two men involved in this, then.

Deep down, there had been a faint hope that somehow she could outwit the intruder, even if she couldn't outfight him. She wasn't going to be taken by surprise. Maybe she could whack him over the head with something while he wasn't looking or . . . her imagination stopped there. But it wasn't going to happen. There were two men involved and she wasn't going to come out of this alive.

"Phone." This man's voice was just as calm, just as cold as the other man's. Cut out of the same mold. Alert, icy and deadly.

Her hand shook as she held the cell out to him.

The man gave a short jerk of his head. "Get in."

Never get into the car.

One of the cardinal rules for State Department families in countries where kidnapping was a major industry. Never get into the car. Make a run for it. Attract attention by screaming. Carry Mace and use it. But never, ever get into the car. If you got into the car, you were as good as dead.

Wonderful advice. Only one thing. The clever men and women running the State Department Security Force seminars never told their listeners what to do when a loved one was being held hostage.

Never get into the car.

She got into the car.

The man threw her cell phone on the ground,

crushed it with his boot heel, kicked it into the scrub off the lot and got behind the wheel.

Never get into the car.

Nicole was in the car and her last hope of reaching Sam was lying in shards on the dark asphalt.

Chapter 13

Sam walked into his office, which looked like Mission Control. Every single light was on, the banks of computer monitors all lit, and four men were sitting around his desk. Harry, Mike and two guys he had no trouble at all identifying as Feebs.

All looking grim.

"Show me what you have," Sam said, sitting down behind his desk.

Silence for a moment, then Mike stirred. "Nothing good. First let me introduce the two newcomers. They're—"

"FBI," Sam said. "Yeah, I could tell."

Two bland looks. "It's the shoes," Sam explained. If they'd been from military security they'd have been wearing boots. If they'd been CIA, the footwear would have been top quality.

A moment's silence. The taller one, obviously senior, nodded. "Special Agent Ross and this is Special Agent Vanzetti."

Sam didn't care if they were Special Agents Mulder and Scully. He'd never liked the Feebs. He just wanted them to cut to the chase.

"So give me the lowdown." He looked each in the eye.

But it was Mike who answered. He'd been staring at a laptop screen. He turned it around so Sam could see it.

It was a page scanned from a military jacket. Prominent in the upper left hand side of the page was an unsmiling photograph of the man who'd broken into Nicole's office.

The man was wearing a black beret, had a skull with two crossed knives flash on his shoulder. Ranger tab on the left sleeve.

Dishonorable discharge, for selling military arms off base.

It was all there, the massive threat to Nicole.

Sam's jaw tightened and he bit down hard on his back teeth as he read carefully. The man's name was Sean McInerny, 75th battalion. Saw action in Iraq and Afghanistan. Dishonorable discharge in 2005.

Sam looked up at the four men. "A Ranger, like you said."

Special Agent Ross replied. "That's right. We've been chasing him for a couple of years. After he got his discharge—"

"Dishonorable discharge," Sam interrupted.

"Yeah." Special Agent Ross's jaw muscles jumped. "After he got his dishonorable discharge he simply dropped off the face of the earth. We suspect he's become a contract killer. There was a partial found at the site of what was made to look like a mugging but was an assassination of a bank CEO. And a security tape caught a half profile at another killing. We were lucky this time, your tape caught him full face. We have no idea where he lives. There is no record of any Sean McInerny renting or buying a house or a car, or using credit cards or entering or leaving the country. We don't know where he is. He's off the grid."

"You do know where he is," Sam pointed out coldly. "He's here in San Diego, obviously on a job. Have you checked the hotels?" He kept outwardly calm but inside he was raging. A Special Forces soldier as a gun for hire. The news couldn't have been worse.

"We've done this before, believe it or not," Ross said. "We're making the rounds now with a photograph, because if he's in a hotel, he's using an alias. We want him worse than you do."

I doubt it, Sam thought grimly. They were just doing their job, wanting to bag a bad guy. It would go on their record, maybe snag them a promotion. He wanted to keep his woman safe. Big difference. He opened his mouth to say something when his cell vibrated, three times in quick succession.

Every hair on his body stood up. He could actually feel them brushing against his shirtsleeves and shirt front, tiny little spears of terror. He froze, unable to move, unable to breathe, panic exploding in his head in a surge of white-hot light.

The two Feebs didn't notice, though Harry and Mike were looking at him strangely. Sam shook his head sharply and they got the message. *Not now.*

Ross was checking something on the laptop, pointing to the screen and Vanzetti was talking quietly into his cell. He switched off and turned to his partner. "We've just checked all the hotels and motels in the metropolitan area. Nothing."

Sam clenched his jaws. Even if they'd started checking immediately, they'd only had a couple of hours. The fact that they'd already checked with all the hotels and motels in the area meant that they'd called in local law enforcement officers, too. Probably the entire SDPF. This was a huge manhunt. All the more reason to get them out of his hair. Right. Now.

His cell was in his hand. He wanted to call Nicole with it so badly it felt like it was burning against his palm.

Sam stood and the two Feebs looked up, startled, then stood, too. A big, theatrical yawn as he stretched. He put on a sheepish look. "Didn't sleep well last night," he confessed to them. He'd slept maybe four hours in the past forty-eight, but he couldn't sleep now if you pumped him full of a triple dose of Valium. Every cell in his body was on red alert. He wanted the two Feebs out on their asses, *now.* "Sounds like you've got an army out looking for this guy, this Sean McInerney. I'm sure you'll get him real soon. When you find him, I have a few words to say to him."

He knew what he wanted them to see. A genial guy who'd had a scare a couple of hours ago, but now only wanted to get back to his bed, where a beautiful woman awaited him.

There was no way for the Feebs to know that under that amiable persona was a man sweating with terror, guts cold and roiling because something was going down *now*.

Harry and Mike watched, baffled, as Sam subtly urged the two special agents to the outer door and saw them off with a brisk handshake.

"Sam," Harry said uneasily when the door closed behind them. "Don't you understand that the guy who broke into Nicole's apartment is a—"

"No time," Sam gritted. "Got a signal from my cell phone—means my home security's been breached. Someone going *out*. Nicole's on the move. No way would Nicole leave my apartment without telling me unless she was forced to." He had Nicole's cell phone number on speed dial. It was busy. Goddamn. "Harry!" he barked. "Triangulate this number for me, fast." He rapped out Nicole's cell phone number. Harry put his crutches to one side, sat down at one of the computers and bent over the keyboard.

Sam switched on a monitor connected with his home computer and saw the big, dark empty lobby of his own apartment complex appear.

"Shit," Mike breathed. "You're hacking your own building's security."

The cameras were high quality. It had been a condition for buying the apartment. No jerky stills every four seconds to save money. Sam went to ten minutes ago, when he'd heard the signal that Nicole was leaving his apartment. He could see everything, including the night guard behind his U-shaped desk. It was 0200 in the morning but the guard was alert, not reading, not dozing, checking in a regular loop the array of monitors glowing brightly on the desk.

Good man.

The guard must have heard something. He turned toward the bank of elevators, hand on his holstered weapon. And there she was, Nicole, looking desperate, nearly running across the lobby. She stopped just outside the huge glass doors, at the limit of the lobby cameras' range. Sam watched her, shaking, slender arms crossed over her waist as if hugging herself for comfort as she waited for something impatiently.

Mike had drifted over to stand by Sam. Harry watched the screen, face sober.

Sam called her again. Busy. She wasn't talking into it. She was keeping the line open because . . . he felt air leave the room. She was keeping it open because someone was keeping tabs on her.

Her head lifted as she saw something outside, then she ran out of the cameras' range. A faint glow could be seen beyond the building's gates. A light on top of a yellow vehicle.

"Outdoor cameras," he ordered and Harry typed so fast his fingers were a blur. It was Harry's building, too, and he knew the codes inside out. The outside cameras flashed onto the monitors, showed Nicole opening the passenger door of a taxi. The plates were in shadow.

Sam called again. Busy.

"Keep that cell phone triangulated," he ordered Harry.

"On it."

The only thing that would force Nicole out would be a threat to her father.

"Mike," he said, striding to the gun locker hidden away in a coat closet. He punched in the code fast and opened the armored door. "Check on those two officers guarding Nicole's father."

"Roger that." Mike was in uniform, radio mike attached to a loop on his shoulder. He spoke quietly into it, static cutting in and out.

Sam stared at the small arsenal he had. *Don't bring a knife to a gunfight. Match your weapon to your mission.* Holy, sacred words that had been pounded into his head by every drill instructor he'd ever had. Matching your weapon to your mission was essential if you wanted to stay alive.

The mission was Nicole. But what was he facing here?

He tried to call her again, on the faintest hope that she'd closed the connection. Maybe now that she was in a taxi . . .

No such luck. Busy. She was following orders.

"Harry," he called over his shoulder. "Where's she going?"

"Heading out along the causeway. Maybe coming into town? No, she's moving inland. Taxi's moving real fast. Over the speed limit."

Mouth grim, Sam turned back to the locker.

If you didn't know your enemy, then you couldn't go wrong with a long gun and a pistol. He chose an HK–91 with an already-mounted scope. He already had his Glock 19, good for close-in work. NVG. Three magazines for the HK, hanging off a belt. Who knew how much firepower he'd be needing?

He bent and put a small block of C–4 and three detonators inside a backpack. A lot of problems could be solved by C–4. Flashbangs, four grenades.

He had a full tactical suit in the locker, they all did. He stripped down to the skin and built a warrior from the skin out. Nomex suit, body armor.

Mike was stripping out of his cop uniform.

"Whoa, whoa, can't come with me," Sam growled to Mike as he zipped up. "You're a police officer. This is an unsanctioned mission." He met and held Mike's eyes. "Internal Affairs will eat you alive if you come in with me. Stay out of this, it's my fight."

Mike lifted out his precious Remington 700. "Fuck that," he said, picking up three 4-round magazines. "You're not going in alone." He met Sam's eyes. "And I'm not going to let McInerney take that great woman down." His jaws clenched. "No way."

"It'll cost you your job." Mike loved being a cop.

"Fuck that," Mike said and calmly suited up.

Mike's head was made of concrete. Once he

made his mind up, Sam knew, there was no changing it. Mike was risking his job, they were both clear on that, Mike above all. Knowing Mike couldn't be talked out of it, Sam allowed himself a little spurt of relief. Nicole was more likely to come out of this alive if Mike had his six.

Armed, they both turned to face Harry. He was standing, barely upright, leaning heavily on the crutches, white-faced with the effort, yet quivering with desire to go with them. The three men looked at one another, understanding one another perfectly.

Harry couldn't go. Sam knew that Harry would give a kidney to be able to go, but he couldn't. In his condition, he'd only be a drag. Possibly get them killed. Sam knew that if Harry had been in even a slightly better condition, he'd have insisted on coming.

His two brothers. Mike, willing to give up a job he loved for him, and Harry, sick because he was too weak to help.

Harry made a low growling noise in his throat and sat back down at the computer. At least he could help that way.

Sam was closing the locker door when Harry called out. Sam turned his head. Harry's mouth was tight, his pale, thin face drawn with worry.

"What?"

"Lost her. The cab drove to the parking lot of the Westwood shopping mall and then she switched her cell off. It's completely dead. There's no way to track her now."

Sam strode over to the monitor and punched in the LoJack code. "Yes, there is. I put a micro Lo-Jack in her portable hard drive. She keeps that in her purse. She has her purse with her, I saw it on the security tape."

They watched as the system processed the new info.

"Boy, that really breaks the girlfriend rule. She'll give you hell for that, if she ever finds out." Harry shook his head.

"I'll take it, as long as she comes out of this alive."

The monitor flashed a map, the grid of streets around the south part of town. A bright point was moving steadily south. "She's on the move again." *Nicole, honey,* Sam thought, heart heavy. *Where are you headed? Where the fuck are they taking you?*

Mike was speaking softly into the shoulder mike on the shirt he'd discarded.

The bright point that was Nicole, or rather her hard disk, slowed and turned into the industrial area around the docks. "Now where the hell—"

"Sam." Mike put a hand on Sam's shoulder. "I just called dispatch. They couldn't contact the two officers, so they're assuming it's an officer down situation. A patrol car is on its way to Nicole's house, be there in five, but it doesn't look good. I think they've been eliminated and I think this McInerney has Nicole's dad. She's heading straight for him. "

Sam stood, mind churning. He was known for thinking fast in the field but right now horror froze him. He never went into battle afraid. You couldn't go into battle afraid, it was like signing your own death sentence. Warriors make their peace with death right from the start, and go into battle with a free mind.

Terror gripped him, made him clumsy and slow. McInerney had been to SERE school. It was meant to train soldiers to withstand torture, but it was run by sadists who loved their work just a little too much. And though soldiers were taught to resist, they were also taught how to beat information out of anyone, even the strongest man.

Sam knew the methods and he simply couldn't bear the thought of them being applied to Nicole. To that soft, gentle, beautiful woman. Or—God— to her father. A sick, dying man. If this Sean had hired himself out as a contract killer, there wasn't going to be anything stopping him, no moral line he wouldn't cross.

Maybe the fuckhead might even enjoy it. Enjoy inflicting pain. Enjoy listening to Nicole scream . . .

Sam closed his eyes, sweat rolling down his face. He simply couldn't deal with it.

He was a good strategic thinker, but right now he had the strategic IQ of a rock. His head was filled with clamoring noise, with visions of Nicole laid out on a table, being flayed alive.

Attached to electrodes. Being waterboarded. Fingernails pulled out one by one. Violently raped . . .

Sam turned swiftly and vomited into a trash

can, emptying his stomach of its contents, but not his mind of its nightmares.

Mike frowned. "It's bad, yeah. You really shouldn't have sent the two special agents away. You could have had the resources of the FBI on your side and you just let them go."

Sam wiped his mouth and picked up his body armor, the one without the Kevlar core to keep the weight down. He had no idea if he'd have to climb or maneuver. It was always a trade-off—weight against agility. Right now, being able to move easily trumped having a bullet penetrate the armor.

He started pulling it on. "Okay, so the Feds have enormous resources, but what's their top priority? What's the one thing they want?"

"Got it." Mike's jaw worked. "Sean McInerney."

"Who's ex Special Forces. He's not going down without a fight. However much the Feds will try to make it go down without collateral damage, their number-one goal is McInerney. If we give them Nicole's location, they're going to go in with a full tactical team, no holds barred. Do the math. Maybe twenty men, one hundred rounds each, that's two thousand rounds that might be fired in the space of a few minutes. There's going to be a firefight, with Nicole and her dad caught in the crossfire. If it's just me, I know what my priority is, and it's getting Nicole and her dad out alive—" He stopped for a second and looked Mike and Harry in the eyes. "And offing this guy. I want him dead. I don't want him to testify or to stand trial.

I want him gone." Sam turned to Harry. "Don't take your eyes off that monitor. Where are they now?"

Harry leaned over and checked the monitor. "Still heading south." Harry leaned over and touched the screen. "You can intercept them here if you hurry. Take the SUV."

Hold on Nicole, Sam thought, moving out, moving fast. *I'm coming for you.*

New York

He looked out his thirty-fifth floor window, at the sweep of Manhattan at his feet. Night had fallen, the skyscrapers were lit up like a false dawn. Cars and taxis made their way through the streets like a restless, irritable, illuminated worm. Something was holding up traffic uptown and the north-bound lanes were stalled. At street level, Muhammed knew, horns would be blasting, drivers and cabbies would be sticking their heads out the windows and screaming obscenities. Time was money and lost time was felt as keenly as the pickpocket's nimble fingers filching your wallet.

The energy and the power of the city was like a strong wind. It could blow you away like a mote of dust if you didn't know how to resist its lures.

Muhammed could. Easily. There was nothing here that didn't fill him with hatred and disgust.

The women, in particular. Wall Street was full

of them now, with their mannish ways and full-out aggression.

He had grown up in a culture where women dropped their eyes, never looking a man full in the face. He remembered vividly when he had turned from a boy to a man. How the street women who had yelled at him, cuffed his ears, suddenly avoided him, spoke to him softly, if at all.

The women in Manhattan would eat a man alive, if you let them. They were casual mothers and wives, discarding husbands and children like unwanted clothes, but deadly serious about money.

Monsters, not women. And Allah, through his servant Muhammed, was about to punish them.

His view took in the entire harbor, the Statue of Liberty, Ellis Island and in the far-off distance, the slow swells of the Atlantic Ocean. The direction from which vengeance was coming, at sixty knots.

Each day was a gift from Allah, and it was a sin to wish a gift away, but Muhammed ached for the day after tomorrow. Only the sternest self-discipline kept his face placid with the bankers, hedge fund managers, CEOs he dealt with daily. Inside, he was exulting. He could see an empty, desolate Manhattan so clearly—smashed windows, grass growing up through cracks in the sidewalks, loose newspapers fluttering through the streets—it confused him that there was still traffic clogging the streets, people walking on the sidewalks, office buildings lit up with workers making deals far into the night.

Soon, so soon, it would all be over, the heart of the Great Satan punched out.

And he—Muhammed Wahed—would have done this. For his people and for his God.

Chapter 14

San Diego

The van pulled out from the parking lot so fast the tires burned rubber. Had it not been the dead of night, Nicole could have hoped that the speed would have attracted some attention.

Or she could try buzzing down the window and screaming at a passing car. Make noise. Wrench the wheel and cause an accident.

Do *something*. Resist.

But they had the highest bargaining chip possible—her father. Who was right now terrified and no doubt in blinding pain, held in a hidden location. The only path to her father ran through this large, cold man sitting beside her.

And probably she wouldn't have been able to do anything to escape this man, anyway, even if he and the intruder weren't holding her father hostage.

The driver was vigilant. His eyes tracked from

the inside and outside rearview mirrors to the road ahead, to her, ceaselessly, in a constant loop. There was only a mere second between glances, there would barely be enough time for her to bunch her muscles for a move, and he'd notice that.

No, her only hope would have been to attract the attention of someone. But there was no one around. The man in the van had waited for the taxi driver to drive off before leaning down to turn on the ignition. Nicole had watched the tail-lights of the cab disappear with despair. There had been no chance whatsoever to communicate with the taxi driver. The phone had been open during the drive and then she'd had to get into the car with the new man and her phone had been destroyed.

It had been her last hope—that maybe Sam could somehow trace her through her cell phone. In the movies and in the thrillers she loved to read, a cell phone was like the bread crumbs left by Hansel and Gretel. In *NCIS*, Tim could trace cell phone signals down to a couple of square feet, and he could do it in the blink of an eye.

If Tim McGee could do it, Sam Reston could. Of that she was certain. If anyone could track her down, it would be Sam.

But not even Tim McGee could track a smashed and dead cell phone and even if by some wizardry he could, she wasn't there anymore. Sam would track her down to some smashed bits of plastic and metal. The cell phone had been destroyed and she was hurtling through the darkness with an unknown man to an unknown destination. The only thing she was certain of was that they had hurt her father and wouldn't hesitate to do it again. She sneaked a glance at the driver.

He was driving fast but well, like Sam. He shared other attributes with Sam. Tall, though not as tall as Sam, very fit, with the gift of stillness and a strong aura of self-control.

But there, of course, the similarities ended. This man gave off menacing vibes by the ton. No doubt Sam could do that, too, but she didn't think he could do that with a woman. And she couldn't—by any stretch of the imagination—imagine him hurting a sick old man.

Where the hell were they?

Nicole tried to keep track of where they were going, with some vague idea of stealing a cell phone, surreptitiously phoning Sam and providing him with an address.

But by the fourth squealing, stomach-churning curve, Nicole was utterly and completely lost. She had no idea what direction they were traveling in and she didn't recognize anything about her surroundings.

They were near the ocean, that's the only thing she knew. They were on a straight stretch of road now and at the crossroads, to her right, she could see a glint of moon off coal-black water. It didn't help her. San Diego was nothing but coastline.

They were in some kind of industrial section, only run down and deserted. She imagined a functioning port area to be busy day and night, loading and unloading the ships that arrived and departed on an hourly basis.

This place had mile after mile of derelict warehouses and industrial plants behind chain-link fencing, the buildings low and utterly dark.

Nicole sneaked a glance at the driver's hard face, then looked away. She had no sense at all that she was in a car with another human being. He could have been a robot-driver for all the emotion he betrayed.

She tried to steel herself for whatever was coming, but waves of panic rolled over her. Even trying to make some kind of a plan—how could she, when she had no idea what was going on?

The driver was not the man who had attacked her. So there were at least two men involved. Two very hard, criminal men. Where there were two, there could be three or four. There could be an army. It didn't make any difference. She'd been powerless against one. She couldn't hope to hold her own against two. If there were more, it didn't really make that much difference.

There was absolutely nothing on her person she could use as a weapon. Whatever they wanted from her, they were going to get.

"Where—" Nicole's mouth was so dry her tongue stuck to the roof of her mouth. She shuddered and tried again. "Where are we going?"

Ahead of them the empty road stretched, dark

buildings on either side. Nicole would have no trouble believing that she and robo-driver were the last humans on the face of the earth.

Silence.

She licked her lips and tried again. "Where are we going?"

Somehow, not knowing where they were racing to added another layer of horror to the situation. If only she knew where they were going, she could, she could . . .

What?

"Here," robo-driver growled and turned a corner so fast she had to cling to the seat belt.

"Shit," Sam growled, banging his hand on the steering wheel. "Can't go any faster."

He was pushing 90 mph as it was. He just hoped he didn't run into any cops, because he wasn't slowing down for anybody. It wasn't that the SUV couldn't go any faster—he'd clocked it at 140 mph on a racetrack—but rather that Harry was triangulating their relative positions. Harry observed the path of the vehicle carrying Nicole and had to calculate the best, fastest way for Sam to get there. It was a complex piece of geometry and Sam had to be able to take a corner on a dime when Harry said.

Mike wasn't paying him any attention. He was staring at the small screen set in the dashboard, listening hard to Harry through his earpiece. Sam was getting the same intel over his.

Mike acted as navigator, quietly telling him

two minutes before he had to turn a corner. If they'd been traveling during rush hour, they'd both be dead in smoking ruins by now.

"Turning left onto Spring Road," Harry said. "Where the *fuck* is he going? There's just nothing there but . . ." His voice trailed off.

"But warehouses," Mike finished for him. "I thought that might be where he's headed." His mouth pressed into a thin, grim line. Sam met his eyes briefly, then gave his whole attention back to the road.

"Not good," Mike said quietly.

No, it wasn't good. It was a section of town destined for demolition. A new residential complex was supposed to go up afterward, though the plans had been halted due to the real-estate crisis. In the meantime, it was an area of derelict warehouses and abandoned buildings. Empty, for miles. Guaranteed privacy, for as long as they wanted. No one would ever hear Nicole screaming . . .

He pressed the accelerator just a little harder.

"Target stopped," Harry announced quietly into their headsets.

Mike pointed to the screen. "We're about ten minutes out."

"Where, exactly?" Sam asked, eyes on the road.

Mike leaned forward, frowning at the map on the screen. "Turn right." The tires' squealing sounded loud in the night's silence. "Left."

A straight stretch. Sam nudged it up to 110 mph.

"Coming up," Harry's voice came over the headset. "Got it?"

Sam flicked a glance down at the grid on the laptop screen on the console, where a blipping light was stopped. It wasn't on the road, but inside an outline. "Got it. What the fuck is it?"

"They're inside a compound. Don't know what security measures they've got set up, though. You and Mike be careful." Harry's calm voice sounded loud in Sam's ear.

"That's a whole row of condemned buildings." Mike ran his finger over the street. The map showed long rectangles of buildings separated by alleys along the waterfront. "You got the number?"

"Says here 3440." Harry's voice was low, calm, but Sam could hear his fingers pounding the keyboard. "It was—yeah, coming up now. Formerly a bonded warehouse. Company moved out in 'oh six."

"There was a big bust there," Mike said grimly. "Arms for cocaine. SDPD bagged a couple of real bad guys. That was before Sam set up shop here, before my time even."

No one to hear her scream. Sam's hands tightened on the wheel and he pressed down on the accelerator. They were going so fast it took all his skills to keep the SUV on the road at turns.

They were on a straight stretch, only a few minutes out. Sam started slowing down.

"Kill the engine . . . now," Harry ordered, and the vehicle drifted soundlessly forward until it came to rest at the curb of a cross street, about ten feet from the street where the car with Nicole had gone in.

The SUV was still rocking when Sam shouldered the driver's-side door open, ready to leap out. A strong hand held him back.

What the fuck?

"Goddamnit Mike, Nicole's in there." Urgency rippled through his veins, prickled his skin. Right now, someone could be hurting Nicole, cutting her, burning her . . . "Let me go," he snarled.

"Wait," Mike said calmly. "We need more intel."

Sam swallowed. He knew this. He knew this on an intellectual and theoretical level. You do not go blind into a situation. But, shit, Nicole was in there *now* and Sam felt like jumping out of his skin with urgency. He was panting, the sound loud in the dark cabin of the vehicle.

Mike pulled his head around and went nose to nose with him. "Listen up here, I know you're worried, but I'm not going to let you fuck this up. I like Nicole, too. And the best way to bury that beautiful woman is to go in guns blazing without knowing the terrain or even where they are."

"Blueprints of the building coming up . . . now," Harry said into their earpiece. The screen darkened, then lit again with the blueprints of an industrial complex.

"See?" Mike said. "There's at least sixty thousand square feet there. How the *fuck* you think you're going to find them? By following bread crumbs?"

Sam and Mike stared at the screen. Sam sure as fuck hoped Mike was taking it all in, because he wasn't. A high keening sound rattled in Sam's head, the sound of panic. He had the classic symptoms. His heart raced, his palms were sweaty, he could barely focus his thoughts, he didn't have a sense of his own body, only of imminent danger to his woman.

This wasn't helping Nicole.

He leaned his head back against the headrest, pressing against it hard, and wiped his mind, concentrating on his breathing, trying to repress the very clear, spotlit image he had of Nicole being hurt that made his heart trip-hammer.

Breathing slowing, heartbeat slowing . . .

"Welcome back," Mike said quietly.

Sam opened his eyes and just like that, he *was* back. Capable and cool, the operator he'd always been.

Panic would get Nicole killed. She was already in serious danger. He was the only thing that stood between Nicole and death. If he didn't get himself under control, she was fucked, and he would lose her.

Sam leaned forward. "How many points of entry?"

Mike looked at him intently for a second, eyes bright blue even in the low glow of the monitor, then nodded. "Seven," he said. His finger pinpointed the doors into the building. "Plus what could only be a big loading bay here."

Sam turned it over in his head. "They won't be using the loading bay. Those suckers have huge doors that take forever to open even if you find the control panel. They'll go in through one of the side doors. They're on some kind of timeline. Whatever it is they're doing, it has to be quick."

Mike nodded. "Makes sense. And I don't think they'd go far into the building, so we're looking at perimeter rooms."

Sam nodded. "Here. And here." He tapped two doors on the blueprint, on either side of the front loading bay.

If the fuckers were at all rational, that's where they'd be. They had no idea that anyone could be tracking them. Entering into the huge maze of the warehouse made no sense.

"Jesus, I wish we had a Predator with thermal imaging," Harry sighed into the earpiece.

Fuck yeah. An aerial image showing where warm bodies were.

"Don't have a Predator," Mike said, reaching behind him for his backpack. "But while Sam was freaking, I was thinking." He hauled a camera-like machine with binoculars into the front seat.

A goddamn handheld thermal imager! And Mike was right—he'd been thinking while Sam was freaking. "I have a thermal imager," Mike said into the mike, for Harry's benefit.

"Sam should kiss you on the mouth for that," Harry said.

"Ewww," Sam and Mike replied in unison.

Mike smiled evilly. "But I *will* take that kiss from Nicole once we get her out."

"Over my dead body," Sam growled.

"Make sure it isn't over anyone's dead body,

except for the bad guys," Harry replied over their earpieces. "Now go get them. And afterward, Nicole has to kiss me, too."

They were in some kind of abandoned industrial building, but Nicole had no idea where. They could have been on the back side of the moon for all she knew.

When the car veered into one of the empty compounds, big gate standing open, her heart sank. The driver got out, growled *don't move*, pulled out a big black gun and kept it pointed at her. He could see her perfectly, since the headlights bounced off the steel walls of the building, lighting up the inside of the car. Nicole could barely see the man, and followed what he was doing by sound rather than sight.

The two big steel gates were pulled closed, a chain run through the handles and a padlock on the chain.

She was locked in.

The man came to her side of the car, opened the door and pulled her out roughly, pushing her ahead of him.

They walked around the right-hand corner, the man prodding her painfully in the back with the gun. Along the side wall was a door, ajar, visible in the backwash of the headlights around the corner. The man pushed hard with the gun. The doorway loomed, empty and black and forbidding.

It was like walking to her doom. They'd driven for ten minutes without seeing a light, without seeing another car or another human being. There was no one around to call for help, no way to signal, no way to call. She and her father were as abandoned as this building.

There was no way out, none. Even if, by some insane series of events, Nicole managed to overcome two armed men—and there might be more—and run away, she couldn't. Her father couldn't walk, she couldn't carry him and she'd never leave him behind.

Another sharp jab in the back, hard enough to break skin. Nicole's heart beat painfully hard as she eyed the open doorway, utter blackness beyond. Something, some animal instinct told her that she and her father wouldn't escape this building alive. The rusty abandoned warehouse would be their tomb.

"Get going, bitch." Behind her, the driver's voice was low, rough. This time instead of stabbing her in the back with the gun, he gave her a violent push that almost sent her to her knees.

Slowly, heart thundering, Nicole walked toward the blackness, stumbling over the threshold, then waited. She had no idea where he wanted her to go.

A heavy hand on her shoulder. "Right," he rasped and she started walking.

There was a faint light in the distance that grew brighter as she approached it. A door slightly ajar, light behind it. She stopped outside the door, suddenly terrified of what might be behind it.

"Move it." A hard push against the door and

she tumbled into the room. What she saw raised the hair on the nape of her neck.

Her father, duct taped to a chair, hands in restraints clasped on his lap, head hung low, dried blood from the slashed cheek all over the side of his face and his pajamas.

There was a large plastic sheet under the chair. For the blood. To ensure that no DNA be left behind. A tense shiver of horror ran through her. These men were thorough. They were not going to make mistakes.

On a stool next to her father was the man who'd broken into her office. A powerful lamp on a nearby steel table provided enough light to see the hellish scene by.

The man's head rose at their entrance and Nicole stepped back at the fierce coldness in his eyes.

She bumped into the man behind her.

He pushed her forward. "Watch where you're going, bitch."

Nicole barely heard him. Her father—she couldn't see his chest moving. Oh my God, was he—

"Daddy?" she whispered out of a tight throat.

Nicholas Pearce's eyelids flickered, opened. His head wobbled up, brows furrowed, eyes narrowed, unfocused.

"Daddy!" Nicole sobbed and he saw her.

In terrible pain, restraints so tight his hands were white and bloodless, duct taped to a chair by thugs, her father tried to reassure her. He made a stab at a smile and the deep wound in his cheek began sullenly bleeding again.

"It's okay, darling," he whispered. "I'm okay."

Pain made her heart miss a beat. She couldn't stand seeing her father hurt. The room swam as tears flooded Nicole's eyes. She rushed forward to hold her father, but was abruptly yanked back by a big, strong hand on her arm.

"Very touching," the man on the stool said, coolly. "Fatherly love. A daughter's devotion. It helps me." He picked up a big gun. Nicole heard a sharp *snick!* A thousand movies told her it was the safety coming off. He pointed the gun at her father's knee. "Now. Do you have what I want?"

Shaking so hard it took her two tries to unzip her purse, Nicole reached in and brought out the portable hard disk.

Please let this be what he wants, she thought. Otherwise he'd shoot her father in one knee, then the other. She met the man's eyes, cold, inhuman. The feral eyes of a creature of the night. There was no mercy there at all.

Still, she tried.

"Please," she whispered, and placed the hard disk on the ground with a trembling hand. The man curled his free hand up in the universal *gimme* gesture. Kneeling still, Nicole sent the hard disk skimming over the floor to him. He stopped it with a booted foot and picked it up.

He put the gun back down. He could afford to. Her father was tied up in a way a strong man couldn't break, let alone a weak, very sick one. She was at least ten feet from him. Even if she didn't have a gun pointed at her back, she'd never be able to make the leap, pick up the gun and shoot. The other man's hand was a second from the gun and he obviously knew how to use it.

She had no options here, none. She was helpless, unable to save her father, unable to save herself.

The man reached behind him, bringing out an ultra-thin laptop. He fired it up. It looked expensive and it was fast. With a couple of beeps, everything was ready. Connecting the hard disk via the USB port, the man stared at the monitor. Nicole couldn't see anything other than the silver back of the monitor and the blue-green wash of light over the man's cold, expressionless face.

"Password," he grunted.

"Nickyblue," she said shakily. Her mother's nickname for her.

He clicked his way through something, following intently, while Nicole trembled. Though it was cold in the warehouse, sweat coated her torso, drops falling between her breasts. Terror made her heart pump so hard she thought it would jump out of her chest.

Utter silence except for the genteel, expensive whir of top-of-the-line electronics, then the man sat back with a sigh. He looked at the other man, next to Nicole. "Got it."

"Great," the man next to her answered.

"Now." The intruder stared coldly at Nicole, picking the gun up once more, placing it against her father's knee again. "Has this information been forwarded? Did you send the file to anyone?"

Nicole had no idea which file he meant, but she hadn't e-mailed anyone in the past thirty-six hours.

She shook her head and he nodded. She had no saliva in her mouth to answer.

The man had the air of someone wrapping something up. It was coming to a head. "Did you copy it to a flash drive?" She shook her head again. "Show me." His voice was low, harsh, affectless.

Nicole lowered her purse to the floor and shoved it to him with her foot, as she had with the hard disk. "In the side pocket," she said, her dry mouth making the words hard to understand.

He extracted the flash drive, inserted it into the USB port and clicked through it. If it was on the hard disk but not on the flash drive, it must be a file that had arrived on the twenty-eighth or later.

He nodded and looked her straight in the eyes. She forced herself to meet his gaze. It was like looking into a dark abyss.

"Swear that you haven't copied or forwarded the file." The man pressed his gun hard against her father's knee. Sweat broke out on her father's face, but he said nothing.

"I swear! Please, oh please don't hurt him!" Nicole cried. Oh God, she couldn't stand this. Her father was so sick, so fragile. He'd been without pain medication for hours. He was in agony, she could tell.

Nicole watched the man's eyes, watched the utter indifference to her father's pain.

A flood of rage swept through her. This man

was like every cruel man who had ever lived. He enjoyed holding power over others, he enjoyed inflicting pain, simply because he could.

He looked at her for a full minute. "I believe you," he finally said, with a nod. "Which means we won't be needing you anymore."

He nodded to his partner and lifted the gun from her father's knee to place it against his head. In the same instant, Nicole felt the round cold circle of a gun muzzle against the nape of her neck.

Oh God. This was it.

She and her father were going to die right here, right now, in a cold, empty, abandoned warehouse with the stench of machine oil and rat droppings in their nostrils, where their bodies might not be found for months. Though, come to think of it, there was the big wide ocean right outside. Weighted down with chains, no one would ever find their bodies.

Nicole wanted to plead, to ask for mercy, but there was no mercy at all in those light brown eyes, as dead and opaque as marbles.

"I guess it's good-bye, Ms. Pearce." The man's hand tightened, white showing on the knuckles.

"No!" she screamed, leaping forward, trying crazily to reach her father, as if she could somehow place herself between the bullet and her father in the time it took the man to pull the trigger.

She was hauled back brutally by the hair by the other man. He knocked her to her knees and placed his gun against the back of her head again.

Crazily, Nicole braced, as if that would help her deflect a bullet.

She looked over at her father through the tears swimming in her eyes. If she could at least have departed this life looking into his eyes, so they could go together . . . but his head lay heavily against his chest, unconscious. He'd slip from unconsciousness into death . . .

Two shots rang in the room and she cried out. In shock, and then, after a second, surprise. It took her seconds to get her bearings. She was . . . she was still alive! As was her father, slumped and pale and broken, but alive.

A pink mist had bloomed around the intruder's head. He had an expression of utter and total astonishment. He sat on the stool for a long moment, a round pink hole in the center of his forehead. Then, suddenly, as if the weight of the gun against her father's head were too great to bear, the pistol slipped from his hand, falling to the floor with a clatter. Then he bent forward slowly, finally tumbling to the floor.

Nicole turned around, heart racing. The man who'd been holding a gun to her head had suddenly disappeared. Just like that, in a second. Shock had her staring at where he'd been, stupidly checking the room. Finally, she looked down and there he was, sprawled on the filthy concrete floor, a pool of red flowing from his head, gun still in his hand.

None of this made any sense.

Two figures stepped forward from the doorway,

appearing out of the utter darkness like ghosts. Strong, substantial ghosts, hard-eyed and carrying rifles . . .

Nicole simply sat there, completely incapable of processing any of this, shaking, mind blank. Her entire body felt heavy with the lethargy of shock.

"Honey," one of the ghosts said, and it was as if that deep voice shattered the chains of shock holding her in place.

Sam! Sam and Mike!

Somehow they'd found her! She drew in a shuddering breath and only then realized that she had stopped breathing. A second later, she still found it hard to breathe, because Sam was holding her so hard.

"Jesus," he muttered into her hair. "That was close."

"Yeah." She laughed shakily. "What took you so long?"

He made a sound deep in his chest. Not a laugh, not a snort, but a combination of the two.

Just feeling him against her, knowing he was there, made her strong. Awareness rushed back in. The men who had threatened her were dead, but her father needed medical care and she had to figure out what was in her computer because there was no guarantee that other bad men might not follow.

Nicole pulled Sam's head down, kissed him, then pushed against his chest, hard. Surprised, he opened his arms to let her go. She turned to Mike, gave him a resounding kiss on the mouth, then ran to her father.

"Hey!" Sam shouted.

"Harry wants one of those, too," Mike called out.

The intruder was sprawled at her father's feet, hand still curled around his gun, finger in the trigger guard. A second later, and a bullet would have gone through her father's head.

Nicole stared down at the man for a moment, hating him with every fiber of her being. She kicked his arm away with disdain and knelt next to her father, frantically touching him all over.

"Daddy, Daddy, are you okay?" She tugged desperately at the duct tape. She couldn't stand seeing him tied up for one second more. But no matter how frantically she pulled, the tape held. Her father swayed in his seat as she tugged harder and sobbed. "Damn it! I can't get this stuff off him!" she raged.

Big hands pulled her gently away. "Here honey, let me," Sam said, pulling out one of those huge black knives she so wanted for herself.

Nicole eyed the man at her feet. "Too bad he's dead. I'd love to cut his beating heart out with that knife."

"Beautiful and bloodthirsty, I like it," Sam said, slicing easily through the duct tape, one big hand on her father's shoulder so he wouldn't fall off the chair. "Though it's not as easy as it looks, getting past the ribs to the heart." He sliced the restraints around the wrists and slipped the knife back into a sheath around his thigh.

"Oh God." Nicole looked up at Sam, tears swimming in her eyes. "He's unconscious. We've got to get him to a hospital immediately!"

"Yeah." Sam bent and lifted her father carefully in his arms. "We can drive him as fast as any ambulance. St. Jude's is about twenty minutes away. Let's get going."

"I'll drive," Mike said. He looked down at the dead bodies, then at Sam. "I'll have to call this in."

"From the road," Sam answered, turning sideways to get through the door with her father in his arms. "We don't have time right now. Let's move."

Nicole scrambled to her feet, light-headed, still shocked at not being dead, and followed them out the door. Mike held a powerful flashlight to light the way.

She was halfway down the corridor when she stopped, cursing. Nearly dying had scrambled her brains. She ran back to the room that had almost been her graveyard, leaping over the man who'd nearly blown a hole in her head, and grabbed the intruder's laptop, her hard disk and her purse.

Mike was waiting for her, a question in his eyes.

"Whatever they were looking for, they were willing to commit murder to get it," she huffed, holding the laptop and hard disk up. "We need to find out what it is. What?" He was looking at her strangely.

They were walking quickly down the corridor, trying to catch up with Sam, who was already at the big steel gates.

"Should have thought of that myself," Mike grumbled. "Couldn't count on Sam to think of it, he was crazy with worry over you, but sh—damn! I should have thought of that. Here, let me carry that for you."

He looked weighed down by about a thousand pounds of . . . stuff. Nicole didn't recognize any of it except for a big black rifle, a big black pistol and a big black knife.

She could certainly carry a laptop, a purse and a small hard disk.

"No, that's fine. I've got it. You just saved my life," Nicole said as they exited out onto the dark loading apron. "You can be forgiven for forgetting things."

"Do your thing, Sam," Mike said, holding out his arms.

Sam gently transferred her father to Mike's strong arms and pulled something small out of a side pocket. Two seconds later, he'd picked the padlock and was pulling the chains out of the handles. He pulled out the big steel gates just enough for them to slip through.

"How'd you guys get in?" Nicole looked around for an alternative route they could have used, but couldn't find one.

"Rappelled," Sam said succinctly, directing the flashlight for a moment over to the right. Two slender ropes hung down, swaying gently in the chill night air coming off the ocean.

They followed Mike out the big gate and around a corner. He was carefully laying her father down on the back seat of a big SUV. Nicole rounded the vehicle, gently lifted her father's head, slid in, then placed his head on her lap. She stroked his face, carefully, because she didn't want the deep slash to start bleeding again. Her heart squeezed with sorrow as she felt the loose skin over bone, the crepe-like texture of his skin. His eyes were sunken deep in their sockets. What was lying on her lap looked more like a skull than the head of a man.

Mike started up the vehicle and pulled out fast. She looked up to see Sam watching her, twisted in his seat, thick arm over the back.

She stroked around the ugly slash in her father's cheek and met Sam's eyes. "I hate that man so much," she said, voice low. "I wish he were alive so I could kill him again. Blow his head apart. Cut his black heart right out with your knife."

She meant every word and it surprised the hell out of her. If anyone had asked, she'd have assured them that she was tolerant and profoundly nonviolent. The feelings that coursed through her were utterly new, unwelcome, fierce.

She wished with all her heart that she'd been the one to kill the two men.

The men had been so brutal to her father, a helpless and sick man. They'd even tied him up, put his hands in restraints. Slashed his face open. It hurt her heart to think of it.

And they had been perfectly willing to kill both of them to keep a secret. "I need to try to find out what they were looking for," she told Sam.

He nodded. "We're vulnerable until we know."

The back of the driver's seat held a pull-down tray, like on airplanes. She placed the intruder's laptop on it, powered it up, and inserted her hard disk.

In seconds, Outlook was open. She blocked out everything from her mind. The shock of nearly dying, her father, Sam . . . In seconds she was in that place where she lived when doing translations, a place of no distractions and utter concentration.

She checked the files that had arrived between June 27 and June 29. Luckily, all in languages with a Latin alphabet. French, German, Spanish, Italian. She knew enough German and Italian to understand the topics of the texts. She went over every single file, one by one.

Nothing. They were perfectly innocuous. All of them.

"Anything?" Sam asked quietly.

Nicole met his eyes. She shook her head, frustrated, went back to staring at the screen. "Nothing."

"Leave it," Sam suggested. "Come back to it later, with a fresh mind. You've been traumatized, maybe you're not seeing it."

She'd been traumatized, that was for sure, but not enough that she'd miss something important. She *knew* these files. Each file was from a customer she'd had for at least six months. One customer—the Port Authority of Marseilles— she'd had for years.

She knew the texts, too. They were iterations of the same texts she'd either translated herself or sent out for translation. The Banque de Luxembourg, for example. They'd sent the minutes of a board meeting, 80 percent of which would be exactly what had been said at the last board meeting. Or the Berlin Buchmesse, a smaller version of the Frankfurt Book Fair. They had sent a copy of their current "Manual for Exhibitors" to translate and it would be very much like the last manual.

She huffed out a frustrated breath.

"ETA fifteen minutes," Mike said, voice low.

They'd be at the hospital in a quarter of an hour. Nicole looked down at her father, still unconscious, so fragile and precious. Sick and vulnerable.

They'd slashed him open and would have killed him without a second thought.

She ground her teeth together and turned back to the monitor. Why? *Why* were they sent to do harm to her and her father? For what?

"Talk it through, out loud," Mike suggested, meeting her eyes in the rearview mirror. "That sometimes helps."

"Okay." She stared into the monitor, as if she could get it to yield its secrets by sheer will power. "I'm looking at twenty files. All by old clients. Not one new one. They are all familiar texts, in that the subject matter is very similar to other texts from the same client."

"Go over them from the opposite direction," Sam suggested. "From the last to the first."

Nicole shrugged. It wouldn't change anything, but still. "Okay." She ran the cursor over the files, one by one, from the bottom up. From the oldest to the newest.

She frowned. "That's odd."

"What?" Sam and Mike said in unison.

The cursor hovered over the Marseille Port Authority file.

"One of the files is much bigger than it should be. Clients ask for a quote before sending me the text, even old clients. Wordsmith charges by the word, sixteen cents a word, or forty dollars a page of fifteen hundred bytes. I remember clearly the quote for the Marseille job—twenty-six hundred dollars for about a hundred kilobytes. But it says here the size of the file is almost eight hundred KB. Normally, if there are illustrations or, say, part of the text is in PowerPoint, that will of course increase the bytes, but they told me it would be all text."

"Open it. Run through it again," Mike urged. They were in an inhabited area and he'd had to slow down for the speed bumps.

"Okay." She opened the attachment and scrolled through the text slowly, the words and the concepts very familiar to her, so familiar she sometimes thought she could qualify for a harbormaster certificate. Suddenly, the font changed size for twenty pages. "Whoa."

Nicole sat back. The file came from the Port administrative clerk, who usually sent her the work, Jean-Paul Simonet. She'd found out that he had lost his daughters in the Madrid terrorist attack, and she had sent him condolences. After that, they often sent each other greetings. He was an odd man, with strange passions. Collecting Tintin comic books, trainspotting and . . . steganography!

"Oh my God," she muttered. Was the laptop Wi-Fi enabled? Yes, she discovered, logging on feverishly, trying to remember a long e-mail exchange with Simonet on his passion. He'd written at boring length about a program called . . . she stopped, fingers curved over the keyboard.

She suddenly had a huge sense of urgency, a prickling in her veins, a feeling that she had to move *now*. Not tomorrow or the next day or even the next hour. Right *now*. Inexplicable, irresistible, almost painful in its intensity.

What was the name of the program? Mike was looking at her in the rearview mirror, frowning, Sam was watching her carefully. She probably looked insane, teeth clenched, eyes closed.

Think, Nicole!

They'd had their last lengthy exchange in December. He wrote that he missed his family a lot come Christmastime. He'd lost two daughters and then his wife. Her heart had gone out to him, spending a Christmas alone. It was cold in Marseille, he'd complained.

Why was she thinking all of this now? Cold . . . *snow*. The small app was called Snow!

She clenched her teeth. "I'm going to try something now."

Nicole was good with computers. She bent down

and a few minutes later, the blue bar had filled up, the app was downloaded, and she clicked on the file.

"I have something," Nicole said softly. Mike watched her in the mirror, Sam had turned completely in his seat to see her. "It was hidden in the file."

She watched as a section of the Port Authority report dissolved, and new text was superimposed on the old. Steganography wasn't encryption. Thank God. She'd never have been able to break a code. Steganography was hiding. Hiding one file inside another.

A message, from Simonet.

Mademoiselle Pearce—je vous envoie le manifeste d'un navire, destination New York, je crois qu'il rappresente un nouveau attentat—un attentat nucléaire— contre les Etats Unis, parce que—

Nicole translated the text, trying to keep her voice level. "This is a message from a clerk in the Port Authority. The message reads: Ms. Pearce, I am sending you the manifest of a ship sailing to New York, I think they intend to carry out another attack against the United States." She looked up and met Sam's eyes. Her voice wobbled. "He says . . . he says a *nuclear* attack. The message ends abruptly. As if he was . . . interrupted."

"Or worse," Sam growled, already punching his cell phone.

A nuclear attack on the United States. Nicole clicked her way through the pages, terror rising. "Here we are Sam, Mike. The ship flies a Liberian flag. The

Marie Claire. Next stop New York, slated to arrive day after tomorrow. The man who sent me the message is very alive to terrorist threats. He lost his family in the Madrid bombing." She met Sam's sober eyes again. "There's something on that ship, Sam. It's got to be stopped."

Sam was already talking quietly and earnestly into his cell. He turned back to her, holding the cell phone up. "Okay, sweetheart, Harry's patched me through to the FBI and they've got the Coast Guard listening too. Give us particulars about this ship."

"Even better," Nicole said. "Give me an e-mail address and I'll send the file. The hidden information is now readable."

"Great idea." Sam gave her three e-mail addresses, all ending with .gov.

As she tapped ENTER the SUV swerved, driving up the well-lit ramp of the emergency entrance of a huge hospital complex.

She picked up her father's limp hand and held it tight. "We might have saved the world. Now let's save my dad."

Chapter 15

Muhammed stood looking out over Manhattan from his privileged perch, holding the Thuraya satellite cell phone so tightly it was a miracle it didn't crush.

He'd been standing for four hours, watching as the sun rose in the sky. Watching as the streets became busy, traffic heavy, gazing into the bustling offices, looking like beehives. Everyone making money, losing money, obsessing about money. Godless infidels, each and every one.

He and his brothers had failed.

Four hours ago the Coast Guard, carrying FBI and CIA agents and in all likelihood a contingent of NEST agents—from the Nuclear Agency Support Team—had boarded the *Marie Claire*. The captain had been unable to stop them. The last image Muhammed had seen was taken by the captain's cell phone, just before he tossed it into the ocean.

The scene was very clear—two Coast Guard cutters, with two gunners apiece sitting in harness behind .50-caliber machine guns. Above, an AH–64D Apache helicopter hovered, powerful rotors whipping the ocean waves. Its cannons carried 1,200 rounds, and just one of the nineteen Hellfire or Sidewinder missiles in its pods would blow the *Marie Claire* out of the water.

Muhammed had studied the enemy's resources well and for many years. You do not defeat the Great Satan head on. It has resources his brothers could never match. Asymmetrical warfare, the Americans called it. What that meant was that the mujahideen pitted their brave hearts and steadfast souls against the huge military and intelligence machine of the West.

Sometimes they lost. At times, courage and faith were not enough. The captain of the *Marie Claire* was outgunned and made no attempt to resist.

They'd find what they were looking for. Not because of the radioactive material. The canisters were well shielded and gave off a level of radioactivity that matched that of the freshly cut granite that was in the official hold of the ship.

The American soldiers would go over the ship with Geiger counters, with tests for bio agents which would come up negative. Then they'd use thermal imagers.

That's what would give them away.

The thermal imagers would show the warm, living presence of the martyrs behind the undetectable door. And the *shaheed* would be betrayed by their own brave, strong, beating hearts.

Muhammed knew that there was nothing on the ship that would lead to his involvement. Had there been anything, anything at all, traceable back to him, the FBI would have knocked on his door long ago. He was free, while his brothers would spend the rest of their lives in captivity, if they survived treatment at the hands of the infidel at all.

The plan had been excellent. Brilliant, in fact. The weak spot had not been gathering the radioactive material. That had proved relatively easy. They didn't need the type of rare element or the technical expertise to build a nuclear bomb. The material in the bomb only had to be radioactive. Radioactive material was everywhere—in hospital waste, as a by-product of nuclear power. All you needed was money and time.

Their weak spot had been bringing the men into the country.

But . . . what if this brilliant plan could be carried out in a country that was *already* full of potential *shaheeds*, martyrs to the faith? A country like . . . Britain. With its large and alienated Muslim population, recruitment could come from within the country.

The martyrs would understand the culture, speak the language.

Britain was an island, nothing *but* coastline. Getting material into the country by boat would be ridiculously easy. And if there were a group of martyrs already in-country—say twenty or thirty—Muhammed could take down the City—London's financial district.

It would work. Muhammed felt the power of the idea course through him. It would definitely work.

They'd have to wait a year, maybe two. Fine. His culture was the opposite of the frantic hurry-up culture of the West. Jihad could take a lifetime, two. More, even. The memory of the Crusades still burned in their hearts. It didn't matter. Allah was eternal.

Muhammed knew lots of people in finance in London. Inside a year, he'd have a map of the buildings to take down and letters of introduction to the CEOs of the businesses. If the City were destroyed, it would have almost the same effect as wiping out Wall Street.

It would work, *imshallah*.

Muhammed picked up the phone and called the travel agency his company used, open 24-7. He wouldn't have any difficulty in persuading his company to send him to London. In fact, his boss had said there was an opening in their London office.

"Hello," he said to the voice that picked up. "This is Paul Preston. I'd like a ticket on the last plane leaving for London today. If possible, I'd prefer to travel British Airways."

He listened to the voice at the other end, blond brows snapping together in annoyance.

"Of course first class," he snapped. "What am I? A peasant?"

San Diego
Early morning
July 3

Nicole opened her eyes, turned her head and smiled at him sleepily.

Sam considered it a major victory that he'd gotten her home, in his bed, after she'd spent forty-eight hours sitting on a hard chair by her father's hospital bed.

Ambassador Pearce would be released tomorrow and in the meantime was lightly sedated. Sam had told her to go home, Harry and Mike had told her to go home, the hospital staff had told her to go home, but it wasn't until her father passed a shaking hand over her hair and told her to go rest that she even considered it. Even then, Sam had had to pry her away.

She'd fallen straight asleep in the car and he'd carried her up to his apartment, undressed her carefully, given her one of his tee shirts and put her between the sheets.

She'd come half awake as he undressed her, looking at him, then at the blue-steeler in his pants. But he kept it zipped. Nicole's beautiful eyes were bruised with fatigue and she was paper white.

Though his body had been raring to go, he'd rather have slit his own throat than expect sex when she was so exhausted. He'd fixed her a big cup of hot milk with lots of honey and a jigger of whiskey and after he'd made sure she drank it all, she'd turned on her side and gone out like a light.

He sat all night in a chair by the bed, holding her hand, simply watching her in the quiet stillness. Toward morning, he stripped and slowly eased himself into the bed.

Moving carefully, he spooned himself around her, one arm under her head, the other curled around her belly. The more of her he touched, the happier he was. Touching her—touching the warm, living flesh of her—was vital to his sanity.

He'd almost lost her, there in that abandoned warehouse.

Lost, as in dead. As in dead forever.

He could barely think about it without shuddering. To his dying day, he would see her, trying to leap to intercept a bullet, yanked back by the hair by a scumbag getting ready to blow a hole through her head.

If Sam closed his eyes, he could see the alternate reality, if he and Mike had come even a second later. Nicole, crumpled on the filthy floor in a pool of her own blood, all that beauty and grace and goodness—gone forever.

Jesus.

His hands tightened convulsively at the thought and that was when she turned to smile sleepily at him.

Oh shit. He clenched his jaw. "I woke you up. Sorry."

She turned completely around, rustling the sheets, until they were front to front. Her breasts against his chest, belly against his, long legs brushing his. He jerked when she brushed against his super-sensitized cock.

Sweat broke out on his forehead. He was trying to be good, here. Trying to be considerate. But how the fuck was he supposed to do *that* when he had Nicole Pearce in his arms, looking up at him with a half smile, so beautiful it hurt the eyes?

How the fuck was he supposed to respect her tiredness when he could smell the perfume of her skin, when she was like a little furnace all along his front? And how about when she breathed and her breasts brushed against him? How about that?

"Mmm . . ." Nicole smiled, eyes closed, and rubbed herself against him, head to toe. Her mound was rubbing right against his hard-on and he shuddered.

He went commando in bed, had never liked pajamas. And Nicole was only wearing one of his tee shirts. It covered her down to her knees, but the material was so soft, Sam could feel every inch of her as if she were naked.

Nicole slid a slender arm around his torso, hand clinging to his back, and buried her face in his neck. When her tongue snaked out and licked him, he thought *the hell with this.*

A minute later, his ripped tee shirt was fluttering to the floor and he was rolling onto her, burying himself deep inside her, held tight in her soft, wet clasp.

He closed his eyes in despair. Did it again.

"Shit," he whispered. Sam levered himself up on his elbows and looked down at her. "I forgot foreplay. Again."

Nicole lifted her head and kissed him. "I was having an erotic dream about you." She lifted her hips and he slid even more deeply into her. She was slick, wet, thank you, Aphrodite. "I think that might count as foreplay."

"Oh yeah?" Intrigued, Sam pulled slowly out, pressed back into her, watching intently as her eyelids fluttered. "What were we doing? How sexy was it?"

"Off the scale," she assured him softly. "We were in your bed and you took off my nightgown . . . actually you ripped it off. And it wasn't my nightgown, it was your tee shirt and . . ."

He stopped her mouth with a kiss, feeling her smile underneath it. He was moving so slowly, like the waves of the sea. Cupping her shoulders, he slid back into her, deep. As deep as he could go. Her smile had gone, her kisses now felt urgent. Mouths connecting like their sexes.

Nicole's legs lifted, widened and she somehow impaled herself even more on his cock.

An electric charge raced down his spine and

his balls tightened. Not good. He had to stop this, stop coming the instant he entered her. Of course, afterward he just kept on fucking, but he had to learn a little bit of self-control around her and try not to come in the first five strokes.

Still, the urge to torture himself was strong. Sam lifted himself on his forearms, so he could watch them as he moved inside her, oh-so slowly.

"Nice dream." He had to work to keep from panting. "I had one too. In this one, I'm fu—we're making love, and we're in my bed. And we're watching me enter you."

In.

"It's sexy as hell," he breathed.

Out.

Nicole looked down too, at the picture they made together. It was almost unbearably erotic, her slender white torso moving, stomach muscles clenching, the puffy pink lips of her cunt visibly holding onto him while he pulled out, as if it couldn't bear to let him go.

In.

She felt like heaven. He'd never fucked before without latex. Even wearing a rubber, sex with Nicole would have been more intense than any other sex he'd ever had. Bareback . . . it was sometimes a miracle he lasted those five strokes.

Out.

Bareback, he could feel every inch of her. He knew her cunt now like he knew the back of his hand. He knew how it became even softer after she came, he could tell in an instant what turned her on, the skin of his cock could feel the extra wetness.

In.

No latex between them. The only thing stopping her from getting pregnant was some hormones pressed into little pills. Had she been taking the pill over the past few days, with everything going on?

Out.

Because, if she hadn't, if she'd forgotten to take them—and who could blame her?—then . . . well, then she could be pregnant right now.

In.

With his baby.

Out.

At the thought, Sam swelled even more, became harder, longer. Nicole gazed up at him, startled. She'd felt it, his almost unbearable excitement.

In.

Because if she were pregnant, it would have to be a little girl who looked just like Nicole. With glossy black hair and intense blue eyes.

Out.

A little girl who would twine her little arms around his neck and tell him she loved him. And he would love her and protect her, fiercely.

In.

Nicole would grow more outrageously beautiful in pregnancy. She just had that look; she'd become rounder and rounder by the day, shining in her beauty.

Out.

He'd fuck her carefully, entering from behind. Oh-so slowly. And late in the pregnancy, he'd be inside her, and his hand on her belly would feel their child, moving.

In.Out.

She could be pregnant . . .

In.Out.In.

right . . .

Inoutinoutinout

now!

Sam exploded, a hot wire drawn from the top of his head that ran straight down his spine and through his cock blew in one pounding, electric second. The top of his head threatened to blow off and his toes dug into the mattress so he could be as deep in her as was humanly possible. He clenched his teeth against a shout, it was so intense.

He came in waves, shuddering and spurting in enormous jets, flooding her with his sperm, collapsing onto her. He was heavy, he knew that, but there was no strength in his arms while coming, everything was concentrated on his cock.

It wiped him out. He lay sprawled on her, breathing hard, waiting for the spots behind his eyelids to dissipate, thinking of absolutely nothing, only feeling. Until consciousness slowly returned.

Shit, she hadn't . . .

Yes, there it was!

She was coming! Sharp little contractions around his cock, breath puffing in his ear, thank you God, because he hadn't done anything to deserve this.

He held himself deep inside her while she writhed around him. It was almost better than coming himself, feeling her pleasure. He'd learned to prolong her climax by rocking slightly inside her while she came and he did so now, small little movements with his hips, barely perceptible, but man, she liked that.

Sam smiled into her hair. He didn't need to look to see her expression, it was imprinted on his brain. On his death-bed, he'd see her face, eyes closed tight with pleasure, long neck arched, luscious mouth open to pull in more air.

The contractions slowed and he stopped his movements. She liked quiet at exactly this moment as she slowly came back into herself.

He loved that. He loved that he knew her so well, knew her body, knew what she was feeling. Nicole never dissimulated, never tried any female games on him. Everything about her was utterly genuine, including her pleasure.

The pleasure *he* gave her.

Oh man, this was the best.

Her little cunt was still now, soft and wet, and her arms relaxed around him. She gave a long sigh of contentment.

Sam nuzzled her temple with his nose, her hair soft in his face. It always gave him a shock to feel how warm her hair was. It was so midnight black, he always expected it to be cool, but her hair, like the rest of her, was warm and soft.

Oh yeah, his woman.

He took the lobe of her ear in his mouth and bit,

gently. His cock hardened in her, expanding within her soft wet walls. He licked behind her ear, hips moving forward to go more deeply into her.

"Sam?"

Another nuzzle in the warm, fragrant waves of her hair.

"Mm?"

"Sam—sorry. I think I have to check my e-mail. I haven't checked it in two days, I can't simply close up shop. Can you hold that thought?"

She pushed gently at his shoulders and, stifling a sigh, he reluctantly withdrew from her warm clasp. The air felt cold and unwelcoming against the wet skin of his cock. If it had been a person, it would have grumbled. It was not happy outside Nicole.

He smiled down at her, though. Even being near Nicole was better than fucking anyone else. She smiled back, cupping his jaw in a gesture of affection that was becoming familiar.

"When you're all caught up, could you translate something for me?" he asked. "There's this bank in Tijuana that wants to upgrade their security. Drug gangs have robbed them fifteen times in the past year, so they're looking further afield than the local police. They put in a request for a bid but all the technical information is in Spanish."

She raised herself up on her elbows and kissed his jaw. "Of course. Be glad to. I'll even give you a special lover's discount."

Sam froze. An opening. An opening he could drive a truck through.

His heart started thudding, a frantic tattoo of hope and panic. He'd thought to wait. A month, maybe two. Let her get over the past couple of days, settle down. He had every intention of being by her side as much as possible, of course. Get her used to being with him.

He knew perfectly well he wasn't the kind of man she ordinarily dated. On the face of it, they were a mismatch.

He was a roughneck, more a beer kind of guy than a champagne one. Nicole was champagne, the finest.

Being with him wasn't going to get her an entrée into high society, though arguably, as an ambassador's daughter, she had that covered on her own.

What he could give her didn't look like much on paper, but was very real, though. Fidelity, devotion, unwavering support. And, presumably, at some time in the future, a normal sex life where he didn't jump her bones at the slightest opportunity. He knew that was in his future, he just didn't know when.

So the plan was to just stick by her like glue. He knew she needed to be with her father, and he respected that. He could drive her to work and back. They could have lunch together. She had to eat in the evening. He'd eat at her house, take her out for an hour, he didn't give a shit, as long as he was with her. The point was to get her used to having him around and then ... pop the question some time down the line.

But life was unpredictable. Dangerous, even. No one knew that better than he did.

He'd almost lost her, twice.

Now.

Sam took in a deep breath.

"I don't know about that," he said, making a major effort to keep his voice cool, casual. "I don't believe in prenups, so when you charge me, you'll basically be charging yourself. Doesn't make much sense to me."

Silence. Total, aching silence.

Sam sneaked a glance at Nicole, refraining from wincing at the totally blank expression on her face.

Shit shit *shit!*

What the *hell* had possessed him to speak up now? Christ, why couldn't he have waited? Now he'd shot his wad and how could he—

Nicole narrowed her eyes. "Was that a marriage proposal I heard in there?"

He didn't have the courage to do anything but stare.

"Well, was it?"

Mouth dry, he nodded.

"Because if it was," she continued, aggrieved, "it was definitely the most half-assed proposal I've ever heard of."

He nodded. Yes, yes, it was half-assed, all right.

"Sorry." He cleared his tight throat. "You're right, I don't know what I was—"

"However," she said, talking right over him,

"I'll cut you some slack since you did save my life. Twice. That earns you points. Do you love me?"

That he could answer. "Yes," he said firmly and waited. And waited. She simply looked at him, a thoughtful expression on her face.

Fuck. She was going to say no.

Well, hell. How could he expect anything else? He knew himself and he knew what he wanted and he wanted her, no question. But not everyone was like him, able to make important decisions fast. He had no doubts at all, but what about her?

She was an extraordinarily beautiful woman. She'd probably had men falling balls-deep in love within five minutes of meeting her since she'd hit puberty. He had no doubts, but she would. She'd be crazy to trust someone like him, put her life in his hands.

She came from a solid, loving family. He was as far from that as it was possible to be and still grow up on the same planet. How could she trust him to—

"It's a very good thing that you're not going to be making any marriage proposals after this one, because you suck at it. However, the answer is yes."

"I know I'm probably not what you're used to, but I swear, you can count on me forever. I'll take care of you. No one will ever hurt you, ever again. I promise you I'll be true, and—"

"Sam," she sighed. "I said yes. And for the record, I love you, too."

His brain seized up, simply froze. He stopped breathing for a moment. "Yes?" he echoed blankly. He couldn't possibly have heard right.

Nicole's eyes rolled in her head and she pulled his head down for a kiss.

Epilogue

It was an unusually cold and blustery day. Nicole shivered as she laid a small bouquet of snowdrops and baby's breath on her father's grave, then stood back.

Sam put his arm around her and she leaned gratefully into his strength and warmth. She'd dressed much too lightly. The morning had seemed almost warm when they'd set out from Coronado Shores an hour ago.

The icy wind whipping off the Pacific felt like it came straight from the North Pole. She didn't even have gloves with her. She hadn't been able to wear gloves for six months now. There wasn't a glove in the world that would fit over the diamond ring as big as a pigeon's egg Sam had insisted on buying her. It was beautiful but enormous, a source almost of embarrassment in the beginning, though she was starting to become quite fond of it.

Nicole reached out to touch the headstone. "Happy birthday, Pops," she whispered. It would have been his sixty-second birthday.

She and Sam had been married by a justice of the peace in her father's sickroom the day after he returned from the hospital, with Harry and Mike and Manuela in attendance.

Before the wedding, Sam had gone into her father's room and closed the door. They'd talked for more than an hour. She couldn't pry what had been said out of her father. He'd only clasped her hand between his cold ones and told her she was marrying a good man.

When the short, simple ceremony was over, instead of giving her a passionate kiss, as she'd expected, Sam held her in his arms and whispered into her ear, voice raw with emotion, "I'm going to make you a good husband, I swear."

He had, too. He'd made her a better husband, actually, than she'd made him a wife, particularly in the first two months of their marriage—the last two months of her father's life.

Sam had bought the small apartment next to his, opened up the door between the two apartments, and turned it into a hospital suite for her father. For the first two months of their marriage, Nicole basically let everything drop as her father began his painful slide into death.

Sam had let her know in no uncertain terms

that her only responsibility was her father, she was to worry about nothing else. Bills were paid, food appeared and was cleared away, doctors and nurses came and went. Nicole barely noticed. Sam took care of everything.

When, after she spent three straight nights awake at his bedside, her father took his last breath, Sam had been there to hold her in her grief. As she moved in a stupor of mourning and exhaustion, it didn't occur to her until later that he had arranged the funeral and had bought the plot and ordered the headstone.

Time had brought a healing. After the funeral, Sam had taken her to Maui for a belated honeymoon and made sure all she did was eat, sleep and make love with him. At their return, she dedicated herself to Wordsmith. Every day, Nicole rode with Sam to the office building and up to the ninth floor, where they worked across the hall from each other. Wordsmith was finally taking off. Mike had quit the force and joined Sam and Harry in the company, which was now officially RBK Security.

Their nights were filled with a passion that showed no signs of slowing down.

Sam was an incredibly loving, though at times annoyingly overprotective, husband. Wordsmith was growing by the day and she tended it the way a mother tended her child.

Well, she thought, rubbing a hand over her belly, almost.

The wind suddenly died down and the clouds

parted. The grass turned a bright green in the sunshine, a gentle carpet edging down to the shore.

Her father would have loved it here. He'd spent much of his career in dry, arid places. Somehow, Sam had chosen the perfect cemetery, and the perfect spot, on a round knoll with a spectacular view over the ocean.

As the sun broke out, the temperature turned warm, almost balmy. Nicole lifted a smiling face to the warmth.

A benevolent presence hovered in the air, a whisper of love. Somewhere her father's spirit lingered and she could almost feel his gentle hand passing over her hair.

Somewhere, she knew, he was smiling. And holding her mother's hand. She'd wanted to wait, but now was the perfect moment. It felt like she had her family's loving blessing from on high.

Nicole jabbed an elbow into Sam's side. "I have a Christmas present for you."

"Yeah?" He smiled down at her, hugging her closer to him. "Isn't it a little early? Christmas won't be here for another ten days."

She leaned against him, rubbing her head against his shoulder. "Well, it's a present that will take nine months to get to you, so I'm starting early."

A cemetery is a sad, bleak place, a place of grief, watered by the tears of those who have lost loved ones.

But that morning, the cemetery rang with the deep sound of a man's delighted laughter.

THE NIGHT HUNTRESS NOVELS FROM

JEANIENE FROST

✠ HALFWAY TO THE GRAVE ✠

978-0-06-124508-4

Kick-ass demon hunter and half-vampire Cat Crawfield and her sexy mentor, Bones, are being pursued by a group of killers. Now Cat will have to choose a side…and Bones is turning out to be as tempting as any man with a heartbeat.

✠ ONE FOOT IN THE GRAVE ✠

978-0-06-124509-1

Cat Crawfield works to rid the world of the rogue undead. But when she's targeted for assassination she turns to her ex, the sexy and dangerous vampire Bones, to help her.

✠ AT GRAVE'S END ✠

978-0-06-158307-0

Caught in the crosshairs of a vengeful vamp, Cat's about to learn the true meaning of bad blood—just as she and Bones need to stop a lethal magic from being unleashed.

✠ DESTINED FOR AN EARLY GRAVE ✠

978-0-06-158321-6

Cat is having terrifying visions in her dreams of a vampire named Gregor who's more powerful than Bones.

✠ THIS SIDE OF THE GRAVE ✠

978-0-06-178318-0

Cat and her vampire husband Bones have fought for their lives, as well as their relationship. But Cat's new and unexpected abilities threaten the both of them.

At Avon Books, we know your passion for romance—once you finish one of our novels, you find yourself wanting more.

May we tempt you with . . .

- **Excerpts** from our upcoming releases.

- Entertaining **extras,** including authors' personal photo albums and book lists.

- Behind-the-scenes **scoop** on your favorite characters and series.

- **Sweepstakes** for the chance to win free books, romantic getaways, and other fun prizes.

- Writing **tips** from our authors and editors.

- **Blog** with our authors and find out why they love to write romance.

- **Exclusive content** that's not contained within the pages of our novels.

Join us at
www.avonbooks.com

AVON *An Imprint of* HarperCollins*Publishers*
www.avonromance.com

Available wherever books are sold or please call 1-800-331-3761 to order.